Truitt's Truth

Escape to an Era Where True Love Prevails

Other Books by Julia David

Love's Pure Gold Series
Truitt's Truth.
Morgan's Medicine.
Ian's Empire

Leaving Lennhurst Asylum Series
Available on Amazon and Kindle Ebook
Love Covers *Book 1 Elias*
Love Flies *Book 2 Patience*
Love Protects *Book 3 Anna*

Other Historical Romance Books by Julia David
Mighty One Series
Available on Amazon and Kindle Ebook
Burgundy Gloves
Broken Chain
Black Coat

Come visit: https://www.juliadwrites.com for behind the scenes, photos, videos, newsletters, release dates and fun giveaways.

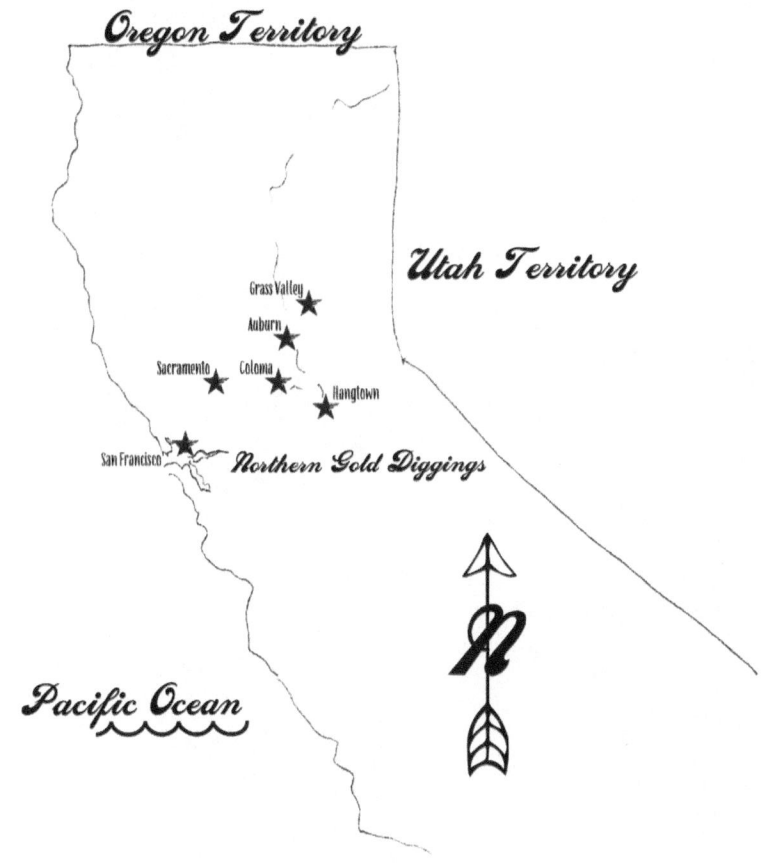

Oregon Territory

Utah Territory

Grass Valley

Auburn

Sacramento   Coloma

Hangtown

San Francisco   *Northern Gold Diggings*

Pacific Ocean

Truitt's Truth

A Novel By

Julia David

Field Runner Press

 **Field Runner Press**

Published by Field Runner Press
Redding, Ca.
Printed in the United States of America

"Truly, your message of truth means more to me than a
vault filled with the purest gold."
Psalm 119:127 TPT

"There is gold in every piece of your story."
Magnolia

One

Utah Territory,
Fall, 1850

CASSIDY O'RYAN GAZED with tear-filled eyes across the dry, empty desert. A lone tumbleweed drew her attention as it rolled across the flat and parched landscape. The few folks left in their small wagon caravan had unceremoniously moved on to California without them, and now Mr. Dingle was dead.

She had no partiality for this United States territory called Utah. After miles of yellow and green prairie grass guarded by breathtaking snowcapped peaks, nothing pleased the eye in this new, desolate land. Stepping away from the stifling sun and hovering in the few inches of the wagon's shade, she popped her fan open to cool her face. The early morning air brought little reprieve to her aggravated state. No trees. No water to be had as far as she could see. The sand felt more taxing than the miles and miles of prairie she'd walked. The small hot pebbles brought no kindly distractions to her feet, legs, or being. And what kind of self-respecting mountain would have flat tops like that rising up from the sand?

Sighing, she laid her hand on the empty water barrel hanging from the side of the wagon. Months and months of planning had brought her here to this place. A new life awaited her. Her old identity tying her to Boston died on this journey. The only two men who knew her secret didn't matter any longer. Mr. Dingle, the dear man, was to be buried in a grave with her past, and for that, she should be truly grateful, aside from losing the poor man. Joy was now truly nowhere to be found, besides the older man's death, to think they all might die of thirst anyway. Poor Mr. Dingle, to come this far and die in such a dreadful place.

Ethel Finnegan, Finny as Cassidy always called her, could now trade places with her as planned. She'd not been responsible for the old man's death, yet because of it, Cassidy could finally get what she wanted. More despondency overcame her, and she blinked slowly with exhaustion. Her salty tears flowed over her dusty cheeks.

"Miss O'Ryan."

Cassidy jumped at the sound of the wagon driver's voice.

"Yes, Mr. Coffey." She quickly drew her sleeve over her wet face.

"I find it pure toil, ma'am, to dig in this sand." The short man pulled his hat off and slapped it on his filthy pants. "My oxen be needin' a drink soon." He shook his head and plopped on his hat. "I can't dig worth nothin'. As soon as I pull a shovel of sand out, the sides just fill back up."

Cassidy inhaled a sturdy breath. "I can feel the poor fortune of one dying in the desert." She stilled, frowning. Being alive, *how* could she feel his misfortune? Tucking her loose hair behind her ear, her shoulders drooped. Unlike Finny, Mr. Coffey never noticed her blunders, so she carried on. "Mr. Dingle had been with my family for over forty years. Certainly, I owe him a proper burial."

"I felt kindly to the man myself," Mr. Coffey sighed, looking out across the miles of scorching desert. "We lost a few days for the dyin', and now everyone's moved on. I don't like being so far behind." He frowned, pulling on his black and gray beard.

Cassidy despised the day she'd vowed she could do this trading identities with Finny and naively leaving Boston on a wagon train west. Planning and scheming for the switch while pretending to all the kindhearted wagon folk they were just two honorable young women from Boston. Her pernicious selfishness had caught up with her. More tears escaped, she should have stayed and married the first suitor her father pressed on her. Her mind drifted to the older, red, square-faced colleague of her father's and closed her eyes, suppressing a shudder.

Finny leaned out the back of the covered wagon. "Do the best you can, Walt. God rest his soul." She disappeared just as fast as she appeared.

Cassidy's blood and body wilted. Finny carried no consciousness of her blunt speech. Before she could speak, Mr. Coffey had already turned the corner. Sliding down the side of the wagon wheel in a heap, she peeked over her shoulder. Poor Mr. Dingle wrapped like a mummy in canvas, lying underneath the wagon, waiting for his final resting place. "I'm so sorry," she whispered. "You were a good man and served my family well. You don't deserve this." Her throat constricted and the tears pooled again. She dropped her head onto her knees and covered her head with her arms.

That afternoon, Cassidy, Finny, and Mr. Coffey gathered around the shallow grave. Mr. Dingle's shoe tips made the tan, burial canvas peek out from the sand.

"Them—Those stiff black shoes were downfall himself," Finny announced over the silence. "Gave him those blood blisters, aye, they did." Her curt Irish brogue spilled out. "Them black devil socks leaked their poison right into them, sure and it's true." She pursed her thin lips and decisively bobbed her head, eyes flashing the truth of what she said. "And then he died." A swift, hot wind kicked their skirts around their legs. "Or that he was just old." She shrugged, holding Cassidy's parasol tight against the swirling wind. "God rest his soul."

Finny gestured for Cassidy to steal a glance at Mr. Walter Coffey. The short, burly teamster closed his eyes, showing his reverence. Finny pinched her nose closed and scowled. Cassidy knew well enough the man never bathed, and as much as they appreciated his wagon expertise, his body odor would reroute a stampede. They both stood on the wrong side of the wind for this modest funeral.

"Did you go through his things now?" Finny asked.

Mr. Coffey's eyes shot open, and Cassidy wished she could grab her parasol back and smack her opinionated companion. "I'll be sayin' a prayer," Cassidy announced, hoping to change the subject.

"Dearest Father in Heaven." How did the priest at Second Street Parish say it? She took in a deep, convincing breath. A woman could pray aloud. Couldn't she? "We thank you for the life of Mr. Dingle. Thank you for taking his spirit to heaven yesterday." Did he go straight to heaven or—oh, lolly, she should have paid more attention. "May you receive him and give him a—a nice chair, and home, and everything—that you do for—for—for thine is the glory forever and ever. And your kingdom come forever. Amen." She thought she heard Finny snicker at the rushed ending.

"God rest his soul." Finny lifted her fingers to her forehead, down to her chest and touched each shoulder in the sign of the cross. "Amen."

"How 'bout ya play one of those nice church hymns with your fiddle, Miss O'Ryan," said Mr. Coffey slapping his hat back on.

Finny waved the parasol in the air. "Sweet Mary, Mother, and Joseph, why don't we start a fire and make skillet bread while we're at it. I'm thinkin' we had little water, and you were in a hurry to get to California, Walt." Finny spun on her heel. "I know I am. I have a rich fiancé waitin' for me." She snapped the sun-beaten parasol closed and spun back to Cassidy, pulling her from the gravesite. "We need to get a move on. Those oxen get one whiff of Mr. Coffey, and beast and man will all be dead and buried in this cursed sand."

The next day Finny slept as Mr. Coffey led their wagon across the punishing desert. Cassidy sat crossed-legged on the bench looking down at her assigned lady's maid asleep on the padded pallet in the middle of the wagon. Wanting to find her usual dislike for the young woman who'd agreed to travel west and marry the man her father picked for her, she shook her head.

Cousin Arnold Snider, to be specific, a cousin by marriage who had been groomed by her father these last years to start a new branch of cargo and shipping from the bay of San Francisco.

Her father would have nothing less for her than a profitable business match. She hadn't seen Cousin Arnold face to face since she was eleven and he was twenty. Little mind did they pay to each other back then.

Heaven above, the closer they got to California, the more she wondered if she'd lost her good sense on the long trail west. Maybe it was losing Mr. Dingle, the only one who knew for certain she was the oldest daughter of one of the most successful shipping tycoons in the east. And by all social standings, he alone understood Finny was her lady's maid.

Mouth dry as cotton, she licked her cracked lips and pulled her fingers through her thick coppery red hair. Propriety was long gone from her daily toilet. Finny stopped helping her dress a month after they left Missouri. Like a feral cat set free from a cage, Finny came alive with the thought of being unbarred in this new land. The unmarried cowboys and ranchers certainly had no problem being Finny's persistent source of entertainment and revelry on the trail. She pulled the dirty pieces of hair apart and weaved the thick strands into a braid. Many times she knew Finny teetered on leaving their planned caper for the strong shoulder of a dandy promising her anything she wanted. But the annoying housemaid had sat tight, and Cassidy had to give her credit. For a young woman who'd never had any family, of course, the prospect of wealth and security pressed Finny forward. And she herself would never take for granted the comforts of life again. Little did she know she could survive broken axels, deep river crossings, and steep ascents. What obstacle did she and this wagon not have to contend with? A few sips of water a day would surely be her last test.

The newspapers were calling the people rushing to find gold in California Argonauts. Cassidy believed they were a brave breed of people, worthy of the name. Picking at the threads from a hole in her skirt, she thought about what they were doing. Taking everything they owned, leaving their predictable lives behind, and bearing their children along the way — all for the promise of gold, silver, or land and timber. And many just like her, trying to find independence from life's restraints. She rubbed her hand over her violin case. This was her gold — the love of song, dance, and entertainment. She'd read in the newspaper that the west was open for the arts and performance, even for women.

Mr. Dingle's bedroll swung from a peg. The cost for a hapless-romantic girl's dream west had been so high. *Forgive me, kind sir.* Her mind drifted to his smile and progressive disposition. Just two days ago, she'd tried to give him her sips of water as Finny chastised her for the waste. She'd prayed her drops would keep him going. She held back a groan. The only day she'd seen him melancholy was when the Raymond family split with the wagon train to take the Oregon Trail. He'd had a special friendship with the old widow, Mae Raymond. Knowing this trip was about her blessed freedom, why didn't she offer him his freedom to follow his heart?

Weary in body and conscience, Cassidy contemplated laying back down, but she knew that would just free her mind in favor for more fretting. Searching their tiny, rustic, moving home, Cassidy wondered if any last drops remained in Mr. Dingle's canteen. In these desperate times, womanly preparations halted for the greater need of thirst. Peering down at Finny once more, she wondered how she could begrudge Finny her exhaustion. They were all tired and reduced in spirit. How could she think months of explaining manners and decorum could transform a housemaid into a lady? Though the cowboys, miners, and families along the trail made no such class distinctions, many of them offered friendship to both of them equally.

Folks commented weekly on how they should have been born sisters. Finny's red hair shone in a lighter, not quite as curly style. Cassidy started adding the olive dye to produce a richer, polished copper color. Thinner and longer in the nose, Finny had narrower cheeks than herself. Cassidy ran her fingers along her face, ignoring the small compact in her reticule. She'd no desire to see how thin and weather-beaten she appeared now.

They would get to the end of this desert and rest at the border of California. From there on, she would need to remember to call Finny Kathleen, or rather, Miss Kathleen O'Ryan, or better yet, Miss O'Ryan. And she would have to claim the name, Miss Cassidy Finnegan for herself. It wasn't a bad name, Cassidy. Coming from her days with her grandmother when she asked they call her Cassidy rather than Kathleen. She nodded her head. Finnegan was a strong name in the Irish community of Boston.

Some of her starch leeched away as she thought perhaps the California people would treat her in a lowly servanthood state. But Finny had agreed to address Cassidy as her lady's companion, not as a maid knowing full well that Finny had been a domestic her entire life. They agreed to help each other in their new roles, and now that she'd found Mr. Dingle's pouch and had hidden her family's money with her things, the new Kathleen would have to follow through with that promise. Two hundred dollars for a dowry, her father's money handed to Mr. Arnold Snider upon his day of marriage to Miss Kathleen O'Ryan in the form of Finny Finnegan, the young, eager, overconfident woman standing in her place. Could it get any more confusing?

Two

Damonte Station
California-Utah Territory Border

TWACK! THE LONG handle of the ax reverberated from the hickory wood up into Truitt Emerson's unhealed, broken fingers. Hardening his stubbled jaw, he pulled the ax from the stump and reached for the large pieces that had just been cut in two. Feeling another cool breeze against his sweaty skin, he lobbed the large, cut wood into the woodpile. Two of his swollen fingertips tapped against his thumb before he set another piece on the stump and swung the ax high in the air. *Twack!* The wood split easily mimicking the splitting of his unruly tension.

"Mr. Emerson, sir!" A boy of ten or so who helped at Damonte Station ran toward him.

Truitt nodded and swept the back of his wrist across his brow.

"A new wagon just rolled in, sir." The boy panted.

Truitt felt his temper rise a notch as he slammed the sharp edge of the ax into the round stump. He reached for his shirt. The stragglers had made it to the new California State border. Finally.

The boy skipped next to Truitt's long strides, piping up. "But I'm not sure it's the wagon you're searchin' fer." Truitt stopped cold, and the boy looked back to find him.

"Not to make you upended, sir." The boy glanced toward the station. "I don't see any woman with red hair in that there wagon. A ma and pa and some yellow-headed children as best I can make the likes of."

Truitt bent over and squeezed his knees until his purple fingers screamed with pain. "I'm not sore with you, boy." He stood tall and finished jerking his shirt closed. "Maybe these folks know of something of her and her wagon."

The boy nodded and jogged away toward the corral.

"Wait," Truitt called after him. Taking a nickel from his pocket, he flipped it out to the lad as he caught it.

"What? What's this fer?" The boy said wide-eyed.

"For keepin' an eye out for me. I'm getting vexed with waiting." Truitt murmured his last words while looking around Damonte Station. It'd been five days and no sign of his boss's fianceé. Hard to imagine what would be worse, telling Arnold Snider she'd died on the trail or that she just never showed up. Hangtown's strange businessman had been acting giddy as a new foal as the time drew close to meet his betrothed.

Maybe Truitt should be thankful to be away from the corrupt, pitiful Hangtown, allowing his broken fingers some time to heal. Snider's pay was still generous and all he'd done is chop wood and watch the cowboys break in new horses. The day's ride out to the Washoe Indians yesterday had proven a worthy diversion. Blankets and canvas were in short supply and they seemed hesitantly thankful for the provisions. Many did not trust the white eyes, but they knew of his father and the Emerson land owned near the expansive sky-blue lake. With only peaceful interactions, they seemed to tolerate him.

A woman in the back of the station house pulled a stick laden with laundry from the black boiling pot and threw it over a taut rope. He wondered daily how his mother and sisters fared back in Russia, the mail bringing news back and forth so far and few. His father's land claim, with the fast-flowing river leading to the icy blue lake, could be for them now—if they wanted to come. His sisters had possibly married and were on their own. With the money Truitt made, soon he would build a proper house and at least bring his mother here. But without his father.

The thought of his father's hanging spiked his anger, and he shook his head. Tension rippled through him as he marched toward the corral. If he knew today would be another waste of time, he would have spent the night in the woods and continued to clear his land.

Truitt approached a sandy-haired man and his son as they unhitched the horses.

"Sorry for the interruption, sir. Did you happen to have an acquaintance with a wagon coming this direction?"

"We best had fifteen in our group all comin' this a-ways." He pulled his team forward, and Truitt opened the corral gate. He'd counted ten wagons come through Damonte Station since he'd been here. "It should have held a young woman, I understand, with red hair in her early twenties. Traveling with an elderly man." Truitt pulled the small piece of paper from his pocket. "He is a Mr. Dingle, and her name is Miss Kathleen O'Ryan."

"Yes, I do remember two red-headed gals. I never could tell them apart. Was one of them Kathleen O'Ryan, Luke?" He asked his son.

"Cassidy. The one who played the fiddle." Luke looked up to Truitt. "But the other one with red hair, I don't recall her last name." He brightened a bit and continued, "Everyone called her Figgy or Finny or something like that."

Truitt covered his sigh as he pulled his hand down his rough, auburn chin stubble.

A woman with a blonde toddler attached to her hip came around the corner of the wagon. Her wide-brimmed prairie hat covered most of her face.

"Mama, this gentleman is lookin' for a Mr. Dingle. Do you recall him?"

"I do." She nodded. "Word was he was ailing and they had to pull back from the group to see to his recovery."

Truitt felt more hopeful than he had in days. "Do you know how he faired, ma'am?" Out of the corner of his eye, the father and son struggled with the tongue of the wagon. Truitt reached in to help. The wagon moved easily back and to the left with his strength.

"I'd a feelin' with your size and girth you'd be strong as an ox," the son smiled and tugged at the red kerchief in his pocket.

Truitt nodded back. Since he was this teen's age, everyone commented on his height and thick build. Not many like him in the country, six feet and three inches.

"I'm sorry, Mr…" The wife spoke.

"Emerson." Truitt reached out and gave the men a thick handshake. The young teen smiled and shook his hand, then grimaced as if the squeeze was painful.

"Mr. Emerson, I do apologize," she said. "I have no knowledge of how Mr. Dingle faired."

The father began to untie the boxes from the wagon. "So many of us heard about the forty miles of desert. It was all we could do to keep our rigs movin'. It's a merciless trail."

"I understand. You've given me some hope my waiting is not in vain. Where are you all to next?"

"Heading toward Sutter's Fort. Maybe I can work at the mill and discover my own vein of gold," the father chuckled.

"Good luck to you, then." Truitt lifted a wave as he left. They would need more than luck he mused as his thick legs lumbered toward the bunkhouse. He'd seen too much. One ounce of slapdash man and one ounce of fickle gold never made a life.

A year or more passed since that first hit of gold. People came from every direction filling tents and shacks. Arnold Snider had built his empire on the backs of the eager miners. Hangtown sprouted up quickly, boasting two stores, a livery, a forge, hotels, a bank, restaurants, theaters, and so many others, he couldn't keep track. With great forethought, Arnold Snider greedily slid deeper into most branches of business and ultimately the miners gold pouches living off others' fortune and misfortune. The only thing he couldn't buy was a socially suitable wife from back east.

Snider was never in lack of a woman's affections, but he wanted a wife who would represent the finer things. One who would sparkle on his arm as they pranced around Hangtown like a king and queen.

Truitt stopped before his boot crossed the bunkhouse porch. A light rain began to fall. One large hovering gray cloud had stretched into two. Cold moisture chilled in the air. The clean scent of wind-swept pines overpowered the smell of mossy ground and ranch animals. Chewing the corner of his lip, he turned back to his mountain of chopped wood, might as well stack it fully under this porch in case it poured.

By dusk, Truitt could have eaten the leg off a buck. He stood outside in line with the other boarders and cowboys holding his tin pan. The evening mixture of beans and whatever else was on hand didn't promise a satisfied belly—his experience from the last five nights had taught him that. *But oh, for the buttermilk and biscuits.* Some angel in the Damonte Station kitchen possessed a gift from God. He inched forward with the line, spying over the cowboy hats to the table heaped with the fluffy biscuits, fresh creamy butter, and a pitcher of sweet buttermilk. Looking up at the first star appearing against the fading gray sky, he whispered thanks for the clear night that had pushed those clouds apart. But his truest gratitude came from the faint smell that made his stomach rumble and mouth water.

In an hour or so, folks would build a few fires and sit around and share stories and grand dreams of gold and silver. He wasn't much of a talker and listening always fared better for him anyway. Just as he stepped in front of the black steaming pot, an older man with broken lines creasing his face approached and slapped his back. Truitt nodded and balanced the thick plop of beans that hit his tin.

"Mr. Emerson, I'm told." The man reached his hand out, and Truitt stepped back from the line to turn and shake his hand.

"I'm Louis Damonte. I own this place."

Truitt could see the confidence and feel the strength in his thick handshake. "Nice to meet you, sir. Please call me Emerson. Most do."

"I do know who you are." He smiled, baring crooked teeth. "I was in Hangtown, six months back. Saw you fight at that pole and tent set up."

"Yes, sir," Truitt nodded. "Now that place is all shored up. It's got a bar and gambling room, some rooms upstairs. The El Dorado. We clear it all out now for the boxing matches."

"Good and well, good and well." The older man nodded. "I look forward to coming to another match. I should'a bet more on ya. You've got a robust right hook that could knock an elk out cold," he chuckled. "Next time I will." He slapped Truitt's back again, and Truitt clutched his tin from going forward. He turned to see the line was gone and prayed that—

"Oh," Mr. Damonte turned back. "My grandson told me you gave him a little wage for helping you."

Truitt grinned. "You've got a lot of wagons and folk coming and going. He seems to decipher all the ruckus around here."

"That he does." Mr. Damonte chuckled. "As to why I left two bits inside on the parlor desk. I'd wondered who'd chopped and stacked my winter wood supply. My wife put your name on it. Seems you worked more than what we charge for the bunk and slop."

"No, no need for that." Truitt held up his free hand.

Mr. Damonte started to walk away. "Best eat before it's all cold. Hope your wagon from back east comes in soon," he said.

Truitt came around three cowboys talking near the food table and stopped cold. A blonde tyke, not a hair taller than his belt, wearing her homespun dress with a crooked apron, was startled by him. Large brown eyes locked on his as they both reached for the last biscuit. He held his hand out waiting; surely, she would see his size and offer him the one remaining fluffy square of heaven. But nary an eyelash around those full browns did she flicker. He rarely feared much, but this stoic stare of an unnamed female emotion could make a grizzly back down. And though his stomach ruled over many a mood, he slowly drew back and nodded his acquiesce—the large, last morsel was hers.

Three

WEDNESDAY, TRUITT TOOK it upon himself to keep the bunkhouse fire stoked. Blowing out a huff, he could see his breath in the air. The temperature this time of year was too unpredictable and he didn't like it. Outside, leaning against the bunkhouse porch post, he watched the dark clouds thicken over the sky. Yesterday two more wagons had rolled in, got supplies, and rolled out. The Sierras could be an irritable opponent if the weather turned nasty. Without the sun, it could get bitter cold.

Aggravation chewed in his gut. The waiting took a toll he really didn't want to pay. By noon he would take the horse and ride out into the Utah Territory to see what he could find.

Feeling like he'd had the first worthwhile plan in days, Truitt spent the next hour going over his supplies. After cleaning his gun, he gathered water, food, and his bedroll. Adding one more log to the bunkhouse black wood stove, he looked up to see Damonte's grandson bounding in the door.

"Sir, you gotta come! I think this is them!"

Truitt rose and took in a deep breath as he did right before a fight. The boy took off running and Truitt walked across the grass, keeping his heartbeat at bay. Heaven above, this needed to be them. He had a delivery to make in Hangtown, so maybe he could get them to move on across the Sierras today.

A short dusty man shook hands with a few other cowboys, and he noticed a commotion at the back of the wagon. Two ranch hands stepped up to support a red-haired woman stepping down from the end of the wagon, alive and breathing. "Thank the heavens," he whispered under his breath, stepping closer.

A pale, slight, comely thing, she sported a long regal nose and a dusty green and yellow skirt and vest. Right behind her, another young woman followed clutching a long case of some kind. More nutmeg than red in her hair, her features obviously weary, but this astonishing radiant beauty was impossible to miss. Eyes barely lifted, her hand extended for support before her knees buckled, and she tumbled from the wagon height right into his outstretched arms.

"Miss, are you all right?" He held her firm, thankful he'd been watching her.

"Oh, sir, please forgive me," she gripped the long case, "my—my weakened state. Thank you." Her tender, exhausted eyes met his, and he felt something shoot straight down to his toes.

"Who are you?" He didn't mean to sound so brash, but if this one belonged to Arnold Snider... Well, he just needed to know this instant where the land lay.

"Miss O'Ryan, Miss Finnegan." The short man came around the back. "We've been without water and supplies."

The driver spoke to Truitt as he held the woman with her case in his arms. She looked down to the driver and back up to Truitt. "Are all men in California as tall as you?" she asked, her full lips pinched in a twisted frown.

Truitt smiled, her voice, her womanly frame in his arms, and her question sparked something humorous. "I'm one of the taller." He needed to wipe the smile off his face and pull his thoughts back to order. "Your name, Miss?"

"Could you allow me to walk, sir?"

Truitt noticed several others unloading the wagon and decided he liked this captive audience. Without a second thought, he used it to his advantage and held her a fraction closer as he stepped towards the back door of the large ranch and boarding house. "Is the shorter man Mr. Dingle?" he asked.

She suddenly tensed in his arms and pushed off his chest. "What? Pray tell sir, quickly, how do you know of Mr. Dingle?"

He noticed her once tired eyes now vibrant with soft blue and gray flecks.

"I work for Arnold Snider. I'm here to escort you to Hangtown." He set her legs free on the hardwood floors but held his hand to her back. The servants and curious guests in the main house stared at them as if they were some oddity. For a man to be carrying a lady, something must be afoot. Speculation in their eyes confirmed their deep interest.

She clutched her case to her chest. "Excuse me, sir, I'm indisposed at the moment." She stepped toward the stair railing as Mrs. Damonte came to greet her. "You and the other gal can take the third room on the right. I have Maria heating water, and I will bring a tray up shortly."

Truitt watched the thinner woman go up with this beauty on her heel. He couldn't keep his eyes away. She wore a deep red and gray striped dress. Though it looked worn and dirty, it was store-bought, not homespun. Her thick hair hung ragged down her back, but her face posed a certain grace and confidence about it. Of course, this one had to be Arnold's cousin. Something soured in his gut. A woman so gentle and refined, he knew she would be the fiancée. Her speech alone sounded like no woman in Hangtown. Arnold, once again, could make way for whatever he wanted.

CASSIDY CLOSED THE door and leaned against it. The thin room held two narrow beds with just enough room for the washstand and pitcher in the middle. "Oh, lolly, that man, that man who carried me?" Finny ignored her, pouring water into a cup on the stand and drinking it as it dribbled down her neck. "He—he works for Mr. Snider. He is here to take us to Hangtown. He asked for Mr. Dingle." Cassidy said, clutching her throat.

Finny poured more water. "Here drink this. You're starting to babble." Finny grabbed the violin case from her arms and tossed it on the bed.

Cassidy gulped it down quickly. "He's probably down there this minute talking to Mr. Coffey."

Finny bit hard into an apple and held it out to Cassidy. "Take a bite. I swiped it right off the table and no one the wiser."

"Finny!" Cassidy growled then clapped her hand over her mouth, "I mean, Kathleen."

"Eat!" Finny held the apple inches from her lips.

Cassidy took a small bite. As soon as her teeth crushed the pulp, the sweet flavor erupted more delight than all the fine desserts at her father's table. She chewed slowly, closing her eyes to savor the taste. "More water."

Finny offered up the cup, and Cassidy took another drink. "Who do you want to talk about?" Finny smirked. "That tall slab of solid brisket that enjoyed holding you like a feather? Or stinky Mr. Coffey?"

Cassidy's mouth dropped open in shock.

"Sorry," Finny grinned, not looking sorry at all. "I'm so hungry, I only saw him as meat." Snickering, she bit another chunk of apple.

"He's more than meat." Cassidy brushed her hair back over her shoulder.

"You can say that again." Finny smirked, lifting her brows.

"Finny, I mean, Kathleen, focus with me, please." Cassidy dropped her head back. "They are likely conversing right this moment. Mr. Coffey is telling Mr...Mr...oh, I don't remember his name."

Finny took another bite of the apple and held it out toward her.

"Wait," Cassidy held up her hand and frowned. "Rudely, that man held me close without so much as a proper introduction." Cassidy took a bite of apple and groaned. What was her point? "But he works for Mr. Snider," she said around the apple in her mouth. "He asked me my name."

Finny swayed her head. "And you said…Cassidy Finnegan. I will be sayin'… Kathleen O'Ryan. Is that a thing you can be doin', Cassidy?" Her tone was patronizing.

"I can do that, Kathleen. I will be doing that." Cassidy felt a pinch in her stomach. "But Mr. Coffey knows us by our correct last names," she gripped her belly, another sudden pain stabbed her gut. "How do we lie now?" She winced.

"Do not fret, Cassidy," Finny shrugged, unbuttoning her vest. "We say he has enough drink in him to float a ship. Never could keep us straight." She bent to unbuckle her boots. "You said Walt was going from here to Oregon territory anyway."

"Yes, but Mr. Snider's employee asked demanding questions. He looked upon me strangely, his eyes a little squinty, full of suspicion." She clutched her forehead, "Oh, I don't know," she groaned. Another sharp pain stabbed her belly.

"Mary, Mother, and Joseph, Cassidy. You be havin' the vapors now." They both turned at the knock on the door. A worker with a white apron held a tray full of milk and eggs, biscuits and gravy. "Thank you, oh, thank you!" Finny took the tray while Cassidy nodded a faint smile, closing the door.

"Eggs! Cassidy, milk! I've died and gone to heaven, blimey, I have." Finny sat with the tray on her lap and touched her fingers to her head and chest and each shoulder before she picked up the fork. "Sit mi'girl, eat," her words mumbled around the food. "You'll be feelin' better."

Cassidy picked up the other fork, and it wobbled in her trembling hand. "I think I'm going to be sick." Cassidy set the fork back, laying back on her bed. She covered her face with her arms. "Did you feel the stairs, Finny?" she murmured after resting a few minutes.

"How can ye 'feel the stairs?'" Finny set her cup of milk down, "I can't eat anymore, and I think my belly is going to erupt."

"The wood floors under our feet, how they creaked when they felt our steps," Cassidy muttered. "And stairs, I've haven't gone up any stairs in eight months."

"Aye, you're a strange one, Cassidy O'Ryan, um, Finnegan, leaving your grand home in Boston. I've been climbin' enough stairs, haulin' water, or clean clothes to last myself a lifetime. Only you would be *feelin'* the stairs." Finny swiped her finger through the gravy and popped it in her mouth. "I did notice that big kitchen. I couldn't see through the bags, but those shelves were amply filled with beans, potatoes, rice, and spices, I just know it. I vow never to eat bison again." Finny sneered. "Fighting off the scavenger birds for nothing but bones. No, thank you. I plan on being a plump, well-fed, west coast wife now, and you will be bringin' me trays like this."

"How is that your understanding?" Cassidy rolled to her side, facing her.

"By being my maid and all."

"Lady's companion." Cassidy ground out and sat up. Pushing hard on the pain in her side, she reached forward. "Give me that fork."

Four

AFTER THE BRIEF meeting with his new charges, Truitt spent the darkening afternoon securing the women's trunks and looking over his provisions for two women and no Mr. Dingle. Loading his simple canvas shelter, he figured he would give it to them for sleeping. He'd made shelter under a tree more often than he slept in his fancy room at the Bedford Hotel. Even after pushing and shoving things into place, the space was tight. The women would have to sit on the crates in the back and hold the canvas over their heads to stay dry. He'd no desire to make small talk with the beauty in the red and gray dress, so he arranged the seating with their backs to his back.

Pulling a rope taut and roughly whipping the remainder over the wagon, he squeezed the wagon siding. It was high time to quit working for Arnold Snider. The prize money he'd saved was enough. He was tired of Hangtown and tired of doing Snider's fisticuffs and dirty work. Would the sweet-faced, young woman he'd held in his arms understand the nature of her greedy fiancé? Snider used him for his stature and thick fists to get what he wanted when he wanted it. Today it was the kind-voiced, redhead who was now the latest prize for Snider to flaunt.

Truitt blew out a long breath and stomped around the wagon. He smelled stew and looked up to see the tables being set for tonight's meal. The women hadn't been seen all afternoon, but he needed to plan their departure for the morning. After all the lengths they'd traveled, a few more days to Hangtown would be nothing.

He walked to the corral and found Snider's robust chestnut mare. After a good scratch behind those velvet ears, he bent close and brought the horse's leg up to rest on his thigh as he rubbed it down and picked any rocks from its hoof.

What was the rock in his step today? He was clearly still irritated. It started when Mr. Coffey said the thin-nosed woman was the maid and Cassidy was in the care of Mr. Dingle. A sorry loss that, for the gritty, old man to make it this far and never see the beauty of these lakes and mountains. Truitt moved around and grabbed the other leg. So who was Kathleen? Mr. Coffey seemed confused but happy to take Mr. Snider's money for the safe delivery and be on his way. Now he was the inconvenienced errand boy for these two women.

He released a daunting huff as he recalled the strange sensation he'd felt with Miss O'Ryan in his arms. What kind of schoolboy reaction was that? He'd had a woman in his arms before. Marianna had been soft and warm, making him feel alive at her touch. That familiar, jagged rock in his gut, turned giving him another emotional stab.

If it weren't for the Americans turning on the Mexicans and the Chinese, her family would still be here. That foreign miner's tax, a ridiculous amount of twenty dollars a month, had sent them running. An ethnic stew of foreigners had assembled in the pot called the State of California. Tempers boiled over and the Mexicans had attacked the Chinese miners. Without a word, her family packed in the night and were gone to Mexico.

After his father's death, if there had been a clue to follow, perhaps he would have tried to find Marianna. Maybe he would leave Hangtown and do just that. The thought dug under his skin—to go north to prepare a place for his mother and sisters or head south for Marianna. Either way got him out of Hangtown. The rock turned again.

How many men like Mr. Damonte had slapped his back to congratulate his fast hook and fighting ability? How confident did he feel with a wad of cash in his pocket? But one defect no one saw under his size and strength, he'd always been shy and apprehensive with women, so unsure of letting his heart be soft. Then Marianna had slipped in with her sweet brown eyes and broken English. His Spanish was poor, but she'd taught him a few words. Almost two years since she'd disappeared, his heart still held some kind of jaded hope he would see her again.

He let out a heavy sigh. Her family had never approved of him. He'd told himself a hundred times to leave it be. With each boxing match, he swung and crushed his fists into another oblivious fellow. Her leaving, his father's unfair hanging, the soiled doves constantly poking fun for his attention, and the saloon girls, kind, but always pulling on his arm, all of it fueled the venom that seeped like sweat into each Friday night match.

Truitt finished rubbing the horse down, forked a full pile of hay and tossed it at the mare's feet. Some of the cowboys stopped their work and started forming the chow line. Would the women from back east join in with these simple, hardworking folks?

Likely not.

LATER, AFTER SUPPER, people thinned out from visiting; he called after the Damonte grandson. "Have you seen the ladies that came in earlier?"

"Yessir. They're sitting in my grannie's parlor now sipping tea or somethin'."

Sighing, Truitt squeezed his eyes to stop them from rolling.

"I need to speak to Miss O'Ryan," he waited.

"Well, you been in that back door before," the lippy whippersnapper said. "Just walk on in. Everybody else does."

Truitt fought more irritation at the obvious. It was his responsibility to speak to them. "I suppose I could do that." He took another deep breath and ducked in the back door, wishing his size didn't always draw attention everywhere he went. The women in the parlor looked up, and he noticed the fair one he'd carried earlier stand quickly. Their eyes met and she moved past the other ladies, coming to him like she read his mind, wishing he could speak with her again.

"Kind sir." She nodded to the ground. "I don't think we were properly introduced."

He couldn't help but stare. Without the case attached to her chest, she was a striking, buxom woman with more beautiful features than he'd seen before. Her hair was neat and pinned in a bun at the base of her neck, a few soft light copper strands curling around her ears, exposing a perfect, soft neck. She smelled like rose water and the clean, green flowered dress clinging in just the right places was—

"Sir?"

He looked to the side and found a stately grandfather clock. The pendulum swung back and forth. How long had he been staring at her? His face flushed crimson. Did his eyes reveal all the places he'd been looking? Holding back a groan, he pulled his hand across his rough stubble and righted his thinking. "Apologies, ma'am. I'm pleased to see you are feeling better. I'm Truitt Emerson."

Her eyes seemed to soften, and an awkward silence hung between them. Truitt cleared his throat. "So… I'm sorry for the loss of your man, Mr. Dingle. Good thing you brought your gal, there." He nodded toward the parlor. "I'm sure she is a great comfort being so far from home and all."

She blinked and squeezed her hands in front of her. "As I am…to her." She scrunched her face and looked back to the parlor. "Please forgive me, what was your name again?"

"Truitt, Truitt Emerson." His voice held an irritated edge. "I work for Arnold Snider." He felt his introduction was unmemorable, too ordinary for the likes of her.

Her body shuddered and she took such a deep breath he thought she stretched taller. "A pleasure to make your acquaintance, Mr. Emerson. I'm Miss Finnegan." She bowed and finally exhaled.

"Oh." He blinked and pulled on his ear. "I'm not usually so muddled. I thought Mr. Coffey said your name was Miss O'Ryan, and that she went by Finny." His eyes narrowed, looking around her to the group of ladies still visiting. "Are you engaged to Mr. Snider?"

He watched a shade of red climb up her pretty neck, and her mouth opened without words. Was the woman a bit daft?

"I am not." She lifted a crooked smile. "That young lady sitting with her tea is Miss Kathleen O'Ryan." She reached out and tapped her finger on his sleeve. "Could you shamelessly forgive poor Mr. Coffey?" She withdrew her hand and eyes off him and squeezed her hands in front of her. "He never could keep us straight. But he was an excellent wagon driver. Mr. Coffey said his goodbyes earlier and assured me that our things are safe and stored with you."

Truitt swallowed hard. A flick of excitement tried to compete with his confusion. How does a man drive a wagon for eight months and not know his folk? His tale of the last leg through the desert had been a forthright count of names and days and the death of Mr. Dingle. Maybe he hadn't listened close enough. A small curl of a smile tried to rise and then his eyes squinted in confusion.

"Mr. Snider is very anxious to meet Miss O'Ryan." He glanced over to where she sat. "And you are the lady's maid?"

"Companion. There's a difference where we come from," Miss Finnegan spoke tartly.

"Your quick correction is noted, ma'am." He nodded slowly.

"Thank you, Mr. Emerson, for your patience. We can rest a few more days, and then we'll be ready to see California—and Mr. Snider." Though forced, her smile sweetened her expression.

"We leave in the morning, ma'am. First light."

Cassidy glanced over her shoulder. "Ah, Miss O'Ryan does nothing at first light but sleep and she will insist we get our rest. You probably didn't hear; our delay was a calamity, we all almost died. Well… Mr. Dingle did," she huffed.

Truitt rolled his tongue inside his cheek. "I'm sorry for the harshness of the elements, ma'am. But you have no idea about the Sierras, the temperature's dropping and we don't want to be caught in any snow." He nodded and stepped back. "I already have the wagon packed." Turning to leave, he appreciated the distance that made his voice sound confident.

Miss Finnegan caught up with him before he exited. Her full bell skirts swished blocking the doorway. "Just one day?" She tilted her head to the side, those soft gray-blue eyes looking up to him.

Truitt wondered if she thought he didn't know what women did to get their way. This one, unfortunately, could sway a miner from his gold. "No, in the morning. First light." He stepped around her and away from the ranch house. She brazenly followed him, knowing it was dark and not ladylike.

"Just one thing, sir? Um, Mr. Emerson."

He stopped, this beauty was a far better distraction than a bunkhouse of dirty cowboys.

"Well ...two things for aiding Miss O'Ryan." She pressed her hands together at her chest to plead or pray. "Please, do not mention snow. She read about the Donner Party and has a frightful imagination. And no mention of Indians. There was a horrid attack on the wagon train." Pressing her fingers over her lips, she finally spoke. "Miss, ah O'Ryan was only a few feet away from a man that was parted from his scalp. She is easily vexed with fright."

"Far be it from me to provoke her sensibilities," he said lightly, looking down at her. The shadows from a dying campfire danced off her pure skin and light copper ringlets framed her face. "And for you, miss?" He fought the smile rising. "What manners would you like me to keep?" As soon as it left his mouth, he heard the words sounding unsuitable. Another stumble in his weakness with women.

"I...I..." her shoulder curled up, "am here just to make sure she is settled and safe."

"Then, I will see you two at dawn?" He stepped backward waiting for her answer. Their eyes seemed to lock as he pulled further back. He was waiting for her agreement, but she looked to be watching him, a root caught the back of his heel, and he turned quickly to find his footing.

Awkward and fumbling, he snorted as he stalked to the bunkhouse. Both displays he hated about himself with a vengeance.

Five

SOMETHING JOSTLED CASSIDY in the dark. Where was she? What was that noise? Was someone tapping on the wagon?

A strange line of light shone in from the foot of her bed. Oh lolly, they were in a room at the Damonte Station. She sat up quickly and pulled her blanket around her shoulders. It was dark. He said first light. Her heartbeat was erratic as she rose up and opened the door.

"Miss." The woman who'd brought them a tray was dressed as she was yesterday. She held a lantern, and there was some light coming up the stairs from the kitchen. "The gentleman downstairs is waiting. He asked me to make sure you're awake and ready to depart shortly."

Cassidy could smell coffee. "Back east," her voice sounded like the sandy desert, "We call it morning when the sun comes up."

"The sky is dark with rain, miss. Your driver sounds anxious to leave. What should I tell him?"

Cassidy blinked tired eyes and looked back to Finny, snoring lightly. "Tell him we will be along shortly."

TRUITT SCRAPED HIS fork along the last drip of runny eggs and potatoes. If this wasn't his second helping satisfying a now full belly, he might be provoked to snatch some red hair right off some eastern ladies' heads. When he rose, his wooden chair grated loudly along the long kitchen floor. Enough was enough. He'd sent the cook up once and the maid up twice and wasn't going to be told again they would be down shortly. Rubbing his hand against his holster, he wondered if they would move at gunpoint. Releasing his hand from his gun, he saw the full skirts first as they sauntered down the stairs.

It was the beauty, Miss Finnegan, who caught his eye before she glanced away. "Miss." He stepped closer, seeing the long case from their first meeting strapped over her shoulder. "I have been waiting over an hour. Was I not clear enough?"

Abruptly Miss O'Ryan cut in front of Miss Finnegan. "And after you spoke so highly of him, he seems a bit temperamental."

Miss Finnegan covered her face with her hand and looked to the ground.

"I haven't had the pleasure of your introduction, Mr. Emerson," Miss O'Ryan said.

Truitt met Miss O'Ryan's narrow face and steely gaze feeling his chest tighten as it did before a fight. "I'm Truitt Emerson. I work for Arnold Snider. I have waited over a week longer than expected and now you keep me waiting this very morning."

"I am his fiancée, Miss O'Ryan," the woman smirked. "If you feel your duties will be questioned, I assure you after I explain the dreadfulness of our last week and the terrible weather of today, Mr. Snider will understand." She turned toward the kitchen. "After we have eaten, we can see about this rain and…"

"Oh-ho, no." He turned to a basket on the table and grabbed a biscuit. Stepping back to Sniders's irritating fiancée, he grabbed her hand and slapped the biscuit into it and repeated his actions with the lady's companion, Miss Finnegan, who still didn't look at him. He stepped back. "Get your coats and move. Now!"

Freezing cold rain ran down his neck and back before Truitt slapped his hat on and threaded his arms in his thick oiled duster. Helping them into the end of the wagon, Miss O'Ryan popped her parasol, and the rain pelted Miss Finnegan's once tidy hair concoction. He shook the water off the canvas then lobbed it over their heads. Now an escort, nursemaid, and nanny he grumbled to himself. "A little cold water never hurt anyone," he muttered and stepped up to the wet bench. He harumphed and tapped the mare forward. If the snippy, interfering Miss O'Ryan questioned him again, it was time to tell an appalling tale of the Donner Party. Maybe something about how her being too thin to eat, or once she was frozen in a block of snow. These musings and imaginings entertained him as their wagon rolled toward Hangtown.

CLUTCHING HER VIOLIN case across her chest, Cassidy felt the paper envelope with the money for her dowry tucked in her bodice. She'd heard the women on the wagon trail kept their valuables in "safekeeping" when they didn't trust their surroundings. Without Mr. Dingle or Mr. Coffey, it felt safer to have the money tucked in her unmentionables. *Another peculiar day on the long trip to California,* she mused. Cassidy shivered against the damp cold. "Who told us about the warm sun of California?"

Finny propped the parasol next to her box seat to hold the canvas in place. She curled in a ball, tucking her skirts close, "Some liar, no doubt."

"It was Silas Amble. He said the grand Oregon territory was known for the fertile ground. So much rain, he'd said. And California was known for the sunshine." Cassidy shook her head.

"Mr. Amble also said if I married him, I'd be in want for nothing. Another lie. A sodbusters wife I would have ended up. Excuse me. A wet sodbusters wife I would have ended up," Finny sneered. "Use that violin case to stand the canvas up behind you. The water is gathering around our feet."

"Heaven's no," Cassidy countered. "This case can't get wet or damp."

Finny rolled her eyes. "I hope you won't be sorely disappointed, Cassidy. The wagon train folks were desperate for any reprieve from the elements. They loved your tunes and ballads of Ireland. How some of those women kicked up their heels after walking all day was beyond me." She let out a cold huff and kept her voice low. "Besides, my maid, what will you do if no one allows you to play and sing?"

Cassidy knew not to take her doomsday bait. "I'll travel on to San Francisco. There is a group there called the Pacific Minstrels." They both rocked to the side with the rough pothole in the road. "I read about them, men *and* women performers traveling to theaters and halls."

"More like a gypsy caravan, sounds like to me." Finny scoffed. "Cassidy Kathleen, what would your father say?"

"I left his say when we left Boston." She squeezed her gloved hands together. "My stepmother would never agree to come west. Or allow my father to be gone for over a year. I doubt we will ever meet again." Cassidy laid her cheek against her violin case.

"How will you help me write letters if you are in San Francisco? You know my grammar is poor, and my script is worse," Finny growled. Before Cassidy could reassure her about the letter writing, she said, "Oh, blimey, I'm freezing to the bone." She raced her hands up and down her arms and glared at the big man's back, "He's probably got a tin of hot coals at his feet." She blew into her gloved hands. Cassidy sighed and her shoulders dropped.

"Cassidy, I understand your plight." Finny brushed the last biscuit crumbs from her dress. "Your father was a harsh man who forced you into…something that you didn't want. Though many women would be thankful for it."

Cassidy groaned. Finny reached out and squeezed her knee. "Let me finish. But what about Mr. Calhoun or Mr. Spencer? Both of them were attractive, mannerly, and had fine prospects for the future."

"I had to see this through to California," Cassidy cut in.

"And both those men would have come for you if you'd given them the time of day. Won't you be seein' the possibilites? Yourself's own choice, not your father's, wasn't it?"

Cassidy let her head slide further down on her case." I don't know what's wrong with me. "I've always felt different."

"Your grandmother's at fault, after fillin' your colleen head with choices. Feelin' sorry after your mother passed. Keepin' you in Ireland too long. Aye," Finny's own Irish brogue thickened, and she shook her head. "What woman gets to run free? You doin' those jigs in your grandfather's pub. A grandmother fixin' the problem but did you no favors, did she?" Finny pulled up on the canvas, revealing the heavy rain, dark and gray at midday. "If we were walkin, we wouldn't be frozen. Maybe this road is taking us straight to Oregon." They both peeked further out. "Aye, them trees." Finny looked up. "Almost as thick as your man, your lumberjack's arms."

Cassidy glanced away, allowing Finny's snide words to pass without responding. The wagon rocked hard again, and she had to steady herself. She'd whitewashed Finny's sour humor and matchmaking thus far. She could endure a few more days.

<hr>

WINDING UP FARTHER into the Sierras, Truitt closely watched the cracks and waterfalls run off the muddy mountainside. Like spooked snakes, the water hurried across the road and down the steep cliff on his left. He kept the mare steadied to avoid the damage from the fresh deep cuts in the road. He'd studied this terrain on his way here — likely a forest fire from the last time he'd seen smoke from the mountains. Most of the brush seemed sparse, allowing the water to find no place to rest. Various sized rocks tumbled down with the cascading water. He gripped the reins and led the mare steady on.

"Mr. Emerson?"

Truitt looked back to see Miss Finnegan peeking out from the canvas.

"Yes, miss."

"Being that you gave us little time for morning ministrations," she said gently. "We will need a place to stop."

"Not here." He watched the road and gripped the reins tighter. It hadn't even been half a day's ride, and they were making demands.

"Tell him to stop or produce a chamber pot." He could hear Miss O'Ryan's ill-tempered voice. "He's to do as Mr. Arnold's fiancée requests."

Truitt squinted, trying to hear. What did the companion just tell her? Stop being a tart? He had to smile. The thin one was an ill-mannered handful, but the buxom beauty sparred back reasonably well.

He glanced at the blue-black sky before he spied another slosh of rainwater and mud flying off the ridge to his right. The sooner they could get past this crumbling ravine, the better.

Six

THIRTY MINUTES LATER, Cassidy unexpectedly jumped alert.

"Mr. Emerson!" Finny yelled, rocking toward the back of his seat as Cassidy tried to balance the tarp over her head.

"If you do not stop this instant, I will leap from this wagon and tell Mr. Arnold you are the direct cause of my broken leg!"

Truitt pulled the reins back, and the ladies gripped the wagon to keep from rocking clear off their seats.

"Thank you." Finny snapped. "Cassidy, we can't hold the parasol and canvas. Just hold the parasol while we find a tree." Cassidy came out from her protected canvas and noticed that Mr. Emerson had lowered the back gate. The cold rain pelted her head, and she regretted that she'd never donned the wide-brimmed prairie hats like the other women. Thankfully, her lovely, colorful feathered hats were safe inside her trunks. Holding his hand out, he watched the side of the cliff, never making eye contact. Cassidy and Mr. Emerson helped Finny step down. "We have a problem," Cassidy whispered. "That way up is too steep and rocky to find a tree. That way is straight down." Both women looked left to right off the sides of the road wondering what should be done.

"Hurry up, ladies. I didn't want to stop here. Please make haste."

Finny pranced around the wagon, holding the parasol while Cassidy felt the cold rain penetrate her cape, which was now attached to her dress like glue.

"Sir," Finny marched forward. "You are to keep your eyes from whence we've come." Cassidy followed her up the road. Trying to dance over the deep rivulets of rain and mud was of no use. The cold, squishy water seeped into her boots.

"Finny," Cassidy huffed. Finny marched on like a man going to war.

"I'd like a curve in the road, Cassidy. Maybe a twig of privacy."

"I'm getting soaked to the bone, Finny, please." One of the streams of rainwater tumbled down off the steep ravine, raining rock and debris around them.

"This is good." Cassidy entreated. "Up there, no one can see you. Please stop."

TRUITT GROWLED AND clamped down his hat tighter. Hangtown and the foothills had fairly peaceable weather, but he'd grown up all his days around ice and snow. He could smell it coming like a man could smell coffee. Rain and sleet now pounded his hat and shoulders. Maybe they should have waited a few more days. Was his demanding rush impetuous past his own good sense? Did he take his impatience out on these two? Likely so.

Truitt glanced up the road even though he'd said he wouldn't. They were taking too long and were nowhere to be seen. A large mudslide of water and rocks cut into the mountain behind him, alerting his senses. These ridges were too unstable. They had to keep moving. Before he could step up to the wagon seat, another large river of rocks toppled into the road. The mare started to rear back, and Truitt stepped quickly to the front and took her by the bridle.

"Whoa now, walk with me. You can step over this." He calmly pulled her forward as the wagon dipped side to side to cross the mess of mountain rock and debris. Something tumbled from the side of the wagon and landed with a splat on the left. Truitt recognized it as the long case Miss Finnegan clutched everywhere she went. Dropping the reins onto the bench, he stepped back and reached for it. Just as he was going to lift the canvas and toss it under, he heard something rumble low and potent. Was it thunder? Before his eyes could register the location of the sound, the side of the cliff vibrated and began to break apart. The women were coming toward the wagon, and both froze wide-eyed.

"Run!" He yelled, pointing his finger down the road, speeding toward them. Before they could pull up their skirts, he had Miss O'Ryan by the arm and was jerking her forward, dragging her with him. The ground rumbled and water and rocks poured onto their heads as they sprinted. Realizing he'd left the other woman, he turned to see her fast on their heels. Seeing a clearing, he stopped so suddenly that both women slammed into him. Dripping in wet grime, they all huddled close and looked around. The road was gone, the wagon was gone.

Feeling deaf and mute, he stepped back from their squeals and clutching hands. Winded and shocked, he tried to assess the situation. The smashed parasol and the case he'd dropped when he'd intercepted the women were laying at the edge of a wall of rock and dirt. Looking up where rock and rain waterfalls had been only seconds before, he saw vast damage. His chest constricted. A mudslide of boulders and sludge had changed the landscape. Instead of a cliff-faced ravine, there was only empty space and a steeply sloping mountainside.

"Please, sir, find a way to take us from here," Miss Finnegan cried and stepped to pick up the case and parasol.

Truitt stood frozen, covered in disbelief and wrath. The wagon was gone, pushed like a baby buggy over the side of the mountain. He went to the edge and peered over. He quickly stepped back as the ground broke away under his feet, but not before his gut dropped. The lovely mare lay buried in a mountain of rock. No movement, there was no way she could have lived. He leaned over the side again, still unable to comprehend what had just happened.

"Please, sir, don't leave us," One of them choked out.

Truitt finally looked back. The women stood where he'd left them, huddling against the sleet and rain. Grime covered their faces and fine capes. Miss O'Ryan's bent, useless parasol hung over their heads in an absurd attempt to avoid the rain. The other one, Miss Finnegan, clutched the only possession they'd left. He looked over the side again. Their food, their provisions were all buried under ten feet of rock. It would take weeks for one man to dig it out.

Common sense couldn't register in him at this moment as he walked back to the women. Icy rain dribbled off his hat.

"We must walk and get out of this ravine." He stomped past them. Thankfully their shock was as deep as his, and with only a few gulps and hiccups, all he heard was their steps following his.

After what seemed like hours, Miss Finnegan spoke through chattering teeth. "Sir, do you suppose others using this road will find us in our distress?"

"I can't say, miss." Without looking, he knew they were wet, bruised, and freezing. And it was his fault. He'd been impatient to be gone and he'd ignored the snow smell in the air. He knew it would be bad but he'd wanted nothing more but to get moving after kicking his heels, waiting all those days on these women to finally arrive.

He purposely walked ahead of them to avoid their questions. He needed to think. They would need some dry warmth soon, or they would all go the way of that beautiful mare. He knew some of the Indian trails up and through these woods. A village lay up around the path to the east but all further up and likely blanketed in snow.

"Are either of you hurt?" He glanced over his shoulder as they trailed behind him, Miss Finnegan clutched her case, long-soaked hair lying flat against her shoulders and face. The rain had washed most of the mud from their hair and clothes, but it had also washed away needed body heat leaving them shivering and chattering. He could see her pale, breathless shock lingered as well.

"So kind of you to ask—now," Miss O'Ryan chided. "But I would like to thank you for yanking me to safety over lovely Cassidy. Your loyalty to your boss was evident. I'm worried Miss Finnegan does not see you as stalwart as she once did."

Truitt kept his anger at bay. He was doing a job, and she was the only delivery his boss cared about. Right now would be an excellent time to tell her how long it takes red hair to grow back after a good scalping. Women! Why did God have to curse him with the care of these eastern-bred women?

They'd safely wound past the steep sides of the mountain and found the terrain leveling out. Truitt felt his mind scrambling. Even if it didn't snow, the women wouldn't survive without fire and shelter. Could they keep up with him if he diverted from the trail? What kind of fuel could he use that wasn't soaked in the rain? He glanced over at the woman who clutched her long case. Was there something they could burn in her personal belongings? He counted what he had; a gun, knife, flint, and the Russian Bible his mother had given him as a boy.

He stopped and turned to them. "I know of no shelters along this road. I think it best we position ourselves in the woods. I can build a shelter from branches and try to make a fire." He looked down at them.

Miss Finnegan was shaking so hard her chin shivered up and down with her agreement.

His fur-lined oil duster and warm, dry skin caused a wave of guilt wash over him. "What do you carry in that case?" he asked her. "Anything we could burn?"

Gasping, she shook her head no.

"Yes," Miss O'Ryan broke in. "There is wood in there."

"Wood?" Truitt knew his eyes revealed the shock. "That is truly to our fortune."

"How dare you, you ungrateful string bean." Miss Finnegan found her voice. Her once soft blue eyes turned cold. "No one is touching this violin or its case."

Truitt pondered the family who had said a woman in their party played a fiddle. She'd a strong attachment to the instrument for a reason.

"It's a little hard to play that thing all over San Francisco if you're dead, Cassidy." Miss O'Ryan stared her down and seeing Miss Finnegan's returned expression, he wondered if he would be breaking up their own fisticuffs. Miss Finnegan clutched it tighter, exposing a clenched jaw of regal stubbornness. So Cassidy was her given name. He'd heard it spoken a few times and it suited her. She was tender faced with a touch of starch.

"Ladies, can you both follow me off this muddy road and into the woods? I need to make a shelter."

Miss Finnegan's nose and eyes crinkled as she turned to follow him.

"Mr. Emerson," Miss O'Ryan called as she hurried after him. "Are you familiar with any Indian groups in this area? Wouldn't they be afraid of a man your size?" Her breath was puffy white against the darkness of the day.

He held his hand out and pulled her up a tall mound into the forest. It was too easy. He'd practiced his most frightening Indian tales all the way from Damonte Station. A low growl constricted his throat. This woman was Sniders fiancée, and he needed to watch his step. "None that are on the warpath, miss."

Nor any that like mouthy redheads.

Seven

HIKING FURTHER BACK off the road, a decent grove of trees circled a canopy of thick limbs. Truitt took his knife and sawed and bent the bottom branches away.

"Sir, how long do you suppose before we can go back to the rock slide and retrieve our things?" Miss O'Ryan asked.

"We?" Truitt squinted at her and kept working. "We won't be going back."

"All right, yourself now, when will you go back?"

He tossed a thick limb to the side, glaring at her. "Next spring." Annoyed at her question, he kept working until he'd carved out a decent opening for the two of them to stand under the branch covering. He wasn't going to point out the obvious. The slushy rain was turning to snow.

"Ladies, stand under here. I want to hunt around a bit. Please don't move from this tree area." They crowded in under the branches, and Miss Finnegan elbowed Miss O'Ryan.

"Mr. Emerson," Miss O'Ryan cleared her throat. "I would be remiss not to state the obvious." She sucked in a deep breath. "We are at your mercy and we want to thank you for your assistance on this dreadful occurrence. If it hadn't been my call for you to stop, I have to wonder if we'd be after dead under that cliff. Crushed an' frayed broken bones on us—"

"Fin—Kathleen, please." Miss Finnegan gave her a little bump.

"Aye, now. I'll try again." Finny pouted. "My educated companion often feels the need to correct me." Miss O'Ryan rolled her eyes. "What you may not understand is that my trunks with me are filled with my tru...tru..."

"Trousseau." Miss Finnegan jumped in. "We have dozens of dresses, hats, and shoes from some of the finest shops in Boston."

Truitt noticed her chin trembling from shock and cold. After what just happened, why would a bunch of frills cause her such an alarm?

"They've made it across these mountains, these prairies, these states. From east to west." Miss Finnegan rattled on. "Hundreds of dollars. One gown is a flawless masterpiece from Paris."

Truitt shifted his weight to another foot, trying to look interested. A muddy masterpiece. He hid a grin. "Uh-huh."

Miss Finnegan waited and looked resigned at Miss O'Ryan. "We've said all we can say." She shivered with cold. "If only Mr. Dingle would have lived."

"God rest his soul," Miss O'Ryan huffed and tapped her forehead, chest, and each shoulder. "We've lost him, and after seeing our trunks this far west, we've lost them down a blimey, muddy ravine."

Truitt pulled off his hat and shook the light powder off. His boss's fiancée was a tart, whereas the lady's companion often sounded more proper. Confusing. These two were more bother than a miner without a shovel. Usually, he enjoyed how the forest quieted with the first white, soft, brush of snow — not today. They were the weaker sex, he reminded himself and couldn't be left for long. Without movement, the cold would overtake them. "Just give me a few minutes. Please, don't move."

He picked up the pace and searched the area. Some large granite rocks loomed ahead. He jogged around them until he stopped and looked closer at the sweet salvation. Two large pieces had collided at creation, forming a small cave large enough for them to use for the night. He squatted down and peered inside. No bears or varmints, dry dirt, and pine needles. Perfect.

Gathering his female charges and the large branches he'd cut with his knife, he led them around his trail and back to the small cave opening. He noticed Miss Finnegan had pushed her strapped violin case to her back and held her arms around Miss O'Ryan, securing her to her side as they walked.

"Here." Standing in front of the opening, he slid off his warm oil duster and handed it out to Arnold Snider's fiancée. She nodded in silence, and Miss Finnegan helped her out of her wet cape and threaded her arms through his coat. It hung like a bear hide over a skinny rabbit. Glancing at Miss Cassidy Finnegan, he gave her a small assuring smile. "I'll have a fire to warm you in a shake." He held his hand to steady the ladies as they ducked inside the small opening. Kneeling, he saw them seated and crawled forward himself, avoiding the low ceiling of granite.

"Won't this be quite the c...cocoon?" Miss O'Ryan said, teeth chattering. After straightening the coat and wet dress layers, she leaned back against the rock wall. Truitt sat, his feet to knees extended out into the dusting of snow.

"The branches will be our door tonight." He took out his knife and began to dig a hole in the dirt. "Even the smallest flame can warm us." He grinned at Miss Finnegan, gripping her knees. She looked like Lot's wife must have looked. Instead of turning into a pillar of salt, she was a frozen block of ice.

Her pure and trusting eyes watched him. He doubted there was a wicked bone in her body. He smiled at her. "Here, miss, remove that soaked cape." He stopped digging and pulled his flannel hunting shirt from his body. Trembling, she released her case and pushed the cape from her shoulders. Reaching for the shirt, she wrapped it around her. He helped her pull out her long strands of nutmeg hair and tried to squeeze the water out.

Her eyes widened on his chest and shoulders covered only by his linen short sleeve undershirt. Dare he tell her not to dismay; he was not cold? These were going to be incredibly tight quarters. Waiting for Miss O'Ryan to say something rude about his undressed state, he glanced back behind Miss Finnegan. The thin woman was completely balled up and wrapped in his coat. Lying on her side, not a hair or muddy shoe heel showing.

"Are you alive in there, Miss O'Ryan?" he asked, returning his attention to digging out a hole for the fire.

"Aye, sir," she said, muffled under her coverings. "Far from dead and frozen, no need to be eaten."

Miss Finnegan groaned and pulled his shirt collar over her face.

He suppressed a laugh. At least she'd warned him. Truitt gathered the dry pine needles and pulled his flint from his pocket. He tried to keep his eyes down and focused on making a fire, but he couldn't help notice Miss Finnegan reach her hands inside her skirts and give a pull. Surprised at her cleverness, he watched her produce a wad of thin white cotton trim. After four or five strikes with his knife, a spark landed in the hole holding the fabric threads and pine needles. He could feel the muscles in his back relax for the first time in hours. Miss Finnegan removed her gloves and leaned forward. Holding her fingers toward the small flame, he noticed they were slender and elegant. Something about the young woman wrapped in his shirt sent an unexpected inner warmth through his being. Quickly, he added more bark and pine needles. His little fire swirled with smoke, but he didn't care, it was warmth. Meeting the grateful eyes of Cassidy Finnegan, he smiled and above the glow of the flames, she smiled back.

"I see your purple and yellow fingers there." She nodded at his hand. "An accident?"

He frowned. "No, just a fight a few weeks ago." His eyes lingered too long, he could see the color coming back into her cheeks and she had the lightest splatter of freckles on her nose.

Covering her nose, she looked down. "Are there many fights in Hangtown?"

"Yes, many." He held his fingers over the small flame. "Mr. Snider hosts a fight every Friday night at the El Dorado. Something I've done for a year or so. Simple entertainment for the miners."

"So you are a boxer? That is what you do for Mr. Snider?"

He swallowed and tipped his head to the side, avoiding her gaze. "Yes, and other things."

"Ah, yes, an escort," her pretty blue eyes crinkled.

He scratched his chin stubble. "And other things." He dropped a few more dry pine needles in the hole. "And what of you? How long is your employment to be as a companion?"

"I hadn't really thought of it." She scooted back, gripping his shirt around her and sat cross-legged. I suppose until Miss Kathleen is married and settled."

Something strange flipped in his gut. They were a lot alike — both working for Arnold Snider. The fact she was not the fiancée brought him personal pleasure for some odd reason. "She seems a bit full of spunk." He glanced over, nodding to the woman wrapped securely in his coat.

Timidly, Miss Finnegan leaned close to his ear. Unsure and self-conscious, he fought to hold still. "Do you think perchance he will put up with her…her shrewish nature?" she whispered.

Her soft breath so close, he pulled back and tried to remember the question. "I can't say." He dropped a few more pine needles in the small fire pit. "If they don't take to one another, you've come a long way for nothing." His smile tipped upward when their eyes remained on each other. Turning away for some distraction, he cleared the tightness in his throat.

"Please, sir, take your shirt back. You looked chilled now." She swung it over her side and handed it to him.

"Better for your own things to begin to dry," he said as he glanced over her situation. Her hem was soaked, and the cape might take days to dry. He threaded his arms into the damp shirt and buttoned it up, never looking to see if she watched him or not. An awkward air filled the tiny space and he glanced out to see the snow was getting thicker with the setting of the sun.

"We were impolite to keep you waiting so long at Damonte Station," she sighed. "You've got a family, children waiting for your return?"

A strange sound came from the thin ball wrapped up in his coat. Was Miss O'Ryan choking? "Well played, Cassidy." A crackled voice and snickering escaped from inside his heavy coat.

Miss Cassidy Finnegan turned bright red and twisted to grab her violin case. Leaning back to rest against the rough rock wall, she gripped it tight like she had the first time he saw her. There was so little space for her eyes to land, and her embarrassment was evident.

Truitt rolled his tongue under and over the inside of his cheek. He did not want to laugh or add his humor to her pain. Miss O'Ryan had a bristly wit. He scratched his neck and answered. "No, miss, neither married nor a father."

Eight

CASSIDY SWALLOWED THE ache in her throat. She would not cry. She was tired, frozen, wet, dirty, hungry, and now humiliated. What kind of friend chides her one moment about not entertaining a man's interest and then teases her when she asks a question of a personal nature?

Finny Kathleen Finnegan O'Ryan, that's who, the pretender of ladylike quality and likely full of civility and friendship pretense as well. But who was the one who agreed to forgo her life of wealth and status, freely giving it to a housemaid who was used to housework and laundry duties? The original Kathleen Cassidy O'Ryan did. Regrets ran like icy water inside her cold limbs. She searched her cape pocket. Her hankie was gone. *Oh, lolly, I was just trying to be polite. That's all. He asked me about being a lady's companion. That was a personal question, too.*

Cassidy gripped her case tighter, holding her knuckle to her dripping nose. Trying not to be miserable, she chided herself. *I've seen cholera run through the wagon train. I've lived on the bones of bison and birds; seen a stampede and Indian attack with my own eyes — vultures that circled above us waiting to prey on our weakness. I can do this and—*

"Tell me more about this violin you keep close?" Mr. Emerson's question waved her back into the moment.

"I…my grandmother gave it to me. It's been in her family for over fifty years." Thankfully her voice sounded steadier than she felt.

"And you play yourself?" He had sincerity in his eyes, and she loosened her grip on the case.

"Faster and finer than most have ever heard." Finny chimed in from her thick coverings.

Mr. Emerson made a curious grin and shook his head. "I've never seen a woman play an instrument."

"And she sings like a nightingale," Finny added through her warm layers.

Cassidy looked away and shook her head, still shivering but beginning to warm. "I don't know about that."

"Sing for us, Cassidy." Finny finally pulled the coat edge down. Her hair tousled over her face. "Keep our stomachs from rattling aloud."

"No," she countered.

Finny yawned and pulled the coat back over her head.

"You played this violin in Boston? For your family, your grandmother?" he asked.

"Mostly in Ireland," she said shyly. "I lost my mother when I was four and stayed with my grandparents outside of Kilkee. They had a pub in town where people gathered, and the music flowed most evenings. I suppose I grew up around the tunes and my grandparents never scolded me for the instrument I loved."

"And you..." he leaned on his elbow, giving her a warm brown gaze, "want to play and sing in San Francisco?" He dropped a small stick in the hole.

Feeling another wave of embarrassment, she nodded and shrugged. "I do. I'd read that the new state of California is more broadminded, more accepting than back east."

Mr. Emerson rolled his head from side to side, and she wondered what he was thinking.

"I suppose one could say progressive." He snapped a few more twigs in half with his free hand, adding them to the fire. "The mining towns of Hangtown, Coloma, Sutter's Fort, and such are bursting with people from all over the world. The sailors in San Francisco abandoned their positions. Their ships sit empty in the bay. It's a sight to see them float abandoned. The sailors only have gold on their minds, but I suppose, like my boxing, they all want some entertainment."

Entertainer wasn't an acceptable position for a woman, as Cassidy was well aware. Her father was in the shipping business with her cousin by marriage, Mr. Arnold Snider. Did he know the ships and cargo were not moving? She blew out a breath. "I read that in San Francisco there are groups of musicians that travel. Theaters and halls I would imagine. Have you heard of the Pacific Minstrels?"

"No. No, miss." He seemed to want to say more, possibly holding his thoughts back. "What I can tell you is, it is no place for a woman like yourself. The women who travel in those groups are different than you." He spied around their small shadowy cave. "There's not going to be enough to burn into the night to keep us warm. The ground is saturated with water. I can go dig around. I need to find something to burn."

Cassidy gripped her case.

"I can only apologize for the torrent of water and rock that took our provisions and killed Mr. Snider's horse. But if you want to make it to Hangtown, we may need to burn what we have."

Cassidy felt her eyes widen. "How is it that everything else was swept away but my violin?"

"While leading the horse across some large rocks, it fell from the wagon. I picked it up right before the mountain gave way."

How could she judge him corrupt and uncaring for that? Fate would have her most precious possession buried and gone.

"I'll be back in a moment. He pulled his gun from the holster. "If a bear or anything we can eat comes sniffing around, shoot it." He held it out. Cassidy locked apprehensive eyes on his. "I've never held a gun, sir."

"Can you bend your fingers?" He pulled her hands out from the folds of her damp skirt layers, shocked at how stiff they felt. "Barely, I see." He took her hand, rubbed it warm in his, and placed it around the gun. "Put your finger here. Careful now. When you pull your finger back, it will go off."

"Can you just set it down, for now?" She felt the cold ripple anew over her body. "I'll pray you return quickly." She smiled and felt the loss of his warm hand on hers. He climbed out and replaced the branches over the opening. Cassidy peered into the little fire hole and rubbed her fingers together across the heat. Looking back at her case, she said a prayer for dry provisions.

Cassidy must have dozed for a minute. Something startled her and before she could reach for the gun, she saw the large body of Mr. Emerson, crouched down, coming through the branches. Looking down at the little hole, she gasped. "Oh no, oh, lolly. I let the fire go out!"

"It's all right." He dropped a small bundle of bark and reached his hand out to calm her. "I can build it again."

Her eyes narrowed on the small pile they had for fuel and then looked long at the white falling snow against the evening gray night. A new shiver ran up and down her spine. That meager pile would be gone within the hour. The realization set deep remorse and regret over her being. Burning the case and possibly the violin would keep them alive. Coatless, Mr. Emerson shook from the cold and began to strike his flint to the new fuel.

"My grandmother may forgive me for my folly, but my father never will," she mumbled. "God has cursed me as I deserve."

As the fire crackled anew, Mr. Emerson sat back, resting his arms on his skyward knee. "Why would you be cursed, miss?"

"I've been a restless youth, selfish in my desires to play my violin, and I...I... rebuffed the suiters he wanted me to marry."

"I'm sure many a daughter would like to have a say." He glanced up at her; some white snow still hung on his sleeve. "God does not curse one for that." He waited, wanting to hear more. "None of them to your liking?"

Feeling like her body was lulling her back asleep, or was this all a dream? She sighed, wondering if God could have forbearance for her? Knowing that not agreeing on a suiter was the least of her sins, she finally answered. "No. None would accept a woman who was also a musician." It was only a partial truth. That is what she assumed was true. She didn't know if the men or her father ever cared to know the real Cassidy.

"I see." His tone held such gentle understanding and it brought unwanted pools to her eyes. Ridiculously leaving her identity behind, what a fool to think she could find acceptance and carve out something for herself out west. "Sir," she pulled the case onto her lap and raised it up. "The case is wood." A blasted tear ran down the side of her cheek. "There is fabric over it, but underneath is wood. You may burn it and my violin."

Alarm sliced his handsome features. "Miss Cassidy—I, I mean Miss Finnegan…"

"Please." Her upturned face was streaked with her tears. She pushed the long case into his hands. "Call me Cassidy. I would dearly approve of that. Finnegan just reminds me of my callous decisions. Do women and men use first names without faulting propriety in California?"

"Umm." Setting the case aside, he rubbed his jaw with his bruised hand. "In the working class they do."

"As now, I work as a companion." She swiped her dripping nose and cheek. "That's all." Her foolishness had cost her enough. "I *am* working class," she said with conviction watching his strong, determined features twist a frown. "What?" She squinted.

"The working-class women in Hangtown work in the laundry or on their backs or sometimes both." He drew his thumb across his chin.

"How does one do laundry on their back?"

He pinched his lips closed over his snickers. "No, you misunderstood me. Hangtown has gals that work at the laundry. So Chen is the owner, she is a woman. And the other group of working ladies work at the brothels or saloons. Some just dance. Most are prostitutes."

He paused long enough for Cassidy to connect the reference.

"Oh." She pulled at her collar, face flushing.

"But I would be honored to call you Cassidy, and Miss Finnegan around others."

"Fair enough." Cassidy knew every town had painted ladies, she just never in her lifetime had ever entered into a conversation about them. Mr. Emerson possessed such frankness about it. Did he frequent those hotels? The thought gripped her belly and she gathered her legs up and wrapped her damp skirts tight around them. Oh lolly, he was strong as an oak tree and handsome in a rugged unkempt way. As a fighter, surely he'd the esteem of many working women.

Chewing on her bottom lip, she tried to avoid pining after her violin case leaning against the rock wall. Their cave was dark, except the small flickering firelight, and staring at it only made her eyes heavy. Would he dismantle it while she slept?

Nine

CASSIDY SAW A thick steel knife skillfully carve into her upper arm. Awakening, she opened her mouth to scream and jerked up. Her left arm was pinned against the jagged rock wall and her head. She rubbed it up and down and the pain subsided. Glancing up, Mr. Emerson's stoic eyes watched her before he looked away. It mattered not how long she'd slept, the case was gone, and a stack of small splintered wood was all that was left of her beloved violin. Her head swam in dizzy emotion, a flash of her grandmother's smile as she'd tapped her elbow to keep her bowing arm up. The gray-haired folk around the wagon train campfires, clapping and singing along; old man Rodney loved tapping those spoons as she played. Mothers and fathers danced in circles with their children, laughter erasing the harsh conditions; people thanking her for moments of merriment. Her tears and ache overcame her before she could find control. Deep sobs spurt and groaned unquenched, and her hand couldn't dam them as she tried to cover her mouth.

"Here, here, Miss Cassidy."

With only inches to spare, Mr. Emerson found a space next to her and wrapped his thick arms around her. The comfort was immediate. How could she blame this man? He was trying to keep them alive. Her eyes started to drift toward the small fire-hole, and she pressed them closed and buried her face into his chest. Even with Mr. Dingle's death, never such a hopeless display had she demonstrated thus far. But something about the way he stroked her hair and held her tight made her cries acceptable. Months of weary weight tore out of her body. Oh, lolly, she was feeble against it.

Knowing her spectacle of womanly sentiment must be making him uncomfortable, she covered her face with her sleeve, sat up, and gripped her knees. Though she tried to control her cries and move from him, his arm remained fixed on her back, his hand lightly caressing back and forth.

"Stay here." The warmth from his hand and kindness in his voice was sincere. "Just go back to sleep, we have a long walk tomorrow." His face and words were only a breath away. "And you keep me warm." He whispered hoarsely. She dropped her chin and felt an unusual warmth herself.

Pulling into a tight ball, she settled into the cove of his large frame. He smelled like pine needles and campfire, and she carefully pulled one of her hands free and rested it on his shirt. Something sagged in his pocket.

"What is this?" She drew her hand over his pocket.

Truitt pulled a small narrow book out. "It's a Bible my mother gave me. He laid it on his thigh. "I've been tearing pages out of it for the fire."

Cassidy jerked away from his chest. "Say no."

He stiffened, and they both quickly looked away, they were so close, only a whisper of air between them.

"You have sacrificed your greatest passion. I will share in that misfortune." His hand slipped away from her back, leaving only their shoulders touching. "And before you find words to commend me, half of it was in Russian. I only burnt that half. I can't read it."

"You can't read?" She whispered.

"No, I can read." He squinted at her.

Weakened by their conditions, she didn't want to take her eyes from his impressive brown hues, so she didn't.

"But not Russian. I can't read Russian."

"Oh." She grinned. "Is your home, your mother, in Hangtown?"

"No. She and my two younger sisters remained in Russia. She has a large family there. My father was American. He'd mined the icy rivers way up north. He said he was tired of the long winters so he and I came south to stake a claim. We were to work the mines until we had enough to send for them."

Cassidy waited, the distance between them closed to nothing in these last minutes. Would it be trustworthy to tell each other their inner secrets? Could she trust him?

"And I still plan to do that." He brought his knee up and wrapped his arm around it. "My father was a tough man. He used to say my mother was a wonderful woman but impossible to live with." Mr. Emerson huffed a regretful chuckle. "He thought that was funny, but I often wondered if he was truly ever going to go back for her. Before I could find the truth, my father was unjustly hung by the neck. The name of the town, is justified, Hangtown." He glanced over at her. Her eyes reflected shock.

"Famous night of corruption in those parts. Hung without a proper trial or sentencing," he huffed, dropping a few pieces of wood in the hole.

Pulling her hand down her chin, she gripped it around her throat, Cassidy heard his words, while watching the flames burn her precious family heirloom.

"There were three of them that got into a brawl outside the tavern," he began. "My father certainly spent too much time there. That was nothing unusual. But then someone said my father and the other two planned to follow the man with the most money and gold winnings that night after he left. Said they would beat him and rob him. Of course, I wanted to believe he would never do that. But witnesses said he was part of it. Then someone piped in that these same men were all wanted for murder and robbery somewhere else, which was a complete lie." He sighed, shaking his head. "Within thirty minutes, before I'd even gotten a word about the incident, he was hung from the tree in Elstner's Hay Yard." He stopped cold. "That morning I ate hot oats with him in the shanty, before midnight he was six feet under."

Cassidy gripped her hand over her mouth. This is the town she would be going to? "Dear Lord, how shocking. I'm so sorry, Mr. Emerson." She shook her head and whispered. "Aye, I pray a glorious reunion for your father in the heavens."

"You can imagine it didn't sit well with me. It still doesn't. I knew there would be no justice, so I started more fights, causing extra damage anywhere I could." He rubbed his fingers under his scruffy jaw. "I wrote my mother that there was no demand to come, no husband, no home. I guess I was vengeful and angry, sorrowful to be alone. And not interested in reading this anymore." He tapped the top of the Bible. "About then Mr. Snider asked me to come work for him. I got paid to threaten the miners who owed him money. I can knock over shanties in a couple pushes. Make them sorry they ever puffed their chests at me." He huffed, rubbing the back of his neck. "I get paid to bounce a few rash men to their backside on Friday nights. And now, because of a few broken fingers, I am an eastern lady's escort." He popped the Bible back in his pocket and shook his head.

Cassidy felt a chill, wondering how this information changed the way she saw him. "I would safely say, we have all found ourselves more desperate than we thought possible."

"Humph." He nodded once. "The work gives me enough to send money in my letters home. Lately, I've been thinking it's time I left Hangtown. It's likely the contrary of anything I want."

"How long have you been living in Hangtown?" she asked.

"We left Russia next to five years back. I wrote about my father's death, over a year ago, with no word in return from my mother."

"I'm so sorry." Knowing the loss of a parent and the disconnection of the other one, she reached out and gently touched his hand, meeting his soft brown eyes. "So much loss for you." Realizing what she was doing, she quickly pulled back her hand. "When my father insisted I leave Ireland and return to Boston, I felt lost and out of place. Boston never felt like home. Thank you for sharing your thoughts on Hangtown. I feel terrible for all that has happened to you."

He nodded, watching her. "You may hold my hand." The corner of his lips curved upward. "You were just being kind." He held his hand out to her palm up.

She met his rogue grin with one of her own and looked to his thick palm. Unable to find words for the heart-stirring he caused in this little cave, she used her finger like a quill and drew the letters on his palm. N—O.

Taking her hand in his, he opened her palm and repeated the motion with a Y—E—S.

Flattening her smile, she drew more letters, watching his eyes simmer brazenly on her, she wrote on his palm. S—L—E—E—P.

"Sheep?" he teased, squinting at her.

Cassidy smiled and brushed her hand over his like an invisible eraser. Slowly she spelled "sleep" again. Like their little fire, every part of her warmed as his palm held hers. She dared not look into his eyes, their little game heightened their bold familiarity. Oh, lolly. Hadn't she already thrown propriety to the wind leaning on his broad chest earlier *and* putting her hand on it?

He pulled back, laid on his side, and rested his head on his bent elbow and hand. His frame blocked over half of their branch door. With his finger, he pointed to the narrow space in front of him. "Your dress is still damp, and you need to be closest to the heat."

Cassidy bit her bottom lip and glanced over where Finny slept. Tucked in his warm coat, Finny O'Ryan was lulled by the safety he'd created and slept soundly. Humph. She about to have every convenience and luxury intended for Cassidy. Good, nothing stung. She'd only wanted her freedom to be her own person. The charade was still her desire.

Stomach growling with hunger, she laid down on her side, her back lightly touching his chest. Resting her head down on her bent arm, she felt his hand find her hand and open his palm onto hers. Every tingle awakened her body, and she opened it flat while he slowly traced the letters. T—H—A—N—K Y—O—U.

In the brashest thing she'd ever done, she closed her fingers around his, and they entwined finger between fingers, resembling someone's betrothed. Pressing in close to her back, he wrapped his arm around her waist and pulled her close. Reeling from the sensations his arm around her caused and staring at the small flame inches in front of her, she forced her eyes closed. It was either absorb all of this tender moment, the offering of comfort, warmth, his strength, and compassion or watch the remaining pieces of her cherished violin burn to ash.

Ten

TRUITT WOKE AT first light but neglected to move. Each night he'd fallen, exhausted, into his nice soft bed at the Bedford Hotel, but now he was well aware of the womanly comfort he'd been missing. Releasing her hand carefully, he leaned up on his elbow and watched her sleep. Her long, thick hair claimed his attention. It shimmered with copper, yet streaks of light brown feathered throughout. He touched a strand hanging off her back. He'd never seen such a color. Her waist dipped from her side. Even asleep, her perfect hourglass shape beckoned his hand a place to rest. And heat, the woman possessed exceptional warmth, fitting perfectly with his…

"Are you going to seduce her or eat her?"

Truitt jerked up so fast, he nicked his head on the cave ceiling. "Miss O'Ryan." He rubbed his fingers through his sandy brown hair. "Good morning." Heat crawled up his neck.

Cassidy rolled to her back and looked up at him, "Oh, my." Sitting up slowly, her eyes shifted back and forth, finally resting out the cave entrance. "It's not raining or snowing."

He cleared his throat. "The sooner we get moving, the better the chance we might find help from the road."

"We left the snow in Boston for snow in California." Miss O'Ryan tried to finger her hair back into a low bun. "And last week we were dying from heat and no water in the desert. Could

California be purgatory, Mr. Emerson? Tempting us to our limit as humans, seeing if we will just curse God and die?"

Truitt thought she might have a point, but since he'd no idea what purgatory was, he shrugged. "I can't say, miss."

Cassidy gathered her cape back around her shoulders, never looking at him. Miss O'Ryan did not offer him his coat back, so he pushed the branches aside and helped the women from their shelter. The cold air caught in his lungs then puffed around his head as he blew out the breath imitating the high dense clouds he observed.

Starting down the trail, the few inches of snow crunched under his boots. Within a moment, he could hear they were following. The strangest urge nudged him to turn and watch Cassidy. If Miss O'Ryan wasn't such a curt one, he'd find the woman's soft hand from his sleep and tuck it in the crook of his arm. What a strange thought, yesterday he barely tolerated both of them, but today he felt protective and benevolent. He snorted at the thought.

"Cassidy!" Miss O'Ryan's voice rang out, "Your case. We've left your violin."

He turned back as Cassidy timidly shook her head. "It's gone. It burned to keep us warm."

Miss O'Ryan put her palms up in the air. "First Mr. Dingle and now your violin." She slapped her hands on her waist. "God rest their souls." She touched her forehead, chest, and both shoulders. "Aye, tis devilment, sure. Oh, you poor, sweet ninny," she sighed, putting an arm around Cassidy.

They all seemed to respect the need for quiet and walked an hour until Miss O'Ryan broke the bliss. "Tell me more about my fiancé," she said as they stepped back on the snow-covered road.

"He is very smart and very shrewd." Truitt could see his breath in the air and prayed the clouds rolling above would hold back their moisture.

"Humm," she said behind him. "What else. What does he look like?"

"He's a bit taller than you. He likes fancy suits and shiny shoes." The women walked on his right, with linked arms.

"Does he have hair?"

Truitt looked over at her and back to the road.

She turned to Cassidy, "You said he would be about thirty. That happens sometimes." Miss O'Ryan nodded. Strange idea to pose the question to her lady's companion.

"As a matter of fact, he has little hair," Truitt said.

"Umm." She twisted her lips to the side. "That's all right. Does he prefer a bowler or a top hat?"

Truitt opened his mouth and closed it. "Bowler, I suppose."

"Made of silk?"

"I can't say, miss. You'll have to ask him yourself." He shoved his hands in his pockets wishing Cassidy Finnegan was up close to his side.

"What of this protection you spoke of? His assets need protection or his person?"

"Both."

"Why does he need a security man and protection? Is there no law in Hangtown?"

"There is no *real* law in Hangtown," he said, the familiar anger rising as he remembered the night of his father's death. "Yes, there is a sheriff and a couple of thugs. But lawlessness is rampant." He finally caught Cassidy looking his way.

Chewing on the corner of her bottom lip, she looked to her feet. Was she ashamed by their closeness last night or the knowledge of what happened to his father?

He'd no time to talk to her this morning. And what would he say? Thank you for listening to me and letting me hold you? He soured, considering they'd just met, and he knew he was terrible with women. Those words sounded weak and pitiful. She'd stated clearly she'd turned down respectable suiters to be her own person. Boxing surely was not respectable for the likes of her. Anyway, hadn't he decided it was time to leave Hangtown?

"Your size and strength are intimidating." Miss O'Ryan was back with her hundred questions. "Is the town afraid of you or Mr. Snider?"

"Both." He liked his standard answer. But that wasn't quite true. Mostly they were afraid of him. "Mr. Snider poses like…like a man at the bank. He loans the miners money to buy supplies from the store he owns and they sign a paper that if they can't pay back the loan he's entitled to their claim and all the contents. Few rarely read the paper and some can't read at all, so they sign and usually within three months—" Truitt exhaled, running his fingers along the brim of his hat. "Mr. Snider can legally take them for nonpayment. He makes five times the money on supplies and reselling the claims over and over. He's a very shrewd businessman."

"And he has a large home?"

Truitt wondered if anything he said sunk into the mind of this skinny petticoat.

"Yes, it's the biggest house in town. Sits at the top of Hangtown. Three stories with thick staircases, flocked wallpaper, moldings, and five fireplaces, from the last count. Some of the furnishings came over on your father's ships."

"And servants, I'm sure he has many servants." Finny nodded.

Truitt's jaw shifted, weary of her questions. The man was a snake. They would probably be perfect for each other. He nodded over his shoulder and looked back quickly. Did he hear a limb crack in the woods? The snow wasn't heavy enough to break branches. Resting his hand on his gun, he could only pray it was something they could skin and eat. Their steps were quieted by the snow and he spied left to right. With any luck, no two-legged animal wanted to prey on them.

"Stay close to me," he said sharply. A second later, he felt their fingers grip his shirt. His face tensed and their steps slowed as he searched between the trees. Maybe it was nothing, but he sensed someone watched them.

"What, sir, please?" Cassidy held on to him, looking all around. The crimson red of her cheeks highlighted her distress. Miss O'Ryan's eyes widened. Sucking in a breath, she opened her mouth to scream, but her eyes rolled back. She collapsed to her knees, passed out cold while reaching in vain toward Truitt.

He quickly grasped under her arms before she hit the ground full length.

Truitt gritted his teeth and swept her up into his arms to keep from dropping her into the snowy mud, then he turned toward the cause of her distress. Right before them stood three horses carrying three Indian braves.

"Cassidy," he whispered low. "Get my gun and hold it in your skirts." His waist was hidden by Miss O'Ryan's thick layers. He could feel Cassidy's hands jerk his gun from his holster. His heart drummed in his chest. He couldn't hold this woman and defend them.

Speaking to the men, he nodded down at Miss O'Ryan. "Can you help us?" He eyed the oldest man with silver in his hair. Saying something to the other two, they kicked their horses forward.

"Washoe?" Truitt asked.

The older one tipped his head.

"To town." Truitt gestured his head down the road.

They spoke amongst themselves and the youngest one with the buckskin cape jumped off his white pony and led it to where they stood. Searching the forest first, he eyed Truitt and reached out for the limp Miss O'Ryan. Truitt transferred the woman over and watched as the young man nodded to his horse. Truitt grabbed the mane and jumped, swinging his leg around. The Indian brought Miss O'Ryan against the horse, and Truitt reached down and pulled her in front of him.

Was he too trusting? Were they helping them or capturing them?

He wanted to reach back and keep Cassidy walking close to him, but the young man led her to another horse holding a shirtless, greased brave. The tip of his gun handle peeked from her pocket. He took a deep breath, tried to balance Miss O'Ryan and watch Cassidy's every move.

The bare-skinned man leaned down, offering the crook of his arm. Face stricken with fear, Cassidy looked at Truitt for assurance. Trembling, she linked arms with the stout buck and was pulled up behind him. The youngest jumped up behind the older man. The horses began to trot through the woods. He would know soon enough if his trust was well-placed. Would they turn toward Hangtown or Washoe Indian territory?

Eleven

FROM SEARCHING AND remembering all he could about these foothill trails, Truitt felt relief down into his bones. They were heading west. Praise to the Almighty, Hangtown was west. Miss O'Ryan began to squirm in his arms. Before she could release a squeal, he clapped his hand over her mouth and pulled her head back against his chest. "You're safe, miss. Make no noise."

He felt her body stiffen, shiver, then regain her composure. "They are taking us toward Hangtown." He released his hand over her mouth. "I believe I've seen the older man before. I took some supplies to a village last week while I was waiting... waiting for you ladies."

Miss O'Ryan wavered, sucking in a deep breath. "I don't feel well Mr. Emerson. My stomach is in pain, and my head is spinning like a top."

Truitt nudged the horse forward, and made a gesture to the older man for a drink. The Indian pulled a skin pouch from his horse's side. Miss O'Ryan had dug her face into his shirt as the horses trotted on. Reaching out, he took the waterskin.

"Here, drink this."

"I cannot drink from *that*." She almost retched. "What if— these men, these Indians..." she peered out from his chest, spying them. "No, no thank you."

"Suit yourself." He tipped the pouch up and took a large gulp. Pulling the horse to the left, he passed the water off to Cassidy. She followed suit and his ability to form words stuck in his mouth as he watched her drink. What was this strange urge he felt to say something chivalrous to her, something admiring? For he surely admired her plucky acceptance of terrible situations. Feeling remiss for the travel conditions leading to the loss of their wagon and belongings, he clenched his jaw. Not forgetting the burning of her violin, and the fact that she now sat behind an Indian brave, he felt she needed some words of reassurance, "We are heading the right direction. They are helping us." Sounding inadequate, he knew it wasn't enough to appease the dread in her face. Meeting her red-rimmed eyes, he wouldn't blame her if she never spoke to him again.

Sprinkles began to fall from the late afternoon sky. It was too warm for snow and as Truitt looked around, he knew this Indian trail would lead the back way into Hangtown.

Within the hour, the braves stopped and set them all on their feet. He was a tiny bit thankful for Miss O'Ryan's weakened state. It added to his advantage because she clung to him without a sour word after he'd said his thanks to the men. As they turned and rode away, the thin woman could barely look up. Her fear was so great she could not see they had helped them get this far. He spoke confidently, "Maybe only about another thirty minutes and we will arrive." He pulled away from Miss O'Ryan and noticed both women were starting to shiver. "We'll keep a good pace and you'll stay warm."

CASSIDY WRAPPED HER arms around Miss O'Ryan. "We will keep up, sir. Thank you for leading."

"And I insist you sneak us into the hotel," Miss O'Ryan finally spoke. "I don't want anyone seeing me like this."

"As I am able." Truitt moved out toward their destination. *Sir?* How easily all was forgotten of their cozy night in the cave. One woman barely deserved his protection and the other one had nestled right into his gullible, male longings. He released a long huff. With each one of her steps behind him, Cassidy was probably remembering that he'd burnt her beloved violin to ash, and now the same sweet woman he'd held in his arms called him sir. He chided himself foolhardy and trudged on.

Within the hour, they stopped and the women rested against a large tree. Truitt could see the buildings of Hangtown, and to his benefit, there was an empty road that led toward the back door of the hotel.

"This is the town?" Miss O'Ryan frowned, stepping near him. "We are in California now?" She rubbed her temple.

"We are, miss," Truitt said. "Look up and over at that far, gray line of clouds." He pointed. "There is a line of sunshine. Can you see the stream of yellow and pink?"

"Barely," she huffed.

"The sun is setting. You ladies made it to the west." The corner of his mouth turned up in a small smile. Glancing at Cassidy, she looked as stricken as Miss O'Ryan. "I know the man at the hotel; his name is Newton. He will have a fine meal in minutes for you."

Cassidy's eyes flashed on his. "Sir, we will be indisposed. Mr. Snider won't be waiting there, will he?"

Women and their propriety. Did she hear him at all? A nice meal would be had soon. "I doubt it. Come, let's find our way." He started down the small hill to the back road and turned back to see if they needed assistance.

They both stood unmoving, wide-eyed and frozen.

CASSIDY FELT THE tears rising. They had come so far. Why did this paralyzing fear make this the most challenging step she'd ever made? Finny must have felt it too. She'd locked her hand around Cassidy's.

"We are still doing as planned?" Finny's tone was as hushed and uncertain as Cassidy had ever heard.

"Yes." Cassidy's voice wavered.

"Then—then let's get on to our future." Finny's brows rose and her jaw tightened. They both stepped forward, and Cassidy heard Finny murmur. "How delightful to meet you, I'm Kathleen

O'Ryan from Boston. Please, you may call me Kathleen. Kathleen O'Ryan. From Boston."

A HEAVY SET woman with a thick German accent helped them to their room. She'd seen Truitt tip his hat to her as they took the stairs. Would she ever see him again? It had been such an unusual night, should they forget their tenderness ever happened? Could she forget? Not likely. The door opened, and the older woman explained that the owner, Mr. Snider, had a wall taken out to enlarge the room.

Though long and narrow, it was a lovely room with two beds at the opposite ends, folding dressing screens, and soft, sumptuous, inviting bedding. Three large windows faced the street with soft, white, ruffled curtains framing them.

While the maid helped Finny undress, Cassidy watched the busy street. Dusk was settling in, and people scurried by while some folk stopped to talk. Horses and clanking wagons rolled by; a man pulled a large black and white cow down the street right in front of the hotel. Thinking of what happened to Mr. Emerson's father here, she tried to restrain her judgment of these newly formed mining towns.

Her breath caught in her throat; Mr. Emerson walked across the street. His broad shoulders and back proclaimed his muscled strength. She gawked like an owl from a perch at him. A young, blonde woman in a light green dress called out to him from down the block, waving her hand. He raised his hand in return and she broke into a run then dashed into his arms. Cassidy jerked back from the window.

A strange feeling rushed through her stomach. She peered through the curtains again. Mr. Emerson lifted and cradled this young woman in his arms, her petticoats flouncing for the world to see. Clinging unashamed against his large frame, they smiled as he ushered her into the saloon. Cassidy continued to gawk for a long moment after they'd disappeared inside.

Covering her mouth, she pulled in a deep breath. Of course, he had his special women. This should be no surprise. He was tall and robust, ruggedly handsome and mostly kind. She rolled her eyes then her gaze fastened on the door of the saloon.

Working for Arnold Snider brought him all kinds of advantages. She and Finny were just business to him. That's all — just business. He had done his job, and now he was back to his life.

"Good," slipped from her pursed lips. She was ready to be clean and fed and to work on the most essential task: avoiding Cousin Arnold while he developed an attachment to Finny. Ugg, she dropped her head. Kathleen. She *must* remember to call her Kathleen.

After food and clean nightgowns were brought up, the two women snuggled in their clean beds. The sconces on the wall illuminated the reds and greens in the carpet and in the ornate picture of a fruit bowl that hung on the wall.

"You'll be happy to know that Mr. Snider invited us to breakfast," Finny said before she yawned, but Cassidy sat straight up. "But you know how I cherish my sleep. I told Mr. Newton to tell him brunch." Finny ran her fingers through her clean hair. "My, my, word does travel fast. I don't think we'd arrived but fifteen minutes before he was contacting me."

Cassidy thought to make some remark about the blonde woman who quickly knew Mr. Emerson was back in town, very *happy* to see him return. "Yes, word travels fast here." She closed her eyes to the warmth and then they shot open. "I cannot attend, even if Arnold asks. I—I suffer from bunions from all the walking. Say something about the poor health of my feet. Or a cold. I've caught the sniffles from the terrible cold trek."

"Yes, Cassidy, I will make your excuses. You are certain he will not remember you?"

"I was a child. Just returned from Ireland. He never even spoke to me."

"Sweet Mary, Mother, and Joseph, he'd better not recognize you. I've come a long way to be you."

Her curt words rolled troublesome over Cassidy. Without her beloved violin, she'd lost her spark, her desire. Settling into the warm pillows, she thought of one thing that was a bit of comfort. Remembering Mr. Emerson's hand warming hers lifted a little of her melancholy. She'd have to have ice in her veins not to notice how his mouth curled upward when he talked. Or how thick and comforting his arms were when they had surrounded her while she cried. They both must've been weary as he'd spoken about his family and she'd hung on his every word. What a strange night it had been. The familiarity, the soft white snow, the small fire, and riding behind the bear greased brave. Was any of it real?

"Servant wench." Finny snapped her fingers. "Douse the lights, please."

Cassidy flipped her lovely bedding back and walked to the lights. Giving Finny a glare that spoke loudly of her disdain, she turned her back. Finny smiled sheepishly. Cassidy blew out the lamps, and the room went dark.

"Come near," Finny whispered.

Cassidy sighed and approached Finny's bed. Her odd temperamental friend reached out and grabbed her hands. "We made it, Cassidy." She squeezed them tight. "You and I made it all the way to California. Can you scarcely believe it?"

"I suppose not." Cassidy pulled her hands loose and walked over to her side of the room.

"The devil be gone, you will rally, friend," Finny said, hopeful. "As soon as we can get our trunks and me settled. Aye, I will help you, too."

Cassidy climbed back under her warm covers, doubting Finny's intentions. The linens reminded her of her grandparent's lovely home in Ireland and she closed her eyes. A strange cold trembled up her back. Why now, after all these months of overcoming every obstacle, carrying such vision and hope with her every step, she suddenly felt confident of nothing.

Twelve

THE NEXT MORNING, Mr. Newton wrestled the large standing mirror into the corner of their room. Cassidy held it straight as Finny twisted and turned at her reflection.

"Have you ever seen such a fine piece of furniture? I can see my entire bodice and skirt." She twirled again. "Do you think this green is a good color for me?"

"Yes, with your eyes it—"

"Mr. Newton. You said he hadn't arrived yet?" Finny never listened for Cassidy's response. Eyes drooping, Cassidy breathed in a deep breath as Finny flitted from getting ready to back to the beautiful standing mirror. The fair-skinned woman could intimidate a herd of buffalo, but this morning she seemed unusually nervous and fidgety.

"It was most grand to have these gowns sent up." Finny walked past her and grabbed a teal taffeta from the chair. "Should I wear this one?" She held it to her chest and turned toward the mirror. "What about my hair? You did my bun a bit low. I don't want to look like some dowdy matron."

"Finny." Cassidy closed in on her and took the large heavy gown from her. "You look mature and refined. Now if you could just keep your bold and mischievous speech in order."

"You've never seen an actress as grand as me, Miss Finnegan." Finny pinched her cheeks, gazing at herself again. "If this production doesn't work out, we can travel town to town in your gypsy show. I will play Lola Montez and dance with my skirts flipping up while you saw away on your—" Finny stopped and blanched. "Forget it." She fingered the fabric of her fine dress. "My fiancé will be filling me with gifts all the way to the altar and beyond." She straightened herself taller, turning to face Cassidy. "That homespun blue is nice, too. The little touches of black piping give it more than the average service dress. Are you sad that I'm wearing this and you are wearing that?"

"No." Cassidy sighed. Dresses were the least of her concerns. Tricking Cousin Arnold into marrying the wrong woman seemed a bit more pressing in her worries. Maybe she should have given him a chance? Just because all the men her father introduced were old and stifling didn't mean that cousin Arnold wouldn't allow her some freedoms.

A rap on the door made Finny go wide-eyed and pale. Cassidy opened it to find Mr. Newton. "Mr. Snider is downstairs, waiting for Miss O'Ryan."

"Thank you, sir, she will be down shortly." Cassidy turned to see Finny gripping her face, turning it a bright red.

"Relax." Cassidy pealed Finny's hands away. "You'll muss your hair. Now take a deep breath. He's not the enemy or an…Indian. And you are a fine young woman from Boston. What is your name, dear?"

Finny's chest rose and fell. "I am Miss Kathleen O'Ryan from Second Street in Boston. I am mature and demure. My new gloves!" Finny's tone shot to the ceiling. "Devil may care, do you wear gloves for brunch?" Finny spun in a circle, searching.

"No, no gloves. Not for a meal. If he takes you for a stroll," Cassidy found them and put them in her new matching reticule. "Then wear them." Cassidy grabbed her shoulders, handed her the reticule and faced her at the door. "One more deep breath, it's time to meet your betrothed."

Finny swished out in the finest attire the woman had ever donned, and Cassidy could feel the air in the room settle like those spinning whirlwinds in the desert, losing their form. For a few minutes, she stood staring at the closed door.

They had spent almost every waking moment together for the last eight months, how strange the silence and sudden stillness affected her being. She had longed for her freedom and now the first moments to herself felt overly disconcerting. Chewing her bottom lip, she glanced at the array of clothing Finny had left on the floor and began to tidy the room. Why was her father so set against her returning to Ireland? It had been the only place her heart had been free.

She knew the answer. Her stepmother had only produced three more daughters to her father's disappointment. At least Cassidy was of age for marrying a suitable businessman. Cassidy dropped Finny's folded nightgown onto her bed and stopped in front of the fancy mirror. The pale blue dress was fine; she brushed her hand down the simple bodice. A sliver of sulking crept into her expression, before she remembered this was a mining town for heaven's sake, not uptown Boston.

Earlier, she'd pulled the hair around her face back with a few pins. Looking over her shoulder, the soft waves hung free down her back. She turned and spied her hair roots. She would need more olive oil to keep the lightness resonating through her copper locks. Patting the dark circles under her eyes, she sighed. No wonder so few women made it to California, it was the most daunting thing she had ever endured.

Poor Mr. Dingle. How that man had smiled and found goodness in each tedious day. His life brought a fair balance to living with Miss Finny Finnegan. Cassidy turned a circle in the room and then stood a few feet in front of the window. The sounds and sights of this new town tried to tug her closer. She shook her head and walked away.

It was catching sight of Mr. Emerson that truthfully pulled at her. Now she knew full well here was a true annoyance, trying to catch a glimpse of him at every turn instead of enjoying her new-found peace and quiet. Oh, such nonsense. She pounded her new pillow and laid it perfectly square on her bed.

A knock at the door jerked her straight up. Cupping her hand over her mouth, she looked around the room in a panic. Had Cousin Arnold already rejected Finny? Was the charade already up? The knock sounded again, mimicking the pounding of her heart.

Trying to swallow the fear in her throat, she turned the knob and peeked out, seeing Truitt Emerson filling the doorway she pulled the door open with sudden relief.

"Oh lolly. I was...was... Is something wrong?" she stammered.

"Only if me paying you a social call is wrong." The air tingled around her at his voice and the glimmer in those warm eyes. He'd shaved and wore a clean tan shirt.

"No, I meant with Fin—" she dropped her head to the side, "Miss O'Ryan."

He shook his head once. "She looked fine to me. You expecting her to run screaming?"

"No," Cassidy sighed. Social call? Did he say social call? Goodness, he looked fine.

"I just wanted to see if you needed anything. I have time to give you a tour of Hangtown." He gripped his hand against the doorframe leaning an inch closer.

"I'm not sure about a tour." The last thing she needed was to run into Cousin Arnold and Finny. "How far is the dry goods store? Is there, perchance, a mercantile where I could get a few things?"

"There is." He dropped his large hand from the casing and offered his elbow. "Let's go shopping." There was a roguish glint to his smile and Cassidy couldn't help but smile back.

CASSIDY INSISTED THEY not disturb the new couple. Avoiding the dining area, they found their way out the back door. She didn't want to give the wrong impression as she settled her hand in the crook of his arm. But the truth was, he was easy to hide behind and blast it, he smelled like fresh pine needles and soap.

"What do you know?" The question of her wonder slipped out as they started down the sidewalk.

"What?" His eyes narrowed.

"To hear a wooden sidewalk under my feet. First the Damonte Station and now this. It's so strange after so long."

Another grin inched up the corner of his mouth. "And taking a stroll with me. And maybe having food in your belly and a warm bed to sleep in last night?"

She smiled up at him as a man in a tattered jacket stopped in front of them.

"Whose ya got there, Emerson?" The man smiled, showing crooked yellow teeth. "A new gal from the Golden Bar?"

"No." Truitt gripped her hand and pulled her closer than proper. "See you Friday, Cecil." He circled them around the man. Cassidy felt indignation pinch her insides. Golden Bar was the sign over the saloon entrance. She'd seen it from her room. Frowning, she looked down at her gown, did she appear as one of his saloon girls? She clutched her free hand to her high collared dress. Her first time out in California and that was the impression she gave? A loose woman from a saloon? Her face burned red and she removed her hand from the crook of his arm.

Being seen with Truitt just put her on the dark side of this town. How long had they been out in public? Five minutes? Walking faster, she moved in front of him and spied a mother with children coming from the storefront. The simple, sturdy woman looked up from her brood and gaped curious at Cassidy. Finding a small smile to give to the children, Cassidy walked around them and into the store.

Barrels of goods and full shelving of jars and canisters filled the store with sights and smells. Trying to focus on what she needed, she felt Truitt close on her heels as she attempted to shop.

"Mr. Emerson." She turned so quickly he almost bumped into her. "I know this is not your forte. Please feel free to go on with your day." She turned and fingered a table of ribbons. "Finding my way back to the Bedford Hotel will only take me a few minutes." She walked around the table and he followed.

"What's wrong?" He gripped her arm, and she froze. Cassidy felt the sudden heat from his fingers and the serious way his eyes locked on hers. His strength was overwhelming. No wonder so many women desired his attention. But she had not come this far to be branded by such desperation. An entertainer was bad enough, but she was not a loose woman. "Oh, lolly." She'd slept wrapped in his arms only two nights ago. Carefully pulling his fingers from their grip on her arm, she cleared her throat and stepped away from him.

"You say, 'oh, lolly' a lot. Does it mean something?" he asked.

"It was something my grandmother used to say. Probably only people in Ireland know the true meaning." She stepped up to a shelf with soap and oils. "Really, you can go." Her voice held a lighter tone.

"I can't go, Cassidy."

He used her name like they'd had intimacies, familiar and sure. Her eyes closed before she looked around the store. The other shoppers hadn't noticed. Releasing a held breath, she spied his taut expression.

"You can't wander this town alone. Or with Miss O'Ryan." He waited for her agreement. "I'm truthful. Alone, women are not safe here."

"Well, I am not alone, there are people everywhere." She reached out and smelled a bar of soap as another thought hit her. "I suppose this is about business, being Mr. Snider's bodyguard and all. Today you are on assignment." She chided herself for being so naïve. Having some school girl infatuation with the man towering inches from her. "And the offer held something about a tour. I can only tour with a guard at my side?"

"Yes, and many a young woman would be thankful."

"So you look out for many young women here in Hangtown? I've seen how thankful they are to you." She returned a bottle of oil in its place. "Jumping into your arms, likely you're her weekly beau? Humph. Guarding a woman, is not what we call it back east."

His eyebrows peeked as he cracked a short laugh. "Whoa. You judge me corrupt?" Ignoring him, she turned to another corner shelf, and he kept on her heels. Now his voice held no humor. "I'd waited a week longer than planned. But I was relieved to see you ladies, alive. I couldn't control the rain and mud. I apologized about the loss of your personal things. I'm sorry for your violin. I would have never burned it if we were not wet," he growled low, "and... freezing." Cassidy knew his girth blocked her escape from the corner she'd put herself in; what stupidity to stir his ire. Crossing her arms, she looked in every direction but his.

He stepped back. "Well done, Miss Finnegan, now that you have no need of me, your evaluation of my character is duly noted. I could ask for ink and paper if you would like to list my offenses." The scorn dripped from his words, and she remained aloof.

He released a short huff. "I'll wait at the entrance and see you back when you are done."

Thirteen

CASSIDY CLUTCHED HER small paper bag and kept her eyes down as she hastened back down the wooden sidewalk to the Bedford Hotel. She knew he followed not far behind as left to right someone called out a greeting to Emerson.

Miss Finnegan, he'd called her. That was appropriate after the way she'd judged him. What had come over her? Jealousy? From seeing a woman showing her petticoats? She rolled her eyes. She didn't even really know the man except to be alone and comforted by him.

Oh, lolly, she scurried around the corner of the brick hotel and leaned back. Waiting, he must have stopped following, anxious to get away from her wrath and judgment. For months, Mr. Dingle had been her escort and guard. She'd never forget the way Mr. Dingle wrapped his arms around her as she'd huddled under the wagon from the Indian attack.

What if Mr. Emerson was just doing his job? Why did that offend her so? Her eyes began to fill with ridiculous tears. Yes, she should be thankful. Like when she'd seen him at the door and a rush of pleasure had run through her. She felt genuinely secure in his presence. And now in a strange, rough and tumble town, she had cruelly dismissed the only hospitable person she knew. She tapped her head over and over against the brick as the dismal tears ran down her cheeks.

"You doin' that on purpose, miss?"

Startled, Cassidy straightened up. It was the blonde woman with the same light green dress from yesterday. Her hair a tangled mess and a rash of some kind circled her mouth. She popped the chopped end of a carrot into her mouth.

"Get some good fixins' from the back of this hotel." She chomped another bite.

Cassidy looked at the pile of trash that the cooks threw from the back door. Swiping her face dry, she reached out her hand. "I'm Miss Finnegan and you are?"

"Just Janny. Janny Long's my name. But nobody calls me Miss Long." Cassidy felt the grime and looked away from the woman's dirt-filled nails. A rank odor assaulted her senses. "Would you like me to call you Janny or Miss Long?" Cassidy forced a smile.

"Oh, a nice lady like yourself, please to be callin' me Janny."

This woman was like a child. Cassidy felt the tears rising again that she had judged Truitt so harshly. A scavenger, the poor thing. "Janny, are you hungry?" Cassidy remembered the pain of an empty stomach. "I would like to bring you food from the kitchen."

"No, no," Janny spied the back door and backed up. "I got to get to Miz Chen 'bout now. "She keeps a pot of rice soup on for us girls, but some days it just tastes like water."

Cassidy smiled and Janny let out a little giggle.

"Please, call me Cassidy. Until we meet again." Cassidy curtsied, and Janny let out another snicker as she ran from the back of the hotel. A grown woman running with carrot greens dangling from her grip was a strange sight indeed. Maybe it had worked well for her survival here in Hangtown. A wave of gratitude for her safe and sound condition seemed to distract her earlier moments of remorse. Carefully peeking around the corner, Truitt was long gone. She sighed as she walked in the back of the Bedford hotel.

TRUITT STALKED AROUND Arnold Snider's office. The secretary, Mr. Hansen, eyed him.

"I doubt he'll be back soon. He's still out with his new love interest." The thin man scrutinized him.

"I know what he's doing. I just don't know what I'm doing." Truitt stopped and glared out the large front window.

"I've got two evictions you could do today," Mr. Hanson said, looking for something on his desk. "One is the mining site past Eureka Road. They're behind two months in payments. The other is a hard one, a family with a bunch of kids. They don't speak much English, so it's hard to tell them they are going to be booted out on their backside unless they make their payment." The secretary shook his head. "Manifest Destiny at its finest." He placed two notices on the corner of his desk. "Here you go."

Truitt wasn't in the mood to ruin people's lives today. Years ago it fit in, all in a day's work. He didn't hold much sorrow for folks after what happened to his father in this town. Many a time, making them move on, he'd likely done them a favor.

He stared out the window at the afternoon hum of Hangtown without seeing it. Miss Cassidy Finnegan didn't want his attention or favors. Apparently, she liked his attention to see her through the unpredictable Sierras, but now she didn't want to give a low-life like himself the time of day. His fists curled at his sides. Women and Argonauts, he was disgusted with both groups.

Why had she looked at him with soft appreciation at the door this morning? What were her assumptions about him then—that he was a scoundrel with women? He blew out a long huff. How could the woman be more wrong? She had seemed fine when she'd taken his arm at the hotel. They hadn't even stepped out a few minutes before she was trying to get rid of him. Maybe it was Cecil asking if Cassidy was a new girl at the Golden Bar. The blush on her cheeks registered as a likely reason and he scratched his jaw. Even with her agreeable temperament the thought of that occupation could have set her off. Might be helpful to understand women's feelings before he saw every move as rejection.

"Hey there, Emerson." The secretary waved at him. "You keep growling like a grizzly. And with Arnold's new preoccupation, I've got a lot of work to do."

Truitt sucked in a deep breath. "I'll go by both claims." He snatched the notices from the desk. "And then I'm gone for a few days." He reached for the door, developing an idea worth his time.

"Good, be back for Friday's fight. You'd have thought the town was dry of whiskey when you were gone. Not having their Friday night brawls brought business at the Round Tent to a halt."

Truitt smirked. It was a two-story building called the El Dorado now. Agitated with people and this town, he lumbered out.

THE NEXT EVENING, Finny kicked off her boots and flopped onto her bed. "Cassidy, you're going to have to come with me sooner or later. I want to see the house."

Cassidy sat on her bed, running her fingers through her hair. The olive oil dye had covered her deep copper tresses. "I don't know. What did you tell him was wrong with me?"

"I can't remember. We've spent two days talking about me and our future. Do you know he has more money than anyone in this town? And that house!" Finny crooned. "To be the woman of such a fine house. I have to see the inside." She sat up. "It will take me time to prepare. You said you would help me."

"I have been helping you. I posted a letter to my father yesterday. You said what a difficult journey it was and how sorry you were to see Mr. Dingle perish in the desert." She frowned. "And how thankful you are that Cousin Arnold is a fine man."

"Good, good," Finny said. "And you have the dowry money?"

"Yes, the pouch was tucked in my bodice when the wagon went over. Did Cousin Arnold mention it?"

"Yes. He is very business minded. He tells me I will never be in want for anything. I believe the money was to help with his shipping in San Francisco. Something about trade routes that will benefit them both."

Money and marriage shouldn't have to go together. Cassidy couldn't tolerate another minute. Her father's disregard for her feelings and the deception seemed to eat at her regularly now that they were here and playing the parts. "Why can't Mr. Emerson be your chaperone?" She forced her voice to stay calm. "He will protect your reputation."

"Something about him being out of town." Finny crawled into bed. "I told him we would be ready at ten."

Cassidy began to undress. Of course, after looking out the window for two days, she hadn't had one peek at him. She hung her gown in the wardrobe. She couldn't avoid Cousin Arnold much longer. Dread pulled at her shoulders and dipped into her belly as she slipped her nightgown over her head. Tomorrow she would need to be Miss Finnegan body and soul.

CASSIDY STAYED BEHIND Finny the next morning as they descended the stairs. A glance over Finny's shoulders revealed a small balding man in a detailed black suit. Pulling a strand of copper red-streaked hair over her cheek, she eyed him. He was taller when she was a child, but now she appeared to be eye to eye with him — such a difference after being next to Truitt Emerson. He took Finny's hands and kissed them.

"You look lovely, my precious."

Cassidy stared at her shoes. *My precious?*

"And you are the lady's maid, Miss Finnegan?"

Before Cassidy had to make eye contact, he bowed quickly. "So thankful for your assistance to my sweet cousin in the perils of this long journey." She nodded with eyes down.

"And glad to hear you are recovering from the dysentery that can affect so many travelers."

"Dysentery?" She reached out to pinch Finny's arm just as the fraud moved forward and wrapped her arm inside of Arnold's cozily.

After an uneventful walk down the left side of Hangtown, the street forked leaving his fine house center stage. Taking the stairs quickly, Arnold proudly opened the front door to the three-story Victorian. The wide porch looked down on the long dirt street. Like a shiny centerpiece of adornment on an old burlap sack, Cassidy thought.

The entrance was stunning and she stepped carefully across the threshold. The hardwood floors shone with soft hues bouncing off them, while the grand staircase and thick railings engulfed the right side of the foyer. A thick blue and gray carpet lay on the floor, with a coat and hat stand nearby. Spying inside the parlor, she noticed that the house was eerily similar to her family's in Boston.

"It's beautiful." Finny gasped.

A stiff-looking man appeared from the front hall and took their coats and hats. Finny looked back at her and gave a small wink.

"Coffee or tea in the parlor, sir?"

"Yes, Nelson that would be fine. Shall we continue the tour, ladies? Arnold held his hand out and led them from room to room, telling them about each piece of furniture or decoration he'd gathered from all parts of the Americas and Europe.

Now she remembered what a boring conversationalist her cousin was. She covered a yawn. Finny held on his every word, like a child who'd never seen a candy store. The three rooms up the stairs all had tall, dark headboards with beautiful bedding and matching wallpaper. The room on the right was the most elaborate and Cousin Arnold's face turned crimson.

"This is the master bedroom," He smiled at Finny, his expression coy.

Eyes bouncing quickly from the sight of the large bed, Cassidy felt her stomach roll up. "I'm going to check on the tea." Very cold tea, she growled under her breath and grabbed the wide banister and let herself down into the parlor.

Nelson brought a new pot, and Cassidy sat on Cousin Arnold's red velvet settee and had one cup, and then another, and then another. Faint laughter flowed down the wide staircase. Cassidy got up and paced the room. *Finny you better be discussing household responsibilities up there.* Memories of an unabashed red-haired maid and all the cowboys on the wagon train caused her to set the china cup down harder than usual. Was she to be the nanny for these adult children?

What was taking so long? She walked to the thick windows that faced downtown Hangtown. Now *she* was the chaperone. Poor Mr. Emerson. It wasn't a job she would wish on anyone.

That familiar gloomy cloud settled over her. Would she ever have a chance to apologize for her harsh and duplicitous assessment of his character? Mr. Nelson walked in and took the teapot back to the kitchen. This was a refined house but it felt cold and lonely, and she had been ready to leave hours ago. The wooden staircase creaked as the lovebirds descended.

"Finally." She heaved a sigh.

Fourteen

CASSIDY FELT HER nerves were about to boil over, similar to the watery stew they'd had on the wagon train once. Being with Finny and Arnold all afternoon had made her feel like that crusted burnt pot.

"Finny, I don't want to talk." Cassidy unlocked the door to their room. "I just said you were up there far too long. You are giving him the wrong impression. A lady would never visit with a man inside his bedchamber."

"I seem to remember the night you and Mr. Emerson were cozy—far cozier than a lady should allow." Finny scowled, as they walked in.

"I said I don't want to—" Cassidy's raised voice abruptly halted. A long case lay on her bed. "What is this?" Still annoyed, she squinted at Finny.

"I didn't put it there."

Cassidy scanned the room and saw nothing else out of place. A card folded in half lay on her bed.

This is close, but I have something that will make it better.

Truitt

Feeling a light spin in her head or possibly the room, Cassidy lifted the clasp and lid to reveal a pristine Italian violin. "Oh, my Lord!" She covered her mouth and stepped back.

"What is it?" Finny approached and took the card from her hand. "Well, I'll be. Blessed right he should replace it. Burning it to ash like the devil, he did." Finny tossed the card on Cassidy's bed. Cassidy still could not move.

Where would he get such a fine instrument? She'd seen Hangtown. The Studebaker wheelbarrow shop was its finest claim to woodwork.

"He was gone for days," Cassidy murmured looking back to Finny. "Probably to San Francisco." The shock was making her words tremble. Why? Where would this man find such generosity after her cold treatment of him?

"I would consider the feather in his cap has your name on it." Finny turned in front of the mirror. "And now a gift to make it stand out? What a tease."

He's not a tease, Cassidy thought as she picked up the violin and bow. His eyes always shone with benevolent sincerity. She ran the bow across the G and D strings. It was purer than her grandmother's ever was. She felt the tingle in her fingers to play something. Lowering her chin on the chin rest, "Amazing Grace" flowed out without a thought. The room hollowed a sweet presence with the tender pristine sound — something she had not felt in months.

Finny interrupted the last touching note. "Now that you have new violin. Maybe you won't be so irritable."

Cassidy gently laid the violin back in its case, fingering the new wood. "Excuse me, I have to see to something." Focused, she opened the door and ignored Finny's comment about not staying in his room too long.

The Bedford Hotel claimed more than thirty rooms. He said he stayed here. Asking the doorman didn't seem proper. Yet he'd come to her door days ago and somehow entered their locked room today. She descended the stairs and froze. His height and well-toned form could not be missed, standing in the foyer talking to a man in a striped suit. Something akin to panic arose, and her foot tried to retreat up the stairs. He saw her and it was too late. Their eyes locked. With that small roguish twinkle in his eye, he stepped forward, and she had no choice but to swallow her nerves and meet him. The other man's eyes widened, and his large-mouthed smile greeted her.

"Ahh, Emerson. You know this lovely rose?" The man's thick French accent was impossible to miss. "A zephyr swept into the room at her presence." He reached out and kissed Cassidy's hand.

Cocking half a smile, Truitt crossed his thick arms, unimpressed with the display.

"Mr. Pierre Doré, this is Miss Finnegan. She is the companion to Miss O'Ryan who is engaged to Arnold Snider."

"Ahh yes, the women from back east. The town is all abuzz at your arrival." His large smile revealed a row of straight white teeth. A thin black mustache lay straight over his top lip. "What a delight to have you join our fair city. I run the fabulous El Dorado." His eyebrows sprang up and down. "Most people know it as the Round Tent." He waggled his head. "But the tent is gone and a building to hold hundreds is in its place. Emerson's boxing here is our highest attended event."

Truitt glanced at her and back to Mr. Dorè and filled in the gap of her awkward silence. "Miss Finnegan is a violin...ist? Is that how you say it?" She couldn't answer and her nose tingled like right before she cried. His extravagant gift of knowing her heart spoke directly from his perfect lips. After her behavior at the mercantile, why was he even speaking to her and sharing her deepest dreams publicly? She couldn't take her watery gaze from his.

"That is so? Mademoiselle?"

"Yes." Nodding quickly to the man, she patted the corners of her eyes.

"Ahh. Women are so underrepresented in the arts. How very interesting that with your humble station you were allowed to develop an ear for the music."

"May I play for you sometime, sir?" The words were out before she could catch them.

"Oh, oh-oh." His body flinched back, and he chuckled, glancing to Truitt. "I would be honored. What day may I call on you for this private symphony?"

Cassidy's mouth twitched and she chewed on a corner of her bottom lip. "I would rather come and see your new El Dorado." She glanced out the sides of her eyes to Truitt. "Would you be free to take me tomorrow?"

"I suppose." His expression gave her no reason to expect a warm compliance.

There was a long pause, and Mr. Dorè looked back and forth at them. "Ah," he said, and bowed and kissed her hand again. "Until tomorrow, then. Say noon?"

"Yes, thank you." Carefully, Cassidy tipped a smile wondering what she had just done. Another couple came in the large double doors as Mr. Doré exited.

She looked up at Truitt. "I was surprised to see you in the foyer, but you were the reason I came down." With a light touch to her elbow, he led her to the large empty rock fireplace. "I want to say I am sorry about the other day. I was rude and judgmental. And...and I wanted to say that before I saw the gift."

His eyes crinkled with a flash of humor and he pressed his lips together. Should she say more? Did he think her sincere? "And the violin was too extravagant Truitt. I...I...shouldn't accept anything like—"

"Now I am Truitt?"

Cassidy sighed. "Only with your permission. I've noticed everyone else calls you Emerson."

He peered down at her and scratched his chin. "Your hair is different." Truitt leaned to the side and studied her then he walked around her. "Yes, I think it's your hair."

Cassidy looked away, nervously pulling her hand down her locks.

"You are confusing to me, Cassidy. He squinted and crossed his arms over his chest. "And now confusing to this town."

"Do you say that with malice?"

"Oh, no," his brown eyes widened. "Quite the opposite."

Cassidy felt her skin tingle and she glanced toward the staircase.

"If you ask a man if you can play for him. He might think you are offering special favors."

She went to open her mouth but Truitt raised his hand to stop her words. "Which I know is not what you are doing. But if Mr. Snider gets wind of you playing at the El Dorado without his permission, he might ship you back to Boston."

Cassidy bristled, wondering if Truitt knew about her father's shipping business. "I assume he and Miss O'Ryan will be married soon and I will be freed from being her companion. I need to work. Thanks to you and your gift, I can." Her eyes drifted to the floor. "I know I'm asking for the stars," she sighed, "but I had hoped that out west a woman who had a non-provocative talent could be seen as respectable."

TRUITT PRAYED UNDER his breath that those round, soft blue eyes would not fill with tears again. He knew he was powerless against her womanly emotions. Things like tears had not bothered him in other women, but with Cassidy it was different. "I have something else for you." He reached into his pocket and pulled out the coil of four strings. "From your other violin." He held them out to her and her face crumpled with the sentiment. "While you were asleep, I took the violin apart and saved these. Can you string them onto the new one?"

"Your note. I see. Something even better—my orginal strings." Her chin quivered, and she glanced around the empty foyer. With blinking eyes, she shook her head and took them from his palm. It was like holding a piece of all the goodness of her beloved Ireland. Like God had seen the pain of her heart and offered a token of healing. "Yes, of course, I can use them," she whispered. They stood in silence, and she dabbed the corners of her eyes. "I forgot my handkerchief," she sniffed.

He couldn't repress a small smile. He had done a good thing. "I am sorry for all you've had to go through. If it seemed I was ill-tempered in the store, I apologize." He went to touch her arm but quickly brought his hand back, shoving it in his pants pocket. The other thing he had for her felt like hot coals at his fingertips. The music store where he had purchased the violin had a paper about the Pacific Minstrels. It wasn't that hard, just pull it out and give it to her. Something squeezed in his chest. He pulled his hand out empty.

"Shall we just forgive and forget the past?" she asked.

"I believe in the power of forgiveness because the Almighty has said to. But I lack the power to forget." Digging the hole to bury his dead father or hearing Marianna had gone back to Mexico. They had been very hard things to just forget.

This young woman before him wore a new dress tonight and sported those deeper russet locks in her hair. Being away from her for only two days had been difficult. His blood raced, thinking of the crowded cave and holding her in his arms—certain things he didn't want to forget. Like the way she stood before him now in all her soft beauty and forbearance. His gaze dropped to her lips and then quickly to the ground. "Can I see you back to your room?"

"Yes," swallowing, she lifted a weak smile. "Finny will wonder what's become of me."

He took a few steps away and stopped at the stairs.

"Who is Finny?"

Fifteen

CASSIDY ASCENDED THE hotel stairs faking a small cough.
Peeking over her shoulder, Truitt Emerson's question hung
as close as he did. "Sorry, I was choking. I said finicky.
Miss O'Ryan can get finicky when I'm not near." Oh lolly, that
didn't even make sense to her own ears.

"So it seems to be going well with this new engagement?" he
asked.

"I would say very well," Cassidy noted. "I expect an
announcement soon."

"And then the understanding is you will no longer be
needed?" They slowed and stopped in front of her door.

"I don't suppose so. I've been to the house. He has staff
and...and people. Why, he has you!" She chuckled. He didn't
show any enjoyment from that thought, looking more troubled.

"I want to say something more about how dangerous it is for
women and respectable employment in these mining towns, but I
know I've said enough," he waited, eyes narrowing.

"Yes. I'm not so naïve to think that I will be the only
exception to the rule. But how will I know unless I try? I'll tell
you, our understanding of coming west was just a vague notion
to the reality of the true difficulties of the journey. But I made it.
Sometimes I wake up in that soft bed and can hardly believe it.
Most of my hope was slipping away until I saw that violin

tonight. Your gift has renewed my hope. It has given me a chance to try. I *have* to try."

He nodded. "I admire your belief and hope. I will come for you at noon."

Cassidy felt warmth in every fiber of her being. To have a man like him hear her and commend her. His gift was more than she could've asked for or imagined. Throwing etiquette to the wind, she grabbed his hand and opened his large palm. Biting back a smile, she took her finger and traced the letters T—H—A—N—K Y—O—U.

He turned his wrist with hers and opened up her hand. G—O—O—D N—I—G—H—T. She looked up and saw red creeping up his neck before she could find her breath. Squeezing her hand in his, he let go and took his leave down the hall.

FINNEY'S NEW DRESSES and toilette turned into a two-person undertaking going later into the next morning.

"Stop now, Cassidy." Finny grabbed her arm. "You are practically dancing. Tell me, what happened with Mr. Emerson. I swear on my rosary, I will not chide you. Did you go back to his room? I need details, what did he do?" Finny gave her a shake.

"No, you ninny. I did not go back to his room!" Finny's disappointment shone in her frown. "I am not here for a husband, you are. But if you swear on your rosary you won't tell, I will tell you a secret."

"Sweet Mary, Mother, and Joseph, yes, tell me." Finny entreated.

"Today at noon, I will be playing," Cassidy squeezed her hands together, her shoulders raised with excitement, "hopefully *auditioning* for the manager of the El Dorado." Her voice thrummed with exhilaration.

Finny held her mouth open. "That's it. You mean your violin. You're going to play for the manager?"

Cassidy clapped her hands together. "Yes!"

"That's the grand secret?" Finny whined, rolling her eyes.

"Please, Finny. I'm going to ask you not to say anything to Cousin Arnold. I don't want to stir up anything to annoy him until you are married."

"And then you are free to annoy him?" Finny huffed and walked back to her bed. "I will tell you a much more important secret, dear Cassidy. Arnold Snider has a lot of say in this town. He snaps his fingers and people jump. And if they don't jump, they will find themselves on the wrong side of Mr. Emerson's fist. If you knew the things Mr. Emerson does for Arnold, you wouldn't think so highly of him."

Dark foreboding covered Cassidy's excitement. "What kind of things?"

"All these stupid easterners and foreigners come here with nothing but the rags on their backs," Finny sneered. "Arnold helps them, gives them tools and supplies to stake their claims. A few make enough gold to pay him back, but most can't rub two sticks together so he can legally take their claims. Then he sells them over and over to the next senseless miner. Of course, they don't like that, and that's where Mr. Emerson comes in. I won't repeat how to your delicate ears. But he does more in this town than those Friday nights exhibitions with fists flying and sweaty bodies."

Cassidy sat back on her bed and looked at her lovely gift. From the first moment she landed in his arms she had been attracted to him, and yet that next morning he had practically shoved them into the wagon like cargo with nothing but a canvas. She'd seen rough men on the wagon trail and had known he was a tough man back then. Why would this information upset her now? He carried his mother's bible and spoke of the Almighty. The way they continued their childish handwriting game was full of a tenderness she wanted to believe was meant for her alone.

Finny walked near and peered out the window. "We are supposed to go for a drive today. You should see his black leather buggy. There wasn't room for you, too. I'm so sorry your stomach is feeble again." She cast Cassidy a clever smile.

VOWING NOT TO make the same judgmental mistake as before, Cassidy greeted Truitt kindly and clutched her violin case close. He wore clean working-man denim trousers, boots, a green striped shirt, and thick suspenders. So broad of shoulder was he, if he wanted to be an Oregon territory lumberjack, he would likely fit right in.

"Thank you for taking time away to escort me today." She glanced down at his large hands. Had he punched any miners today? "And tonight are the fights you participate in?"

He nodded.

"And those yellow and purple fingers have healed?" She felt herself rambling.

"Yes, thank you, Miss Cassidy, for your concern."

There was that eye-creasing grin again and she wondered if he was having fun at her expense. She was the foolish ninny for taking his hand in hers last night, brazenly writing in his palm. He likely thought her a schoolgirl tease. They stepped off the sidewalk and crossed the street. Men on horseback and some just walking by stared at her as before. She suppressed a growl; she should've never worn the matching lavender hat with her dress. Did she appear to be putting on airs?

"Doin' well today Emerson." A man's voice called out across the street. She wanted to turn and sneer at the insolence but caught Truitt smiling. After a trip across America on a wagon train, surely she could walk down this street with a bit more confidence. The El Dorado was two more blocks up the road on the right.

"Mr. Doré is French, and yet the name of the El Dorado is Spanish?"

Truitt nodded and touched her elbow as they moved a wide berth from the heat of the blacksmith shop. "There is a little of everyone here. Over there," he pointed across the street and down a bit. "That is So Chen's place. I told you, she runs the laundry and bathing house. She came here from China. Her husband died after the first year, and she and her sons created a business. Even dirty miners want a bath and clean duds every couple of weeks."

"And she employs other women?" She looked up to him. "I met a young woman— Janny, Miss Long. She was scavenging behind the hotel."

Truitt shook his head sighing, "Janny has had a rough go. Rumor is, she was traded off in a poker game as a girl. Her mind is still like a child. So Chen keeps an eye on her." They walked on.

"As well as you?" Cassidy said gently.

Casting a glance across the bustle of Main Street, he nodded, "I do."

His eyes held a steady gaze forward and Cassidy felt the contradiction within. Truitt Emerson was a complicated man. Today, she chose to see him as benevolent.

They stopped in front of wide-open double doors. The El Dorado was a bustle inside, and Cassidy felt her stomach knot. Her grandparent's simple pub and the vast open prairie had been her only stages so far.

Cassidy paused just inside the door. The place seemed to swarm with activity. Men were rolling round tables to the side, while others stacked wooden chairs. A woman was mopping the floor, and another was setting out spittoons. She noticed a long bar against the back wall, and Mr. Doré with his back to them leaning on the bar. A simple stage was on the central wall with long red curtains hanging from the side. An upright piano sat against the right side of the curtain.

"This is where you hold your fights," she whispered, wondering where she had left her eastern upbringing and God-given common sense.

"This is it," Truitt said, walking toward the bar.

Mr. Doré turned to them and hurried over with a broad smile. "Oh, *oui*, *mademoiselle*, you are here with your violin?" He bowed and nodded to Truitt. "You look *tres belle*, and I am guessing I will not get a private concert?" He winked taking her elbow and walked her across the wide wooden floors. "Would you like to play on my stage?"

Cassidy's throat constricted. Men worked all around them, talking, scraping wooden chairs against the floor. A sudden panic tried to freeze her feet together. "What would you like to hear, sir?" Her stomach pinched as she set her case on the stage.

"Something an audience might like?" He pulled on his string of a mustache.

Cassidy bowed slightly and slipped up the four steps to center stage. Her heart pounded against her ribs. At least he understood she was interested in playing for an audience. She ran the bow over the strings and tried to settle her chin in place. Her quickened breathing made the new violin rise and fall. She glanced at Truitt. He watched her intently. Acknowledging her nerves, he nodded his head with an encouraging smile at her.

Sucking in a deep breath, she began a fast reel that was full of high and exaggerated notes. Her fingers moved over the strings like flickers of light over fast-moving water. Feeling the echoes of the room tapping and sliding along the wooden floors like invisible dancers, Cassidy whipped her bowing arm back and forth, losing herself in the familiar tune. She leaned to the left and rose on her toes as the notes brought a crescendo to the energetic melody. Pulling long on the last note, she had to smile. The folks on the wagon train would whoop and holler to their delight when she played this. Opening her eyes, all she saw were the workers, Truitt and Mr. Doré staring wide-eyed at her. The room was silent. Every eye stunned and fixated on her alone. After a prolonged awkward silence, she stepped to the edge of the stage.

They apparently didn't appreciate such a rambunctious jig here in California. "Would you prefer a hymn or ballad of some kind? Something slower?"

Truitt finally closed his mouth and began to clap. The workers followed suit and clapped. After a few minutes they returned to their work.

Mr. Doré brows crossed and he scratched his chin. "That was…was…like nothing I've heard before. This was taught to you by…or who…you are from Boston, *mon cher*?

"And Ireland. My grandparents… In my childhood, I lived with them in Ireland."

"Oh, *oui*, and you have more of these tunes to your knowledge?" He scratched his short black hair and patted it. "Some that won't turn this town into a hot backwoods frenzy. *Oui*?"

"Yes." She smiled. "Many that are slower, couples could even dance."

Mr. Doré turned to Truitt. "*Mais oui*," he smiled. "We lost our piano player a month ago. The miners, they have been getting quite unruly without the dancing and the singing." He clapped his hands, "We must see to this ex—exqui—how you say? Exquise. Exquisite musician to play for us…" he turned on his heel with excitement in his steps.

Truitt looked up at Cassidy while he rubbed his knuckle under his chin. Finally he spoke. "Well, I guess you are hired."

Sixteen

TRUITT AND CASSIDY stopped outside the double doors of the El Dorado. The sunlight and fresh air brought a wave of relief and she exhaled, smiling.

"I'm not sure that was the right tune," she said, twisting her lips to the side. "It's a popular one for dancing in Ireland and the folks on the wagon train would dance and spin their children in circles." She waited as Truitt looked up and down Hangtown's Main Street. "Is it too scandalous for Hangtown?"

He looked past her and dropped his chin, then eyed her curiously. "Everything in Hangtown is scandalous."

Cassidy's nose wrinkled from a swirl of dirt as a wagon passed in front of them. "Mr. Doré said to come tomorrow. I could play other songs. At least, I think I heard him say that as he waved a hand at me."

Truitt shifted his weight to his other foot and looked like he often did, wanting to say something but trying to hold back his opinions. "I'm sure he did." He raised his hand signaling forward and they walked back towards the Bedford.

"I shouldn't be reading your mind," she said breaking the silence.

"Lord Almighty, I hope you don't." He nodded to a man who expressed his excitement about tonight's fight.

Cassidy longed to revel in the glorious moments she would

have playing on that stage. Barely a week in this new California, and the winds of change carried her fingers and joy higher than she could hope. But she cared about what Truitt thought. The man was obviously well versed in this robust mining town. She trusted his experience here. Hangtown had been a sorrowful place for him, but he seemed to know everyone.

"Then I won't guess. Tell me what you're thinking," she blurted out.

Truitt cleared his throat and rubbed his forehead as they walked. "I think you should put that new violin away and stay with the job you have."

Cassidy wished she hadn't asked. Why did his opinion carry such weight? "And yet you were the one who bought me the violin and an expensive one, I might add."

"That was because I felt bad for what I did and all you'd lost." His brows furrowed. "And it was before I'd heard you play." He shook his head, conveying something disconcerting. "There was a certain fire in you. Like a starving man who found his first gold rock. I thought those strings were going to start smoking."

Cassidy let his words calm her disappointment. "So if I played something more refined?"

"Oh, no." He scowled. "Hangtown would be stomping off the walls at whatever you played. Word will get out fast and every man with two legs and critter with four will come to watch you."

Delight shot through her, overwhelming and mortifying. He rolled his lips and raked his fingers through his light brown hair. A few more men patted his back as they passed. Excitement for his Friday night fight seemed to follow him block after block.

"Now I understand." They stopped at the Bedford Hotel front doors. "You are worried your audience will trade fighting for my music."

Growling, he pushed the door open and led her inside by the arm.

She glanced up at the storm gathering in his expression and said, "I was just teasing you." She tried to make him smile as they stopped at the stairs.

"Two things." He held his eyes closed, shaking his head, he opened them. "Don't read my mind and don't tease me."

"Yes, sir." She stepped up one step and narrowed her eyes like his, now eye to eye. "This is business." She held her smile back, feigning seriousness.

Truitt's jaw edged to the left and his tongue quickly ran over the corner of his mouth. Cassidy had an intense fear he would angrily reprimand her folly or pull her female form into his rock chest. Both made her shrink back and she took another stair backward.

"Forgive me. I must check on Miss O'Ryan." She pulled up on the thick layers of her dress.

"Cassidy." He gripped higher on the thick banister, but thankfully didn't follow her. "Talk to Miss O'Ryan about you playing at the El Dorado. Without Arnold Snider in agreement, it will only end in disaster. If you can get him to listen, be sure he knows he will get a cut of any profits. You might have a chance."

She stilled at his words, marveling again in his willingness to help her.

LATE THAT AFTERNOON, Finny arrived back at their hotel room and announced her news. "Arnold has arranged for his suit maker and tailor to meet us at the Ohio House in one hour." She beamed. "I am to have four new dresses tailor-made for me." Cassidy glanced up from her small stacks of songs she had broken into musical categories. "That's nice," she murmured.

"Did you hear me? Four!" Finny spun in a circle. "Do you know these frocks he had for me when we arrived he had ordered from San Francisco before we even got here? They were just gifts waiting for me." She straightened her hair in front of the mirror. "He didn't know we had lost everything in the mudslide. How grand that I shared with you, but now I'll have four more, tailor-made, just for me." She squeaked a squeal.

"I was able to audition at the El Dorado today." Cassidy glanced out the window closest to her bed. "Truitt, I mean, Mr.

Emerson believes I should inform Cousin Arnold of my intentions."

Finny swung and faced her, "You never told me, he is not your blood cousin." Her tone curt.

"My Uncle Donavan married a woman with a son. I've never not thought of Arnold as my uncle's son." She wondered about Finney's sour expression.

"Well the devil knows, he wasn't treated like family," Finny spouted "It seems your uncle barely tolerated him, putting him in his place at every turn. Abusive, I would say from such well-bred people."

"Abusive? Surely you exaggerate."

"I may have spent most my life in a plain black dress and thick working apron, but a step-father din't remind me I was good fer nothin', did he?" Finny countered.

Cassidy could hear the Irish brogue and see the flush in Finny's cheeks. It was the wrong time to remind Finny she'd no family to speak of. "It sounds to me as if you care for him."

"Well, o'course, I do." She tossed her head making her hair loosen across her brow. "We be talkin' about a wedding date. Possibly spring."

"Spring?" Cassidy moaned.

"I told him it was too long to wait. And you'll be happy to know; he could care less if any of your folk come from back east. It would take 'em five months by ship. I don't want to wait, and neither you nor I," she gave Cassidy a hard stare, "want family attending."

Cassidy's stomach clenched. "No, you must marry sooner than that," she whispered, contemplating how soon she could leave her deception behind and move to the new city of San Francisco.

DARKNESS WAS FALLING as Cassidy took a seat at the Ohio House's large dressing room. The suit maker and tailor were men and her knees and feet were hurting from doing all the necessary measuring for them. Finny played the part of the blushing fiancée standing behind the large screen in her underthings. The woman, who had no fashion sense, had turned into the queen of England with every little tuck and pleat to her favor.

"Ask them about the lace, Cassidy. Can we have white on the bottom and do a different piecing on the collar?" Finny peaked around her screen to find Cassidy holding her chin in her hands.

"Finny, I'm tired. We've been at this for hours." Cassidy looked up as the men still took notes on their notepads. "Isn't Mr. Snider wanting to take you to dinner soon? You'll never make it at this rate."

"He's attending your man's boxing match tonight."

Cassidy raised her head quickly and eyed the tailors. Thankfully neither seemed to catch the woman's brazenness. "Gentlemen, would you mind bringing out the samples of lace and collars one more time. It seems we need to keep looking."

Two hours later the older suit maker bowed to the women and appointed the younger tailor to walk the ladies back to the hotel. Cassidy and Finny stepped out pulling their capes close.

"The evenings are cool here," Cassidy said as they both turned toward a loud rumble from down the street. "The El Dorado looks packed." She watched. The building almost shook with light and manly cheers. She bit her lip, wondering how Truitt faired in this evening of fisticuffs.

"I think I should check on my fiancé tonight." Finny hooked her elbow through Cassidy's. "Make sure no wanton floozy is hanging on him." Finny pulled her toward the noise.

"Oh, no, Finny." Cassidy tried to pull her in the opposite direction, "No. We can't." She looked back as the quiet man followed behind them and Finny pulled her forward.

"This will only take a moment. We won't go inside. Just a quick peek." Finny glanced over her shoulder, flashing a smile at their escort.

Cassidy pulled Finny to an abrupt stop as a man came flying out the open doors of the El Dorado. His face skidded to a stop in the dirt. "Finny." Cassidy hissed, jerking on her arm. "This is a bad idea. We…we… can't…" The man covered in dirt finally pulled himself up and staggered toward them with blood pouring from his nose and mouth. "Finny! Please, we shouldn't do this. I'm sure Arnold is on the straight and narrow." They gave the bloody man a wide berth as Cassidy tried to pull her in the opposite direction. Suddenly, they stopped the tug of war, as a roar of men shouting shook the ground.

"They won't even know we are near." Finny pulled her arm free and made her way from the light of the open doors and to the right. "That window there."

Cassidy looked around. Everyone seemed to be pressed inside. Even their escort was looking past them to see inside. Through the wavy glass, men moved and leaned to see the fight. Some sat on each other's shoulders holding fists of bills in the air. The packed crowd swayed and moved as the fighters danced in and out of the circle.

"I see Arnold. There on the left, standing on the stage." Finny rose up higher on her tiptoes.

Cassidy's eyes glanced away from her search for Truitt and saw her cousin standing with four or five other well-dressed men. Like a rocking ship, the crowd swirled to the right and Cassidy peered through the cracks in the sea of men.

A sudden jolt widened her eyes. Truitt was bare-chested, large thick arms holding fists in front of his red face. Hair wet with sweat, he eyed his opponent like a hungry hawk. Truitt paced back and forth and swung a swift blow to the other man's jaw, knocking him to the floor. The crowd roared and shook, Cassidy could feel the sound reverberate within her chest. As fast as the man hit the ground, he jumped back to his feet spitting blood on the floor. The crowd whirred to the left as the two men ducked and jeered each other. Cassidy squeezed her hand over her open mouth. "Oh, my Lord," she panted. "Watch out, Truitt. Now he's really mad." Four thick arms collided and the two men became one being with arms swinging and punches landing in every direction.

Cassidy felt her simple dinner roll up in her throat. The crowd moved back toward the window and then away. Cassidy lost sight of Truitt and dug her fingernails into the window casing, leaning closer. Before she could find a new breath, the men separated, and she saw Truitt return to his full height. His fist jerked back, and he lifted his chin just enough to—eye her through the window.

Seventeen

CASSIDY SCREECHED AND jumped back at the same moment she saw the angry fist slam into Truitt's jaw. "We have to go. Now!" The crowd went wild as Truitt disappeared from view, apparently landing somewhere on the hard floor. Finding the agile running legs of Janny Long, she pulled her skirts up and ran with her full might. Women didn't roam alone in Hangtown. She could still hear Truitt's words echo his strong warning in her head. Forget the tailor and Finny, Truitt was going to rise off that floor, march after her, and hold her down with those large hands all the while giving her a tongue lashing. Like a drowning sailor finding shore, she saw the Bedford Hotel in the distance. Out of breath and stamina, she finally made it inside the safety of its tall doors.

His eyes. Would she ever forget the fiery steel daggers he just shot at her? She should be pierced and bleeding this very moment. Staggering to the hotel stairs, she grabbed the railing. Shocked, she panted, "What just happened?" Without a true breath, she didn't know if she could take one more step.

Taking a frightened gasp of new air, she looked up to see Finny and the tailor at the hotel door. Oh, blessed be, Truitt was nowhere behind them. Finny nodded her thanks to the tailor while Cassidy held her chest from convulsing further.

"That was an interesting flight your large bird legs just took." Finny rolled her eyes coming to the stairs. "I haven't' seen you run like that since the mudslide tried to kill us." She taunted. "We were captured by Indians, and you never ran as such. Oh, Cassidy." Finny took the stairs, passing her. "Mary, Mother, and Joseph, you worry too much."

TOO MUCH WAS an understatement to the worrisome tossing and turning Cassidy did that night hour after hour. Her excuses, no, her reasons for working at the El Dorado at night kept looming one after the other in her mind, and when sleep finally did take over, she dreamed Truitt was holding her down in the snow until the white powder suffocated her. She finally sat up and pulled the covers close.

Releasing a deep breath, she knew the pain from her gut was not from a stupid dream, but real. He had been fair and helpful, sometimes more of a friend than Finny, and yet she did not prove herself thankful nor return the kindnesses. Holding so tightly to her identity ruse was causing her to be someone different, a person she didn't like much at all. Even in the dark of night, she knew he would never hurt her. So why dream such a horrible dream?

And why did she think she could hold her feelings for Truitt secret and close? Maybe because she had no real experience with this kind of tug on her heart? She punched her pillow and sank back down. Mr. Calhoun and Mr. Spencer had both been eager to seek her attention during the long months on the trail. And yet, she never felt such trepidation in her gut over them.

Every evening stroll they asked for often felt like an interview for a wife. But at least their intentions were forthright. Cassidy stretched her neck side to side and rolled over. Mr. Spencer had taken her hand in his during one walk. It felt so uncomfortable and Cassidy remembered smiling nervously as she pulled her hand away. After ignoring him for two weeks, he stopped seeking her out.

Truitt Emerson was undoubtedly the finest looking man she had ever seen. His size and strength were to be admired, of course. But the way he'd put his arm around her in that little cave... She sighed. A sad bubble of warmth caught in her throat — what a ninny. She pressed her hands into her face. His confidence and protection had met her like no other. A tender place in her heart cared about him, and cared about what he thought, and cared that every Friday fists pounded against that perfect rugged face. Oh, she squeezed her eyes closed trying to forget the images.

She'd seen some men fight on the wagon train, but it was from far away, and she hadn't known them. Now, she detested this boxing, this fighting. Anyone hurting another for sport was just barbaric — that was another reason she needed to discount her girlish infatuation with this man. Groaning softly, she flopped back into the pillows and tossed to her other side.

TRUITT STUMBLED INTO his room and fell onto the bed. Rarely did he accept the drinks everyone wanted to buy him at the bar. He cared little for the men's accolades. Winning in this insufferable town was his sufficient reward. To him it was more than a Friday night victory in a saloon. Each landed punch, each body toss to the ground, each grunt he heard from his opponent was a conquest over the presumption of his father's guilt and subsequent hanging.

Six small prickly threads stuck from his right cheek. So Chen was his nurse on nights like this. The four drinks he'd consumed likely took the sting out of her needle going in and out of his skin. He let out a deep breath and put his arm over his forehead. He touched the stitches with his other hand and remembered So Chen's reaction as she sewed him up.

"What happened to you, big man? You not big enough to keep some little man's fists from your face?"

So Chen wouldn't let him speak at first. She had to finish her scolding.

"Why you do that? Why you have this Friday night mashing? What you thinking? Save money and put cold towel on eye. Did you eat, yet? You need to eat. Ai yi yi."

Yawning, he remembered how, after her tirade, he recounted the shock of seeing a woman appearing in the El Dorado window. A ghost?

"Must be ghost," So had said.

Truitt could only wish it had been a ghost. But she'd looked amazingly like Miss Cassidy Finnegan and the distraction had kept him from seeing the blazing fist swooping his way.

Truitt knew he wouldn't be able to sleep just yet, so he told So Chen of the trip up the Sierras to pick up Mr. Snider's fiancée and the troubles he'd had with this woman since.

So Chen rarely smiled, but Truitt caught her snickering as she cleaned his other wounds. "No woman since your one lady left?" The pesky little Chinese woman had to say, pulling Truitt to standing.

He'd told her no, but what did that have to do with anything?

Standing on her tip toes, she dabbed the blood off the underside of his chin in a motherly way and had said, "Save money." She jabbed her small finger at a gouge in his arm that looked like it had been made with a fingernail. "Find nice girl and leave. Better for you."

He should have taken the stitches before those drinks. His eyes drifted closed remembering how something had moved from the baskets of laundry lined on So Chen's floor. Truitt expected a passel of kittens, but it was a round infant face watching him. The baby was swaddled tightly, and after inspecting him, closed its eyes to sleep. Likely, its mother was off working tonight.

Truitt tried to turn over but something pinched a muscle in his back. He groaned, or maybe his whole body was still tense from seeing Cassidy's sudden appearance. It had cost him a lot of money and a pouty sneer from Arnold Snider. He didn't lose the fight and didn't care what Arnold thought. It was the stakes. How many men bet Friday after Friday that his backside would never touch the floor? Tonight he had gone down hard. He could feel it in every lumbering step back to the Bedford.

As usual, he'd tried to pay So Chen from his earnings, but she'd always wanted the same thing from him ever since she'd started her laundry and bathing store—for him to watch out for the Chinese and protect them when he could. They worked harder than anyone coming to the gold country, but often were killed without reason. She housed a number of widows, orphans, and soiled doves within that small establishment, giving from her own profits.

His eyes dropped closed. Hangtown had so few hidden gold treasures like her, it was no bother for him to keep the wolves from her doorstep.

Yawning, he twisted and pulled the blanket over his body. Usually, he read from his pocket Bible before going to sleep, tonight the alcohol and the aches dulled him right out of his usual need for redemption.

TRUITT PEELED HIS eyes open. Someone was pounding on his skull. Or just his door. He awakened and swung to standing.

"Mr. Hansen." Truitt's voice sounded like mixed rock and dirt. Opening the door wider, Arnold Snider's secretary walked in.

"So last week I told you Mr. Snider wanted you to evict the Basque folk? The family with a bunch of kids?"

Truitt scratched his chin and winced at the tender bruised area. "Yep."

"And you never did." The thin man looked up, blinking bug eyes at him.

"Yep." Truitt held onto the open door and his stomach rumbled. He could only hope there was some breakfast left in the kitchen.

"So Mr. Snider wants to give them an extension. I guess the two oldest out of the brood are girls. One fourteen, the other gal older."

Truitt stepped back shaking his head then grabbed it with one hand, rubbing the top of his head in an effort to staunch the pain radiating from there. He already knew where Hansen was going with this.

"Mr. Snider will offer the girls jobs; teach them proper English. They can pay some to the debt and some will go to the family," Mr. Hanson said.

"Jobs to work and learn proper English? You think the Basque family will believe that?"

Mr. Hansen scoffed. "How should I know? He said his new wife will need lots of domestic help in the house. Maybe those girls want out of that tent. Learn to cook and clean in the finest house in town."

"And she doesn't even live there, yet." Truitt stopped his other rebuttals. His back hurt along with his head. "No promises, but I'll see what I can do."

CASSIDY HESITATED, WATCHING Main Street bustling with people. Should she do the polite thing and send word to Mr. Doré? But wouldn't he assume she wasn't coming to play more songs—when she didn't show up? Sometime before the pink and yellow sun rose, she had decided to cool the desire to play her tunes at the El Dorado. Without her grandmother's violin, she had already let the dream go and then in a minute's time, it had jumped back to her heart so fast she was like a bull out of a shoot. Still tired in body and soul, she sighed. She should have never played that song. The faces of all the men resembled the shock that Truitt had flashed at her last night.

"Are you ready?" Finny pulled her cream gloves on. "Arnold is busy working all day and said I may freely roam the large house." She held her hand on the knob. "We can explore and take note of all the things I want to see purchased."

Cassidy wanted to ask her about that. The home was sufficiently furnished, she'd seen that for herself. Biting her tongue, they walked out from the Bedford. At least today would be a distraction from her inner turmoil.

Later in the afternoon, Cassidy held a blue and white vase as Finny cut some fall foliage around the large garden. They walked back to the front steps and someone called out.

"Miss Finnegan."

"Yes." Finny turned and replied before Cassidy had a chance. They both looked down the steps to see Mr. Doré at the gate. Cassidy shot her a scowl.

"Mr. Doré." Cassidy tried to lighten her tone progressing down the steps. "Have you met Miss O'Ryan from Boston? This is Mr. Snider's fiancée."

"I have not had the pleasure." He opened the gate and met them at the bottom porch step. Taking Finny's hand, he kissed it lightly. "Welcome to our fair town, *mademoiselle*."

Finny's eyes sparkled from their usual dull state. "And you, sir, run the El Dorado?"

"*Oui*," his gaze shifted to Cassidy. "And I thought we were to meet again today, chérie, yes? It was going to be the highlight of my day."

"I'm so sorry. I was needed..." the vase and cuttings weighed heavy in her hands, "elsewhere."

"May we reschedule?" His face shone light with sincerity glancing back to Finny. "Your companion has such a gift with her violin. I was led to believe we might find a night for a performance at the El Dorado?"

"This was all she could talk about yesterday," Finny blinked smugly at her.

Cassidy unlocked her jaw. "I did—uh—some reassessing, Mr. Doré. I feel with Miss ah...O'Ryan's wedding in the near future, I must devote my time to helping her prepare her home and...and preparations...in, ah general." She said, refusing to acknowledge Finny's rolling eyes.

"Ahh," Mr. Doré said puzzled. "I had thought of one more idea. The mining town of Coloma has been asking me to recommend some local talents for their new town theater. They are growing fast like Hangtown, but may be a bit quainter than the happenings here. Of course, now I think of you, I wonder if your mistress could spare you one afternoon this week. We could travel before the sun sets and see what you think."

Cassidy tilted her head. "I don't think—"

"Yes, I can spare her." Finny quickly cut Cassidy's excuses off. "How about Wednesday? She can be ready at two o'clock."

"Wonderful!" Mr. Doré clapped his hands. "I will pick you up in front of the hotel." His wide toothy smile covered his face. "Until then, I will count the minutes." He turned and let himself out the gate.

Cassidy twisted a hard glare on Finny.

"I know." Finny took the vase from her hands. "Bonny well done. You are half way to your reputable employment. You and your new violin can thank me later."

Eighteen

WEDNESDAY AFTERNOON, WEARING her deep navy blue dress with matching lace and feathered hat, Cassidy clutched her violin case and exited the tall doors of the Bedford Hotel. Mr. Doré tipped his bowler as he stepped from the carriage. Another man rode backward sitting on a shelf on the rear end of the carriage. A long rifle rested over his lap and his legs dangled off the end.

"Ahh, *la belle dame*." He took Cassidy's hand and kissed it. "I would have sent up for you. How prompt to be waiting for my arrival." He stopped, assessing her. "You look radiant, like the deep blue oceans and you bring your violin. *Très bon*." Taking her hand, he helped her onto the thick leather seat. "You will not need to perform for your supper, *mademoiselle*. That will be my pleasure to supply."

Cassidy felt a faint smile rise as he rounded the back and entered on the other side. No one had said anything about dinner. Just looking at his suit and white cravat today, he was apparently well to do for these parts and held the air of a gentleman. She clutched the violin against her chest, her overly personal gift from the rugged, Friday-night-fighter. Without a word from Truitt since the dreadful night-sighting at the El Dorado, her mind wandered in a hundred different directions. Thoughts about him and what he must think of her flurried like a blizzard. Most of them had only left her more bereft in the heart.

"*Belle dame*, please put your case at our feet." Mr. Doré pulled it from her grasp before she could object. Feeling exposed without her covering, she grabbed the seat as Mr. Doré tapped the horse forward.

Cassidy noticed the sparkle of sunlight and a light breeze through the fall trees. The amber and gold swash of landscape drew her in as they ambled out of Hangtown. It looked similar to some of the lovely country she had traveled through. Was any of it safe? "The man who is with us," Cassidy whispered. "He just needs a ride, or is he a chaperone, I suppose?"

"He is along for his eyes." Mr. Doré nodded. "The one thing I cannot do is see behind me." He paused, looking at her before he smiled.

"Mr. Emerson had mentioned that the law is remiss in these towns." Cassidy straightened her back resisting the swaying with the bumpy road. She glanced at her case and wished it was Truitt taking her on the outing today.

"Ahh, the law. It has been known to be ahh…slipshod. I think that is what the Americans call it."

Cassidy wondered if he knew what had happened to Truitt's father. Hung from a tree in town; wrongly accused without even a trial. Oh, the despair Truitt must have felt.

"But you are safe with me. I have taken the utmost care for us." He nodded. "And there is the pistol, no? I keep in my boot."

Cassidy nodded quickly, hoping to change the subject. "Tell me why you came to Hangtown?"

"I come from a very provincial, yet smart people. While everyone else came searching for gold, I came for what they would spend their gold on. Anything that invariably relieves the miners of their gold dust is good business."

Cassidy remembered thinking Truitt Emerson was only doing Cousin Arnold's bidding, keeping his business interests protected. How did her feelings waver so easily? Why couldn't she stop thinking about him?

"And the management of the El Dorado was available?" Cassidy asked, noticing a grove of almond trees and a woman and children filling their aprons with the nuts off the ground.

"*Oui*, Mr. Snider and I are partners. The building is new and we do a fair business."

Her head craned watching the pickers.

"And those are likely miner's people, scouring for food. A sad existence, *oui*?"

"Humm." Cassidy tried to sit back and relax the tension in her back.

"You, *mademoiselle*, have an unusual talent. Are you opposed to earning money for yourself?" His gaze held hers before she looked away.

"Let me ask you a question, sir." She lightly tapped her chin. "Is it possible for a woman to perform, use her talent in a way…that…does not appear or promote a scandalous reputation?"

Pierre Doré let out a deep laugh. "Who, *belle dame*, is to judge you? You perform well and they pay well. What kind of reputation are you in earnest to protect? A lady's companion with high standards?" He laughed again. "This is unusual to me. You must explain."

Cassidy felt herself bristle and scooted an inch away, she picked up her case and rested it on her lap. "I am from back east as you know." She rubbed her hand over the case. "I was educated well and come from a sterling family."

"*Oui*. Who like me, said their goodbyes. What an opportunity for a brave young woman to have a job that takes you so far from home." He nodded and tapped the reins. "So we are much alike. *Oui*? This land of opportunity is ours."

"That is what I had hoped in coming here." Her gaze drifted back to the trees, a group of birds flitted from tree to tree. "But you, as a man, may choose your business as you please." She met his sincere eyes. "I have to be…be prudent…be wise."

"Have a care, *mon chère*," he brushed his finger over his thin mustache. "You are certainly more valuable than a pound of gold and should never to be exploited. You should consider having a partner. Someone wise to help you; you a woman in desire of her upright reputation."

"What do you mean a partner?"

"Someone like me. You have a talent that I imagine many people will find enjoyable and would pay money to see. But I do not think it safe to find this path on your own. Like today, I would be happy to introduce you to owners and set up your performances. Oversee your safety."

Cassidy's mind flashed to Truitt. He had tried to tell her in the mercantile that she wouldn't be safe to come and go.

"I am not ashamed to tell you." His words broke in. "I am in business to make money. I would take a small percentage as your manager. A small amount goes to the owner of the hotel and the rest would be yours."

Cassidy felt a pang of hope; he made it sound so easy. "Truitt, I mean Mr. Emerson, said that I should not pursue anything without Mr. Snider's permission."

"Humph." His eyes narrowed. "Do you receive wages from Mr. Snider? This job as a companion?"

"No, I was compensated by the O'Ryan family. But my...my charge is related to Arnold. So I suppose the dowry and finances we have are family money." Cassidy frowned. Mr. Dingle was put in charge of the money. How strange it had felt to have it in her possession. "Is Mr. Snider to say what kind of performers are allowed in Hangtown or Coloma?"

Tilting his head, Pierre Doré lifted the corner of his mouth. "Not in Coloma."

Cassidy looked down to her case and felt a stab of fear. A foolish dream was one thing to hold, but these were strange towns with mixtures of all kinds of people. It was so easy to entertain others on the wagon trail. No money, no agreement. Just regular folk who asked for their favorite songs around a campfire. Somehow the business end of her dream was confusing. What should she do?

He was right about not doing this alone in these bustling mining towns. There was an undercurrent of unexpected danger and not just for a woman, considering what happened to Truitt's father. She could feel it. Glancing over at him, their eyes met, and she lifted a quick shrug. She didn't really know this man. Often she noted there was devilish mischief in that large smile.

Taking in a deep breath, she watched a few farms and ranches begin to dot the landscape. A creek on the side of the road was growing larger and larger. Men crouched in the water swishing large pans around and around, while others were swinging heavy picks into the rocky, wet soil. Some heard the wagon wheels crunch on the road and looked up, staring at them as they passed.

"I suppose we should see how the day goes. But you are right, Mr. Doré. I am not from here nor a businesswoman. I won't pretend to know the ins and outs of securing a recital or musical event." Her voice sounded forlorn. "Or securing my own protection." Turning in her seat, the man on the back of the carriage pushed a wad of tobacco from inside one cheek to the other. A shadow of homesickness came over her. Recalling Truitt's hand in hers, she began to calm and soften. Her frayed edges started to smooth out and strengthen a bit.

"Oh, *jusqu'ou va ta beaute*," Mr. Doré murmured in French.

The dirt roads and bustling town of Coloma came into view, and she was too distracted to ask Mr. Doré what he'd said. She'd no choice but to trust Truitt to get her safely to Hangtown. She took a deep breath. Now to trust again.

Nineteen

As SOON AS Mr. Doré stopped the carriage, people turned their heads to watch them. Pierre Doré's suit was extravagant. His bright crimson cummerbund shone from his waistcoat almost as flamboyant as his intricately tied cravat. Cassidy clutched her violin close. A weathered-faced woman with a sour expression looked Cassidy up and down before nodding. Trying to ignore the stares, she took Mr. Doré's offered elbow and followed him down the dirt street.

"Highfalutin," a dusty, short man said as they passed.

"We seem a bit out of place, sir." Cassidy tried to steady her breath.

"As we should." Mr. Doré pinched his cravat tighter. "To play the part, you have to look the part." He straightened. "They cannot decide who to gawk at more. You or me." They stepped up on a wooden sidewalk. A tall, brick building came into view. "This is the Gold Dust Building. There is a woman in the kitchen who makes the best mince pies you've ever tasted. But we can wait for that. Would you like to see the theater, the gathering hall?"

"Yes, please."

Mr. Doré released her arm and pulled the tall door open. Cassidy was hit with an unusual smell of floor wax and stale bread or maybe bodies. There was a long thick oak bar that spanned the right side of the room. Four rough and tumbled men leaned against it. All of them turned and looked her over like *she* was a piece of mince pie.

"Not as large as the El Dorado," Mr. Doré said, drawing her attention away from the gray shadows of the room. "But this is the small stage. He touched her elbow and led her between the round tables. Cassidy noticed the simple two-step wooden platform covered with a red and black patterned rug. She stepped up on the first step and tried to find something good about the room. Stomach churning, she stepped down. A small troupe of theater types would fit in well here, she thought.

"Pierre, is that you?" An older, gray-haired man with a towel hanging from his pocket walked toward them.

"*Oui*, Mr. Royce Harkin." Mr. Doré shook his hand vigorously. "I want you to meet the lovely Miss Cassidy Finnegan from Boston."

The man nodded nervously, "Ma'am."

"We've made a special outing today to see you." Mr. Doré said.

Mr. Harkin's eye's widened on Pierre. "You finally got that fighter to agree to come here?"

"Ahh, *non, monsieur*. Unfortunately, he is still in employment with Mr. Snider and cannot break away from that agreement. But I have found someone else that might work for entertainment here at the fine Gold Dust." Mr. Doré rested his hand on her shoulder.

Mr. Harkin's face sunk and Cassidy swallowed a rock in her throat.

"I...I appreciate that she's a pretty thing. But I got women every week kickin' up their skirts for pennies and nickels."

"Of course." Mr. Doré replied overly confident. Cassidy felt her heart thud slower. Mr. Harkin wasn't interested in a true performance. Looking to the ground, she sighed, at least it was a beautiful day for a fall buggy ride.

"But would you give her...say five minutes, *monsieur*?" Mr. Doré placed his hand on her back, and she felt herself taking hesitant steps up the stage. "I think she might change your mind."

"I got five minutes." Mr. Harkin huffed.

"Do the same song you did for me at the El Dorado," he whispered as Cassidy took her violin from the case.

Cassidy scanned the room and took a deep breath. Like playing around the campfire. She rested her chin on the chin rest and warmed up hearing the proper notes in tune. Picturing the faces of the weary travelers standing in the open prairie, she set the strings ablaze into her foot tapping reel. Just remembering how the women would reach for their men to dance and children would laugh and spin with delight. How could she not play the foot stomping tune with love and vigor? Eyes closed she brought the violin up and down and swayed left to right, how could a body not move with the rambunctious melody? Holding out the last notes, she smiled. Most of the staff and a few passerby folks had entered the room. They stared at her, and she recalled a glorious memory. Truitt's astonished expression, eyeing her at the El Dorado pounding his thick hands together to clap for her.

"Can you play 'By the River, my darlin?'" A young man from the back yelled across the room. She looked to Mr. Doré, and he raised a brow and shrugged. Nodding at the young man in the back, she started the soft melody that moved faster and faster until she saw the men at the bar drumming their hands on the bar in time. When she played the chorus one extra time, the young man spun a heavy set woman with a dirty apron in a circle. She laughed and skipped along with him. Just like when she was a child at the pub, people could drop the heavy loads from their care for a few minutes. Her heart overflowed as they whooped and clapped.

Mr. Harkin scratched his head as she placed her violin in the case. Mr. Doré held his hand out as she came down the steps.

Mr. Harkin rubbed the back of his neck. "She's gonna' set this place on its ear. Are you going to be here to manage this, manage her comin' and goin'?"

Pierre Doré looked wide-eyed at Cassidy. "I would be happy to."

Cassidy felt her heart pounding from the exertion. "I...I...suppose yes." What other choice did she have? Mr. Doré had made all this possible.

"*Magnifique!*" He clapped his hands and patted her on her back. "We are in business!"

An hour later they sat at one of the tables, while the young man who had requested a song brought them plates and silverware, bread and meat on a platter. The lady with the dirty apron commented on Cassidy's amazing talent and thanked her many times for working here at the Gold Dust.

Working at the Gold Dust?

Cassidy chatted with the woman while Mr. Doré settled amounts and ideas for her nights of performance. She'd lived in her father's house long enough to know it wasn't proper for her to be in on the business side, but two dollars and fifty cents for dinner and entertainment seemed exorbitant. The woman left and came back holding three slices of mince pie. Mr. Doré beamed his bright, wide smile as she set it in front of him.

He squeezed the waitress's hand. "Madame, this will be my reward." He glanced at Cassidy, "And hearing your heartfelt melodies every Saturday night."

"Every Saturday night, are you sure?" Cassidy tapped the napkin on the corner of her mouth. "Won't the people tire of my jigs and songs?" Cassidy thought of what Finny would say. What if Cousin Arnold heard of this? "Maybe I should start with only one Saturday a month?"

"Ah, *mademoiselle*, you can trust me as your manager," Mr. Doré stated heartily, licking his fork. "I will tell you the details on the way home." He lightly patted her back. "If you do not care for this pie, I will take yours?" Cassidy grinned, never trying a bite. His eyes widened as she pushed her pie over in front of him.

"*Tué š une femme adorable.*" He winked at her.

Mr. Harkin snorted with a sort of sly expression and shook his head. Cassidy had the sudden urge to tell him they were only in business together. They were not a couple. These smiles and pats didn't mean she was with Mr. Doré. She watched as he ate her pie. The Frenchman was friendly, helpful. All his gestures never seemed like overtures for more. Just a friendship. A business arrangement. And who cared what the people of

Coloma thought? This was a job she would love and do until she could find out more about the Pacific Minstrels. This was an experience for her future.

A strange stab of consciousness still pained her chest. What would Truitt say? Didn't she just say to herself, she'd set aside the idea of playing for others? Focus on helping Finny with the house and getting her safely to the altar? As the men continued to talk, Cassidy sighed. Ever since the lies and deception started at Damonte Station, she hadn't felt like herself. Obviously, living a lie will do that. Swallowing a groan, she chewed on the corner of her bottom lip.

Becoming involved with Truitt Emerson was the deeper root. The deception with him constantly gnawed at her gut. Most nights sleep was difficult and her thoughts raced like never before. As the two businessmen talked about advertising, security, and her performance, she wondered who the true Kathleen Cassidy O'Ryan was. Her true identity seemed to be fading from her being and disappearing into uncontrollable imaginings of what she thought she wanted.

Twenty

WITH HEAVY STEPS, Cassidy held her skirts and violin, climbing the stairs of the Bedford Hotel, and turned toward her room. On the ride back to Hangtown, Mr. Doré had made the arrangement sound so easy. She would need to perform five or six songs each Saturday evening. A dinner of chicken gravy over potatoes would be enjoyed by the patrons. After the performance they would spend the night at the Gold Dust. The idea of traveling the road from Coloma to Hangtown in the dark sounded frightful.

Would spending the night in Coloma be worse?

Maybe Finny would reverse their agreement and come along as her companion? She doubted it. Seeing the number of her door, she set her violin down. Her thoughts drifted to Mr. Doré and the firm hold he'd taken of her hand. Before she could pull away or step into the lobby, he'd bent at the waist and kissed it softly then looked long into her eyes, his large wide smile, his leaning toward her too close—

"Cassidy."

Gasping, her head jerked up breaking free of the strange thoughts. "Truitt!" He had a boot on the top step of the back stairs.

"Cassidy." Repeating her name, he rested his broad shoulder against the stairwell and teased her with a coy smile.

"Truitt." This time she could echo without her heart thudding from her throat. Even with a small cut on his cheek surrounded with yellow and deep purple, he looked ruddy, enticing, and far too handsome.

"Should I say your name one more time? This is fun." He brought his large frame up into her hallway. "How was your trip to Coloma?"

How did he know? She'd barely returned. "It was pleasant." He came a step closer, and she backed up against the door. Had he seen Mr. Doré kiss her hand? Searching for the handle behind her back, she stammered for the right words.

"I...I... wanted to apologize for the other night. Ahh, Friday night?" She rubbed the blue collar back and forth at her neck feeling her stomach jump at his nearing stance. She pulled the pin from her hair and slid it into the feathery hat then held the silly thing at the side of her skirt. "It was the strangest thing. One minute Fin...Kathleen and I were finishing up with the tailor. The very next minute, like swoosh." She waved her hand and hat in the air. "There we were standing at the window of the El Dorado."

He twirled his hand in the air towards her. "Like swoosh." He cocked his head to the side, narrowing his rogue gaze.

"Are you going to repeat everything I say?" She straightened taller.

He took her empty hand in his and opened it. Tracing with his finger, he spelled. N—O.

A hundred butterflies started somewhere around her shoulders and ran straight through her body. Without a doubt, her toes tingled. Shocked by the light-headedness she felt, she pulled her hand back. "Miss O'Ryan is...is...needing...me..." Oh Lord, oh lolly, he was leaning closer, and she was trapped by his size and that tempting presence. He smelled like soap and fresh cut wood and those bruises on his whiskered face begged to be soothed. When she could not compact herself any more against the door, it gave way.

Cassidy staggered back then righted herself. With a hand to her throat she said, "Oh, I didn't see you opening the door for me." *Of course, I didn't. I was too busy swooning.* She clenched her teeth together and looked around the room. "Oh, she's not here. Humph." Truitt leaned against the door frame extending her violin to her.

"Where did you play?" His voice deepened, and his eyes rested on her corner bed.

"I played at the Gold Dust." She grabbed the violin case and swished to the side, pulling her nightgown from the end of the bed and tossed it behind her dressing screen one-handed.

"And?" He waited.

"And it went well." She laid the case across her bed. "Mr. Doré has set up arrangements for me to play there on Saturday nights."

"Is that so? Mr. Doré did. And who will see you home on Saturday nights?" His voice was nonchalant but hardened.

"I...uh...spoke directly, uh straightforward, with him. My desire for myself in the entertainment business is to have a respected reputation. We will stay at the hotel as not to endanger ourselves with a dark ride home."

"So you are going to spend the night with him at the Gold Dust?"

She drew herself up into an indignant pose. "Not *with* him!" she exclaimed. Did he listen at all? Closing her eyes, she let out a quick grunt. "I will find a chaperone of course."

"I thought you were here to *be* the chaperone? Where is your mistress?"

"Why do you ask me?" she snapped back. "You are the one who knows all the goings on in this town." She covered her mouth, her eyes wide. Without warning, her tone had assumed a nasty sarcasm just like Finny's.

He looked at his boots, nodding his head. "She's with Snider at the silversmith. Gold bands I think is what they are having sized." He tapped the heel of his boot on the toe of the other. "Cassidy, do you trust me?" His voice was so calm and soothing, like their night in that little cave, she had to force herself to focus on what he was asking.

"I do," she whispered, feeling remorse and longing all at the same time.

"You need to step with care." Looking down, he still tapped heel to toe again. "I told you, Arnold doesn't like things going on without his permission."

A chilled tremor rolled through Cassidy even though the room wasn't cold. "Did he send you today to do his dirty work? Have you been watching all my comings and goings?" Her eyes narrowed, but he still looked to the floor, ignoring her questions. Was Cousin Arnold going to control her every move? How dare he think he could control her choices, too?

Her questions elicited nothing but his silence, which provoked her further. "Are there consequences for Mr. Doré taking business from Hangtown? Are you here to try to scare me?" she accused. "Keeping me close," she muttered, eyes flashing. "All these smiles and teasing, expanding my affections for you...I mean." She tried to calm herself. "Trust in you is...is really for business?" Oh, her tongue was crooked when she was upset.

Nodding slowly up and down, he scratched the back of his head then bent forward watching her from under his eyebrows. "I'm not sure what you just meant or what you want from me." He took in a breath and rose taller. "I wanted to ask a favor, is the reason I came."

Cassidy brushed a loose strand behind her ear. It had been a long day, had she taken all her own fears out on him? Trying to grab a bit of calmness, she turned to the window. The building and commotion of Hangtown had quieted. A man lit the Hangtown lanterns on tall poles. Closing her eyes, she took in a deep breath.

"I apologize for my discord, please, what do you want to ask?

COULD A MAN be any more inept around a beautiful woman? Truitt glanced back to the hallway. It was only a few steps back down the back stairs. Why did he find this so difficult? She wasn't his girl or lover or anything. Just like Marianna, there wasn't any loyalty in her heart for him. Was there?

She turned from the window, and her gray-blue eyes had softened a bit. A cordial opening was all he needed. "There are two sisters who are going to be working at the Snider house," he began. "I don't remember their names. But would you be willing to help them with English? They're from Spain and their father is not doing so well in his mining claim." Just like the dunce who owned the claim before him. Truitt wondered why each prospector assumed they would find gold when no one else had before them at the same place using the same equipment. "So Arnold offered the girls a job at the house. Your mistress likes lots of... help." While Cassidy listened, her hands clutched in front of her deep blue skirt, he continued, "I suppose that she is used to being waited on, having you and all."

Her head dipped to the side, possibly questioning his request. "I would be happy to." She stepped forward. "I will ask... Miss O'Ryan how she would like me to proceed with the young women."

The silence was thick as a granite wall, and he thought he'd rather fight a grizzly this Friday than find the right words for those tired round eyes that studied him.

"You have a fury all your own, Mr. Emerson." A slight blush appeared on her cheeks. "It frightened me to see you in that fighting match." She chewed on the corner of her lip. "When you saw me, I ran like the mudslide was after me. Finny teased me. Which is nothing new." She sighed, and he wished he could understand what really frightened her. "It hurt me to see you in that sport." Her voice softened as he tried to understand what he saw flickering in those sincere eyes.

"Why *did* you run?" He fought the urge to close the space between them.

A crooked smile arose before she looked down. "It's ridiculous now. I—I—"

Cassidy suddenly crumpled, closed her eyes and locked her jaw. "I meant Miss Kathleen. Forgive me, so many on the wagon train got us mixed up. We have these silly names for each other." She rubbed her forehead. "I don't know now why I ran like that. I just thought maybe I could have caused you to lose." She wrung her hands in nervous dismay.

Truitt couldn't help examining her beauty head to toe. One minute feisty and the next so polite and refined. "You didn't," he answered. Did she know her words and the soothing tones of her voice were making her the most strikingly appealing woman? Even more so than her perfect shape and feminine stature?

"I need to leave you." He reached for her door handle. "But hear me, Cassidy. I find no satisfaction in these words." His grip squeezed the handle. "You have taken a great risk and shown pure determination. The very thing people need to survive here in the west," he opened the door wider, "but you are naïve. I'm not the only one who does dirty work for Arnold Snider. There is a rancid, ruthless business in this town that even your ill-tempered mistress would cower under if she knew. You have to stay on the right side of it. I have a notion," he waited till her eyes met his, "just as you don't like to see me in the fighting match, I don't want you to get your hopes up and see your music as your freedom and as easy work. There is no such thing here."

She nodded slowly. "Once again, I apologize. I often misjudge you and yet you still come back to offer gracious help." Her tone was sincere. "I will speak to Mr. Snider so as not to do anything without his permission."

Truitt studied her expression while his jaw rocked to the side and his lips pursed. Then he nodded. "Very well. I will say goodnight." He slowly pulled the door closed and reluctantly let her out of his sight.

He descended to his room, his usual loud boot thuds on the stairs accompanied him. He wondered if that had gone well or not. Besides beautiful, Cassidy was a smart woman, there was no doubt. Did he make her sound insufficient, incapable? Instinctively, he knew she was the one to help the girls handle the fine home. He knew she would treat them with care and concern. That's who she'd always shown herself to be. Any education might help them rise above being Arnold's newest exploitations. The first word she should try to get the two young innocents to say with fervor was, "no!"

Twenty-One

A FEW DAYS later, Cassidy sat at the kitchen table of Cousin Arnold's home with the two teen-aged sisters. Soft-spoken Emery was eighteen and apprehensive Gianna was fifteen. Both were lovely girls with sweet round eyes, rags for clothes, and nervous dispositions. Finny had given her free reign to help them with English as she deemed herself too busy to help.

Cassidy shook her head as she pushed pencils and paper in front of the girls. Finny could have used these lessons as well. Cassidy wanted to start with the first letters of the alphabet and the sounds and then help the girls write them. Reading and writing were as essential as being able to speak the words.

By the end of the hour she could tell they had had some schooling. They were bright and eager, so Cassidy went on to help them say some common items in the kitchen. Both teens were excited and accommodating. Cassidy enjoyed praising them for correct pronunciations and recalling the things they had gone over. Continually they bowed and repeated a heartfelt 'thank you' for her help.

Hearing a rumble outside, Cassidy peered out the window over the sink. Cousin Arnold pulled up in the back of the house and Nelson held his carriage as he jumped out. Cassidy felt her spine stiffen and mouth go dry. It was now or never. She handed the girls a dusting cloth and asked them to clean in the parlor.

Arnold came in the back door and stopped to see her in the kitchen. "Ah, yes, Miss Finnegan. Kathleen said you needed to talk to me today." He peered at the kitchen table. "I can see you are helping the poor Basques." He scratched under his chin. "I want you to remind them of their station, to do as they are told, and they will make money to help their family. If they do not, their family will be evicted from their claim."

Cassidy had always loved going by the name her grandmother had used all her childhood. But hearing Cousin Arnold use her real name, Kathleen to refer to Finny made her bristle. She swallowed his punitive remarks. "That is a lot of pressure for two young teens. Surely their father is providing something?" Cassidy didn't appreciate the harsh consequence for the new girls.

Arnold's brow creased. "Maybe if their father didn't sire a child every year, he'd have enough money to feed them. But you understand, that is none of your concern." He stared down his narrow nose at her. "If they don't toe the line here, I could make them pay in other ways," his tone was menacing.

"Yes, sir." Cassidy wanted favor today not more strife. "I will help them understand."

Arnold's eyes grazed over her body, and she took a step back, looking down. Briefly she wondered what other ways. She didn't believe he was capable of—

"I feel as if I know you," he said. "It happened the first time I saw you. Could you have been employed somewhere in the O'Ryan household, the last time I was there?"

Cassidy's throat constricted. What had Finny said? Would their stories match? "I...I...had a distant relation that worked in the kitchen." That was how Finny found her way there, as an orphan. "I often visited, even developing a friendship with Miss O'Ryan through the years." Her voice drifted with uncertainty at the end. "Our paths might have crossed."

"Humph." Crossing his arms, his stiff black suit rustling with the strain, he stood thinking.

Cassidy attempted to break his scrutiny of her, "I would like to have your permission in an endeavor that has crossed my path recently."

Arnold frowned. "To play your violin at the Gold Dust?"

Her eyes widened and she found a calm voice. "Yes, sir."

"I already spoke with Doré and Emerson. You seem to have found a way to wrap your charm around them and your interests in with theirs. Two men. I must say, Miss Finnegan," a flash of obscene disapproval swept his expression, "since this is my town, I did feel a bit left out."

Cassidy crossed her arms over her chest and felt her fists twitching to point out his crudeness. She scratched her elbow. "Sir, you have been rightly preoccupied. Waiting for all these months for your devoted fiancée to reach California. I can understand what it must be like to finally have her here after all this time. Alive, healthy, and very much enthralled with you."

His cheek twitched a small smile, her words finding their mark. "She's been worth the wait," he said with satisfaction oozing from his tone.

Cassidy felt her body still. His improper tone hung in the air between them. If Finny had partaken in the marriage bed with this man, she would clock him with her violin. Doubting her friend was a blushing victim, all the late nights and excuses for not needing an escort spoke of something scandalous. But any woman worth her white petticoat would know not to go too far. Oh, lolly, her stomach sank, this was Finny she was talking about.

"So here is what I will allow." His words brought her back to the moment. "Remember you are still my Kathleen's servant. And you will at all times represent my interests." He waggled his head. "Though both Doré and Emerson claim you are uncompromising about having a shiny reputation."

"That is true. I believe a performer can—"

"Save your speech," he cut her off. "I've heard it all before. It's my wishes you will keep. So, on Friday nights you will start at the El Dorado at six. Emerson starts around eight. There will be a fee at the door to hear you and a fee for those who want the Emerson fight."

Friday nights at the El Dorado? Cassidy wanted to question as he rambled on.

"Then on Saturday you will travel with Doré and play at the Gold Dust. He said he would represent my wishes and keep tabs on you. Then Monday through Friday, you are to be at Miss O'Ryan's call. She is never to be left alone in this town. If she wants to go outside and see a bird fly you are to be with her. If she wants an item at the mercantile, you are to be with her. If there is ever a sign of any Indians, even peaceful, you are to remove her from the area immediately. Are you listening to me?" he scolded.

Indians? Stunned and amused, Cassidy wondered why he didn't mention her aversion to snow.

"You are here now and where is my fiancée, Miss Finnegan?" suddenly his voice rose with anger.

"I—I—she told me to go on." Cassidy stammered. "She wanted to sleep in."

"Unacceptable!" he yelled, and Cassidy stepped back. Glancing to the Basque girls cleaning, she regretted that the absurd and angry Mr. Snider was their new boss.

"I—I—am aware now of how strongly you feel." The word 'sir' would not leave her lips. He was her cousin, for heaven's sake. How dare he be so authoritative with her? "I'd like to say something." She cleared the tension stuck in her throat. "Since I had no idea you would allow me to play at the El Dorado, may I suggest a Wednesday evening or Sunday matinee. Families and children enjoy many of my tunes. I've seen the Friday nights. It's all men. Certainly, we could find a time where other community members would enjoy a musical soiree?"

"A musical soiree?" his tone dripped his outrage. "The community, the families you speak of, have better things to do with their gold dust. They don't have any need for entertainment. The women should all be working, the children also. That's the only way they can survive. If the men don't like your tunes as you call them, your performing days will end quickly. I suggest you pick your songs with men in mind." He watched the Basque girls dusting. "And make sure they get all the sills and floor corners. This town is one ball of dust, and most of it tries to rest in my house."

A sharp bolt of anger tried to reach her mouth. She was here to teach them English, not take a white glove to their work. Surely his future new wife could rise from bed earlier to see the domestic duties completed.

"I'll have the posters made today. You start on Friday at six." He looked her up and down and sighed. "Thankfully, my Kathleen did not take to your advice on feminine wear. This type of gown is unacceptable for the El Dorado. I'll have something sent over Friday." He must have seen the narrowing of her eyes because he added in a stern tone, "You will wear it."

She went to open her mouth. Her gowns were appropriate for anywhere, stage or—

"And add some rouge to those pale cheekbones." Huffing, he dropped his fist on his hip, and Cassidy bit her tongue till it bled. "And get these two girls something form fitting. I can't have them looking like scalawags that just crawled from the hold of one of my ships. Teach them some grooming while you're at it."

Cassidy blinked back her wrath. Shipping was her family business. What would her father say of the way his brother's step-son rudely flaunted his wealth and power? Arnold grabbed a large cookie from a plate she'd brought for the girls and walked out. She spun in a circle and clawed the air and spun in another circle. Closing her eyes, she rubbed her forehead, listening to his fancy carriage roll out. There was not one street in this town you could not walk to. "How overly pretentious could one man be?" She uttered under her breath.

"Ladies come." She waved them in. "A cookie for each of us and then we are to go shopping and see how much of Mr. Snider's money we can spend." They smiled wide-eyed at the cookies she placed in their hands, likely unsure of the other thing she said. But it didn't matter, though cookie crumbs crumbled from their mouths, they would be proper young working maidens, dressed head to toe in new things. It sounded as if their mother had nothing to look forward to but work. It was high time this woman also got a new shawl and stockings for the winter. Thanks to Arnold Snider. She grinned.

Twenty-Two

"**I** CANNOT POSSIBLY wear this!" Cassidy snapped at Finny, turning in front of the large mirror. "Where did he find this blue costume?" she boomed. "Am I supposed to hold my hand over my bare bosom and play the violin at the same time?!"

Finny snickered, covering her mouth. "And do a jig." Finny pointed out the ruffles in front of the skirt were gathered up, revealing Cassidy's black stockings. "I didn't say anything about the revealing bodice, but I did mention to Arnold you can do those taps and hops while you play."

"On the *prairie*, Finny Finnegan! With all my suitable clothing and children and old folks clapping along." She moaned. "I have less than thirty minutes before I need to be there. This will not do." Cassidy began to twist and finger the black ribbon along the back.

"Wait, wait. Don't throw a paddy now. It's not that bad." Finny came near and grabbed the low bodice and tugged upward. There is a trim of black lace here for your shoulders, and you really can't see that much. Trust me. You should be thankful for your fullness of chest. It will sell more tickets."

"Ahhh…" Cassidy pushed away. "Leave me be, so I can change."

"Cassidy, I have an idea." Finny grabbed her arm to stop her. "Just don't tell Arnold it was me." Finny pulled her white lace-trimmed hankie from her pocket. "This will keep it from gapping, look." Finny folded the hankie in a triangle and shoved the pointy end into the tightly fitting bodice. Cassidy took over the spacing and tucking until she could see that it adequately concealed her cleavage.

"Remember you will be holding a violin. All that bowing and moving you do. No one will see a thing."

"What about my ankles?" Cassidy looked again in the mirror. "My stockings are showing!"

"Look at all these other ruffles and gathers." Finny pulled out the royal blue satin fabric. "The way you move and sway will keep them flowing around, and no one will get a full look." Finny stepped in front of the long mirror blocking her vision. "It's only an hour. Let's pin the front of your hair back and leave the rest down. It will cover your shoulders, and you will feel more like your overly modest self."

Cassidy allowed her to help with her hair, but there was nothing Finny could say or do to help curb her rolling nausea. Cousin Arnold was parading her for profit. Maybe she would squeak out every poor note until they all booed her off the stage. Just like Truitt getting knocked to the floor, her conscience would feel the bruises, but she would heal. Finny moved back, and Cassidy took a deep breath, looking long into the mirror. She didn't feel as humiliated as she had a few minutes ago. "Thank you, Finny, my hair looks better, and your tucked hankie makes me feel more respectable."

"Thank me by getting your cape and violin and showing this town who you are. Remember why you came this far?" Finny provoked. "You walked and rode across America, Cassidy. Isn't this your dream?"

Finny's words pierced a belly of nerves. She had scraped and traveled so far. Even denying her own name and defying her family. How was she to find her confidence in San Francisco if she couldn't find the initiative for playing her tunes in Hangtown? Squaring her shoulders, while holding the black lace trim in place, she turned and grabbed her case.

TRUITT STOOD JUST inside the front door of the El Dorado and scanned the room. Only the usual two poker games on the far left were going. The rest of the tables had already been moved to the side, expecting men to stand like most Friday nights. The long bar was shoulder to shoulder with men leaning on it to talk and order a drink or two. He tried to slow his breathing. The place looked peaceful, harmless enough. Posters had gone up around town — some drawing of a saloon girl playing tonight that looked nothing like Cassidy.

"Suppose you don't own two bits to get in." A tall teen with a sagging hat and missing front tooth caught his attention. "Seein' yous up next." The teen held a bucket to collect tonight's price to get in. Two bits was a lot for a gal playing the violin. Truitt was inwardly pleased most things in the gold towns were hugely overpriced. He didn't want some crowd of men all gawking at her.

He made enough money every Friday night to keep them both in plenty.

The wayward thought rattled him. What kind of woman wants to work and make a wage? Performing in front of others no less? A few more men paid and walked by him. Though she possessed great talent, why had she never spoken of finding a good man and the benefit of settling down? He carefully wiped his hand across the facial stubble that hid his healing cuts and bruises. Obviously, because she hadn't met one yet that turned her head.

And how long would she continue to carry a naïve view of this new state of California? It was one of the things he liked about her. She wasn't ruined or bitter yet. This town, his father's death, and Marianna had surely ruined his disposition. Those dark, foul memories he held close in his chest and right into his fists tonight. He'd a fury all his own, she had remarked. Hidden truth spoke from her remarkable insight. He sighed.

In their short time together, Cassidy could see him so well. Glancing up to the stage, he could still picture her last week when she'd played one of her songs. Undeniably, the woman had spark and a gift for the instrument like nothing he'd ever heard before. But everything about her felt like a gift. Her voice, her touch, seemed to be the only things that quieted his turmoil, settled his restlessness. A group of five dirty miners dropped their coin in the bucket and snapped him back to the upcoming Friday night entertainment at the El Dorado.

"Let's get this frolic started!" One of the men hackled, pounding the back of another.

"So where is this fiddle bloomin' wench?" the other said.

Truitt clenched his jaw and shook his head. This might be the right moment to start the boxing match first.

A few minutes later, like a trapped animal looking for an exit, Truitt paced along the side of the walls, watching the sparse room begin to fill. Some admirer tried to say something about his fight tonight but he never heard a word as Cassidy and Pierre Doré stepped from the back hall and on to the stage. The whistling and whooping started just as he thought it would. She looked like a shiny, crisp apple, more innocent, feminine and desirable than ever before. Softly warming up her notes, the crowd quieted, and he couldn't take his eyes off her.

As Doré talked about what an incredible talent they would experience tonight, her eyes shifted above and around the room until she saw him. He could feel the moment, the impact of their eyes meeting across the huge room. It felt like molasses sliding down into his lungs. With locked eyes on his, the faintest smile rose. Like they were the only two in the room until Doré backed way and she lifted her violin under her chin.

Truitt felt himself holding his breath as she started in on the song that she'd played before. For the first five minutes or so, the room watched in amazement, not knowing what to make of her. Finally, a man at the front of the stage began to stomp his boot and whack his thigh. Cassidy must have felt the shift in the room, as she swayed closer to him and bounced and turned a circle in front of him. Soon five and then ten began to clap along and she wheeled back to the other side of the stage and tapped and danced a jig. The men went wild, and soon the whole room clapped practically drowning out her lively tune. She held her violin and bow upward and strung out the last pure note as the men broke into applause.

She bowed holding her violin across her chest like she had done this all her life. Starting in on a softer mesmerizing song, it sounded like a ballad from the old country. Truitt noticed a few men grabbing their handkerchiefs and wiping their faces. Still, not one person in the room could take his eyes off her and Truitt felt an unusual softening in himself as he leaned his back into the wall. How did she pull the full and the thin notes from the same strings? An untainted melody that would stop a bird from singing.

With each pure note his fortitude was buckling, her tender flair seemed to wash the tensions of the day away. And if that wasn't ruin enough, she lowered her violin and boldly sang the last chorus of the song.

"The curs'ed brigade

Hey, ho anybody home?

Old Shane's misfortune.

My sweet Molly, Oh where have you gone."

Sweeter than one could imagine, her singing held her youth and passion in the same smooth, clean breath. Her eyes flickered to him, and he felt the demolishing of his heart and soul. What beautiful audacity. He released a gruff chuckle. She'd found the intimacy of taking him to a cliff and then, without pause, pushed him off. Helpless against the hitch in his pulse, he listened while she finished out the song with the rich notes of the violin mimicking her last touching vocals.

The men clapped enough to shake the windows, and she quickly regained control by starting a familiar hymn *Holy, Holy, Holy, Lord God Almighty*. That was the Cassidy he knew. The only one who could take a rough and reckless crowd of men and have them all singing along like choir boys at their mother's knee.

"This anit' Sunday, gal!" an old miner yelled from the back.

Cassidy held out the last note and glared at the man like he was about to be cooked in oil. Then her bright smile surprisingly lit up the stage, and she started in on another knee-slapping rambunctious tune. Her hair swung behind her, and she dipped and rose up on her toes. The men followed suit and a few of them hooked elbows and begun to spin each other in a circle.

Across the room, he saw Arnold frowning and his fiancée Kathleen O'Ryan attached to his arm with her matching expression. Neither seemed pleased to see Cassidys command of the audience.

More men began to spin while others were bounced and jostled between the dancing. Truitt saw a man fall to the floor and came up pushing. His shove knocked into another man, and he turned without warning and swung a punch into the unaware man's cheek. That knocked two other men to the floor, and in a blink you couldn't tell who was dancing and who was fighting. Cassidy had stayed to one spot and played while watching the room rock with movement. Out of the corner of his eye, he saw three dirty miners whisper and elbow each other. All three had their sights set on Cassidy's startled eyes. As soon as he saw them approach the side steps, Truitt came off the wall like a raging bull, tossing scrapping men aside like rag dolls.

He'd only one set of light blue eyes, fashioned inside soft lashes and surrounded with copper curls in mind. Turning away fearful, her blue satin dress was moving backward, but never out of his steely focus.

Twenty-Three

"GENTLEMEN!" DORÉ YELLED, jostled by the crowd inches from the stage. Truitt jumped up on the stage and grabbed Cassidy's arm and pulled her quickly back behind the stage curtains.

"Now you've started a riot." he huffed, searching the low lit hallway. "Quick, in here." He pulled her inside a storage closet as her violin slammed against the door jam.

"Truitt! Careful!" She stumbled in and pulled her violin close. As soon as the door clicked closed, they were both sunk into darkness with only a shimmer coming through the top and bottom of the door.

"I can't see. I can't see if my violin's okay."

"Shush." Truitt took the violin and bow from her and set them on a tall trunk. "I'll buy you another." Even in the dim light, he looked away, the white fabric tucked in the top of her dress had slipped loose. The shadows accentuated her ample curves and beauty. "Quiet, until they give up looking for you." He whispered, only inches away.

Did she feel the same impact he'd felt when her sweet eyes fixed them together tonight? It was undeniable, he knew what those coy looks meant to him. They had feelings, extreme attraction feelings. Slowly, he slipped his hands around her waist. She smelled like rosewater, and the little closet closed in tighter. What he wanted was far past a blushing schoolboy kiss, so he pulled her against him. "You were good tonight Cassidy." His voice low and husky. "Too good."

The rounds of her eyes looked long into his and he had no patience to wait for a spoken invitation. Raising his hand and fingers up under her hair, his free forearm felt the lovely warmth of her back and he gently drew her closer until her lips met his. Stunned beyond mere words, his kiss was the only reasonable expression he could offer this beauty. Kiss after dizzying kiss they became more hungry and wanting. Hearing a small whimper from her throat only drove him senseless until he wrapped his arms around her and lifted her off her feet, kissing her neck, temple, and ear as she wiggled in his arms. She was everything a man could dream and more—

"Wait" Chest rising and falling, she pushed against him, and he slowly lowered her down his body till her toes touched the floor. The white fabric fell loose from her bodice, and he went to catch it.

She jolted backward. "You tried to touch my breast!" She snatched the fabric from his hand. "Kissing a woman defenseless in a dark closet is not enough for you?"

"I wasn't…" A wide smile and laugh couldn't be contained. "Wasn't trying to…to take liberties." He rubbed his finger under his bottom lip, hoping they could return to what was happening a second ago.

"I think you were." She choked, shoving the fabric over her cleavage. "Like a miner staking a claim, I suppose."

His good humor stopped abruptly. "Staking a claim?" His eyes slanted.

"I saw the men going from enjoying the concert to something else," she scoffed. "You just happened to get here first."

"I just happened to save you from a mob. Protection Pierre Doré wasn't smart enough to provide," Truitt grumbled. "And if I do want to claim you it's because…"

Twack. The slap of her flat hand caught his cheek unaware. His mouth hung ajar and he rubbed out the sting. "Was hoping you'd claim me too," he mumbled.

"Don't you have a fight to get to?" She pushed against his chest.

"Sounds like I'm already in one." He blinked at the sudden change in her. Good Lord, wasn't she just kissing him back? "Cassidy listen, I…" he groaned. Why was he so confident one minute and drowning in uncertainty the next?

"I know I'm dressed like a floozy." Covering her face, she spoke into her hands. "What am I doing here? Why am I in this El Dorado closet in Hangtown kissing you?" She shook her head. "After I'd convinced myself a performer could be reputable, above reproach?" She moaned, "Oh lolly, what a colossal fraud I am."

"Cassidy." Truitt carefully gripped his hands around her arms as she lowered her covered face. "You're not a fraud."

"Oh, yes." Opening her hands, she regarded him with a piercing, blazing, damp gaze. "I am a fraud head to toe and you should have no part of me. I care for you too much." She whispered, pulling his hands off her arms. "Would you please walk me back to the hotel?" She found her violin and bow and reached for the door.

As soon as the light hit, the familiarity was over. Whatever was sweet and divine was now shock and spoil. As they stepped out, she dashed out the back door and down the few steps. Following the swish of the blue ruffled dress, he thought he heard her say she knew better than to wear this insulting dress. How could he tell her it wasn't just the dress, but her voice and those extraordinary glances at each other that bonded his heart to her tonight. He shook his head. Truthfully it was that and what her kisses did to him. Utterly disgusted with his impulsive behavior with a lady like Cassidy, he wondered how a man's affections could come out as brash actions — certainly dark closets were dangerous.

"I'm sorry for pulling you into the closet," he tried.

The side of her jaw twitched, as she stepped quickly across the dirt street to the opposite wooden walkway.

Someone from down the block yelled, "That fiddle was a burnin' tonight!" *Burnin'*, Truitt grimaced. No recognition or expression moved on her being as she walked swiftly. Was she going to cry?

"You *were* amazing tonight." His long strides tried to keep up with her. "Really. I don't think Hangtown has ever had such a fine show." Her escape, the Bedford Hotel, loomed in front of them.

Fighting frustration, he stepped in front of her and extended his arm in front of the tall glass doors. Cassidy stared into the lobby and he begged the Almighty for adequate words to tell her how he felt.

"I did my part." Her shoulders slumped, interrupting his prayer. "I wore the dress and painted my cheeks. I had the crowd singing and dancing. I even provided momentary favors for the toughest man in town." Frowning, she swayed her head. "Humph," she whined, "oh, lolly, what am I doing? I don't even know who I am anymore."

Provided favors? He tried to pull the door open at the same time she did. *That was a rash opinion.* His hand squeezed over hers. "You forgot your case, can I bring it to you after the fight? I want to talk to you when you're not upset."

"No, give it to Mr. Doré." She tried to pull on the door, but he held it tight. "We leave tomorrow for Coloma." She huffed.

Her cold shoulder was worse than an ice water swim in Lake Bigelow. "Look at me, Cassidy." He twisted her to face him and she looked everywhere but up into his eyes. "Look at me." He gave her a small, one handed shake. The sad blue hues finally met his. "You didn't do anything wrong tonight. It was me. I care for you and I'm terrible at showing it. You are a lady through and through. There is no fraud, no slander to be found." He squeezed the back of his neck. "You didn't provide anything. I took, and I'm sorry."

A lone tear traced down across the red rouge on her cheek. "I'm glad it happened," she said despondently. "We both know how we feel, so there is no more chase to be had." She blinked, and another tear escaped. "I came here to get Miss O'Ryan settled." Her chin quivered and her tongue lightly touched her top lip. "Truitt, I cannot have romantic feelings for you. I'm not who you think I am and it's crushing me." Her eyes pooled thicker. "Please let me go," a hiccup escaped and her hand pushed against his chest. "I'm going to lose my mind if you don't let me in this door."

Walking through the foyer, a man was about to exit, and Truitt moved to hold the door open. Cassidy pushed passed, running up the staircase before he could stop her.

Grinding his teeth, he squeezed the door handle and looked down to the other end of the street where the El Dorado was lit up and waiting for a fight to begin. His nostrils flared as he stomped back toward the saloon.

He should have followed her up those stairs and made her listen to him, made her see the truth as he saw it. His shoulders jerked up and down and flexing his arms, he ran punching his fists in the air. *She couldn't have feelings for him?* Everything in this town turned against him eventually. God had given him the strength and means to leave at any moment. Why was he so stupid? His blood raced with anger, as the crowd roared at his entrance. Arnold Snider sneered at him as he pushed to the center of the room.

What a pig. Arnold wanted Cassidy to play the enticing saloon girl just like he wanted Truitt to play the oversized errand boy and money maker for these fights. Insisting he dazzle and hold back, Arnold wanted the betting going strong and flowing for at least thirty minutes. Before Truitt met his opponent or could get his shirt off, he knew this fight would be over before his challenger could guess what ferocity was coming at him.

Twenty-Four

CASSIDY UNLOCKED THE door and carefully set her unscarred violin and bow on the nightstand. Still reeling, she jerked apart the laces of her blue dress and kicked it into the corner. Thankfully, Finny was not in, so after pitching her boots against the wall and throwing Finny's ridiculous handkerchief to the floor, she flung her body on her bed. Burying her face into her pillow, she released the dam of frustrations and cries. She didn't really feel him touch her breast. His hand had just been close…that's all.

She sunk her fingers like claws into the pillow. Why had she accused him? What kind of friend was she to lean into his embrace, gripping his thick arms and kissing him ardently in return? Indeed, his advances surpassed her own, but what's a woman who's never been kissed with such heated passion, who had never before felt the waves and tingles to her toes, to know? The man left her breathless and quivering an internal fire that she'd never felt before. And the strength to lift her off her feet like a feather only to entwine them tighter together.

Cassidy groaned, wiping her nose and setting her wet cheek on the pillow. "This wasn't supposed to happen," she squeaked. "I was to be a respectable performer. Only Finny was to fall in love." A few ardent kisses in a closet and— a realization stilled inside of her. How strongly had she judged Finny and all the other women with loose morals. Her body had reacted in such a way that she wanted more of those feelings. Much more.

Tonight, she fell head first down the same well. How many times had she thought Finny was a tease and a ninny? But love and attraction were overpowering, sweeping her off her own feet and making all inhibitions fly from reason. She could still feel how his hands clutched her waist, moved across her back and through her hair. His lips had left a sweet nectar she could still taste. What would it be like to be his wife? To share Truitt Emerson's bed in the flickering shadows?

A hard bolt hit her, and she jumped off of the bed and pulled the covers back, staring wide-eyed at the empty white sheets. She trembled as she stood there waiting until her heart came back into rhythm. Finally, her breathing slowed, and she slid into bed, curled up, and threw the covers over her head. "I'm the ninny who thought staying warm with him in a cave would keep me awake at night. Now I've the alluring visions of being his wife!" Admittedly, that was better than being a floozy.

When she couldn't find enough air, Cassidy flipped the covers off her head and sat up staring at nothing in the darkened room. It wasn't the chilled air that brought the goose bumps up her arms. Just when would she tell him the truth about who she was? When would she expose the sinful offensive depths of her deceit? Before their wedding? After their vows? Maybe before the marriage bed?

It was all ludicrous! *Oh, dear love, Truitt, by the way, my name is Kathleen O'Ryan. I am actually the first born heir to the O'Ryan name. My grandparents always called me Cassidy. Funny that? I was sent here with a dowry and my father's wishes to obediently marry Cousin Arnold keeping all the money safely within the family. Do you think my father will mind if I marry you instead?* Cassidy flopped back on her pillow, her stomach hurting. What an absurd mess she'd created.

When she heard a wagon rumble by under her window, she realized no sleep would come. She got to her feet to watch downtown Hangtown. There wasn't enough distraction for her this Friday night. She watched the lights and movement from the El Dorado. How was Truitt faring? Would he be hurt tonight?

Shuddering, she clutched the top of her chemise. Would there be stitches? Broken bones?

"EMERSON!" ARNOLD SNIDER yelled after him as he exited the El Dorado. Truitt stilled in the middle of Hangtown's Main Street.

"What's ailing you, man?" Arnold snapped.

Riled, Truitt looked back, Miss O'Ryan waited beside Arnold. He couldn't take a fist to Snider's jaw while she stood watching them outside the El Dorado's doors.

"You knocked him out!" Arnold spat. "What kind of nose-bender is that?"

"I can't control when a man gets up or stays down."

"You can. I've seen you. You know the bets go higher the more you play the game. The crowd was double tonight when word got out you were knocked to your backside last Friday."

Truitt looked to the ground and heaved a sigh. "I'm done with the game, Snider. You've made enough money off me to front ten Hangtowns. I'm quitting."

The edge in Arnold Snider's voice lowered. "Emerson *talk* to me. I saw you run off after the dancing, fiddle girl earlier. Is it her? Kathleen told me you two might have something. Just tell me. You stay working for me, and I can arrange for her to be yours."

"Oh, right." Truitt mocked. "Hate to break it to ya, Snider, you're not God. Cassidy has her own mind, her own plans."

"She'll have no plans unless I say," Snider ground out. "You stay working for me, and I'll make sure she's safe. It will give you time to win the lass's heart."

Truitt shook his head and started to walk away waving a dismissive hand.

"Emerson. I know more about women than you." Arnold called after him. "Don't give up. She'll come around. Truitt!"

At the sound of his first name, he stopped and looked back.

"Take a week off. Get a horn of baldface and molasses and go back to that land your father left you. Fish the lake before it snows. Or hunt and kill something. You'll feel better, and I'll find a better match for you next Friday. That man was worthless. I could see it in his eyes when you walked in; he was scared spitless."

Truitt could muster no response and stalked away. The land, the trees, river, and the ice blue lake were his reprieve. Though not much else, his father had left him something he valued — something that only changed with the seasons. Even the energy he spent on the wood pile at the Damonte Station could bring more composure than how he felt every waking minute in Hangtown.

God had always shown him the way. He pulled open the door to the Bedford and went to his room. Though he hadn't broken a sweat tonight, he filled the basin with water, stripped off his shirt and began to wash. Seeing his father's mistakes in this town had shown him the way not to go. Why did he struggle to heed God's lessons now? He knew it was time.

But just like tonight, the lure of Snider's words like Satan's lies, tried to cover his own good sense. He wanted them to be true. The way Cassidy felt against him would unreservedly drown out any common sense. The woman was like Mrs. Damonite's biscuits on an icy morning, fresh churned butter melting down inside bones and beyond. He raked the water through his hair with his fingers. He would miss her like his next breath. The toughest man in town, she had called him. Quite the false impression he gave. He picked up his little torn up Bible. More like Samson with his hair cut off.

⌒

CASSIDY ROSE ON one elbow. After months of nights in the covered wagon she often awoke to wonder where she lay. The bed, the coverings, it was the Bedford Hotel. The room was before-dawn-dark, but she could make out her violin and bow. Tonight she'd played her first concert at the El Dorado. In all the commotion, she'd put little thought to the actual performance. The songs seemed to be enjoyed by the customers. She yawned and started to wonder about Coloma.

The bleak silence startled her. Had she been so tired not to hear Finny enter or light the lantern?

"Finny." She whispered. It had to be early morning, the room was freezing cold.

The silence continued. "Finny are you there?"

Cassidy flung off her warm blankets and walked to the other side of the room. Crossing her arms across her chest, she stared. The bed had not been touched. Growling she shook her head and stepped barefooted to the window. Hangtown was silent and remained tucked in for the dark of morning, most likely just like her imprudent friend, Finny, unrighteously impersonating Kathleen O'Ryan.

Twenty-Five

R OLLING OUT OF Hangtown, Pierre Doré's carriage hit a small rut, and Cassidy rocked bumping his shoulder. "Excuse me, sir."

He smiled at her apology. "Pardon the condition of these roads, *ma belle*."

Cassidy grinned half-heartedly.

He kept the afternoon diverting with talk of the Gold Dust and ideas for closing out her musical soiree with a slower melody to avoid the ruckus of last night. The only question that made her want to jump from the carriage was the one where he asked where she'd hidden after the crowd rushed the stage. "By the time I hastened to secure your safety, you were gone," he said. He gave a shrug and lowered his voice. "No one doubted Emerson would see you safely home."

"Yes, he did." She gazed out the side of the carriage. Miners bent over the shallow creeks, swishing their large tin pans. Would she see Truitt tomorrow on her return? What would she possibly say? She sighed.

Would she see Finny at her return? Had the impatient woman already taken up residence at Arnold Snider's large mansion at the end of Main Street? Cassidy felt her stomach churn. "Mr. Doré. Would you—"

"*Si vous plait, mademoiselle*, I would be greatly honored if you would call me Pierre. We are working companions. *Oui*?"

Cassidy went to open her mouth in rebuke, but smiled and nodded instead. "Yes. Pierre."

"Ahh." He placed his hand against his chest. "Lovely words out of your lips, I feel my heart jumping." He laughed. "And you make my heart swell, like after eating a warm croissant filled with chocolate and cream."

Cassidy had to smile at him. Compared to a pastry—that was a first in all the compliments she'd received.

"Your beauty and poise are breathtaking. You must know this. *Oui*? I am likely in a long line of bashful suitors who hunger for your presence."

"Oh, no," Cassidy denied it. "No, no lines." Feeling a bit uncomfortable, she glanced back at the man who rode backward on the end of the carriage. Pulling in a deep breath, she hoped they were soon to Coloma.

"But mademoiselle, you have risen far above your lowly servitude station. How brave of you to come this far to make a mark for yourself." His eyes widened, "No one would know you come from common working class."

An indignant *I don't,* pressed against her closed lips. Finny Finnegan does though. Cassidy tried to contain her frustration with Finny. She'd done it a hundred times on the trail, and she could do it again today. She was a young woman from a well to do family, freely giving away her identity and her status. Position and favor only mattered according to what husband you held on to, anyway. Those things never meant anything to her. It was her dignity she treasured, and it was to be her own, not shackled to someone controlling like Cousin Arnold.

A tinge of annoyance edged her tone as she said, "Sir, there are numerous well-bred ladies who have hit on hard times." It was true, but she felt bad leading him to believe she was one of them. "They have been forced into a companion or governess position to survive." Also true. "There are few choices a lady can make. Being a companion was the only way I could make it out west." The lie made her heart ache. Her stomach hurt. She bit on her lips to keep from blurting out the actual truth. She pressed her hand to her chest. How much longer could she keep this up?

They rode on, but something still bristled in her. "Pierre, I would like you to speak to the manager of the Gold Dust. There was a woman who greeted us last week. I believe she works in the kitchen. I would like her to accompany me to and from my room. I have changed out a few songs for the crowd. Most in attendance will be looking forward to the meal and enjoying the music. Also, I will be wearing my own gowns."

Pierre scratched his neck.

"I will not be strutted like a dance hall girl from the docks."

"No, no, *ma belle*. Take no offense. It's just you have to think of your audience."

"Is this you," her chin tilted a notch, watching him, "as my manager talking or Arnold Snider?"

Pierre's faced scrunched, and his eyes narrowed. "I—I care for your wellbeing, mademoiselle, I hope you know that about me. *Oui*. I know the woman you speak of. I will make sure she's at your disposal."

"Thank you, Pierre."

He released the reins with one hand, took her hand and quickly kissed it. Cassidy quickly removed her hand from his and tucked it back in her skirt layers before she could blink. Using his name was turning him into a scrabbling romantic.

SOMETIME BEFORE NOON the next day, they gathered their things into the carriage and headed back to Hangtown. The same silent man rode backward with his rifle over his legs. Being her second trip in the daylight, Cassidy looked long into the trees and hills around the road. The journey seemed safe enough.

"Your sleep, your breakfast was good, mademoiselle?" Pierre broke into her thoughts.

"Yes, thank you." She held off using his first name. "I saw you speaking to the manager. Was he happy with the performance?" She was pleased the audience seemed to enjoy the tunes. Thankfully, no one raised a ruckus like in Hangtown.

"*Oui, Oui*, he was pleased. And you, how did you feel?"

"I thought it went well. I kept a steadier pace to the music. There were more women with their men in the audience. That was refreshing. Arnold Snider said women are too busy working to enjoy any entertainment. I'm glad to see things are different in Coloma."

"*Oui, oui.*" He waggled his head back and forth. "Your gift for the instrument, your untainted voice is divine. I saw some with tears in their eyes," he nodded.

"The Irish ballads are songs from the old country. I choose to sing only a few of the stanzas. So many are filled with war, pain, loss of love, and loss of home."

"Yes, I can see it in your eyes." His gaze lingered on hers. "You miss this home?"

"I do. Everyday." Cassidy watched the leaves rustle and float down from the trees.

"Are you mourning the loss of your own love?" he whispered over the clopping of the horse's hooves.

Cassidy knew he meant from her past, but she felt her chest squeeze anyway. She was attracted, enamored, and consumed with Truitt Emerson and most likely in love. There was no denial in the way she clung to his chest, allowing his arms to encompass her. She returned his kisses like a woman obsessed with her extravagant lover. Cassidy bit her lip trying to control her breathing. Oh lolly, what if he read that slap to the face as a message of rejection along with all the dismissing words from her mouth? Hating the lies she'd weaved, she shrank back against the bumpy carriage seat.

"You don't have to answer, mademoiselle. That was far too personal."

"I suppose it's best for me to focus on the job at hand." Holding her hand to her throat, she felt her pulse still thumping, "During the week I am to be Miss O'Ryan's escort and oversee the education of two housemaids. I will perform Friday nights at the El Dorado and Saturday in Coloma. That should be enough to keep me occupied."

"I should say. Do you suppose?" He rocked in his seat. "May I call on you? Maybe an evening that you are not working?"

Cassidy felt her body wax cold. "That is a kind proposal," her voice was tight and strained. "I—I—"

"We could keep it on business," he interrupted. "We must meet to have a greater understanding of business owner and artist, *oui*?"

Cassidy was well aware the ten-mile rides back and forth from Hangtown to Coloma allowed plenty of time to discuss her future.

"May I let you know?"

Surprisingly, he displayed his smile and large, white teeth. "Yes, this forthcoming date will keep my shoes in the creek like a miner waiting for the gold to appear."

Cassidy raised a faint smile.

"Oh, before I forget." Pierre pulled a small pouch from his pocket. "Speaking of gold, this is your weekend earning." He held it out as Cassidy reluctantly took it.

"Gold, I'm paid in gold?" she said, testing the faint weight of the pouch in her palm.

"It is real," Pierre grinned. "You may take it to the bank. I don't know if they allow a woman to have her own account, but if they do not, knowing you, you will be the first."

Another rough spot rocked the carriage and she gripped her reticule dangling from her wrist. Pulling the strings apart she dropped her little pouch inside and folded her hands on top of her lap. She wondered how much in coin the gold actually was. Why didn't she have the courage to ask outright how much she was earning? Why did she trust Pierre with managing her contract but not trust him with a more personal relationship? She sighed, then smiled. Her first earnings in the new state of California rested in her reticule. Feeling her nose tingle with emotion, a small knot unraveled in her gut.

She had actually done something unlikely and unusual. By sharing what her grandmother had given her, she found a piece of those priceless years. Years when life was carefree and straightforward; where fault and shame didn't pull her around by the hair. Playing her little tunes was joyful and acceptable. She touched the back of her hand to her dripping nose. *But then I became a woman. Even out west, a woman without a man was unacceptable.*

She glanced at Pierre's beautiful, black suit pant leg and his shiny shoes only inches away from her skirt fabric. How long did she think they could travel back and forth, even after today, thinking it would all stay on business?

She tucked a loose strand of hair behind her ear. Pierre seemed a patient, helpful man, like Truitt. Her mind wandered to the Damonte Station and how he had ordered her and Finny out in the cold rain to sit on the back of a wooden crate. She squeezed her reticule and the little minerals inside.

Then again, Pierre was nothing like Truitt Emerson at all.

Twenty-Six

CASSIDY HAD SPENT the rest of her Sunday preparing for the week. With the room looking as she had left it, there was no sign that Finny had been back. Even a note would have been appreciated, she huffed, looking out the window before dusk. Mr. Newton at the hotel said he would be happy to deliver their wash to and from So Chen's washing and bathing house.

Cassidy chewed her lip looking over her pile. Knowing Truitt often helped out there, she had to admit her motive. She could take the wash and possibly run into him. Peeking up and down the quiet street, she sighed. She missed him. They hadn't separated well.

Every encounter deepened her heart to his but it also became more and more difficult to see any future. She was a liar and imposter and he didn't deserve such deception. Shaking her head, she turned and sat on the end of her bed. She could not, would not enter in a real relationship with him without him knowing the truth. And when he found out the lies she had told, he would have nothing to do with her. Exhaustion and sadness clamored through her. The two performances and the ride from Coloma had left her worn and weary.

A key at the door and its opening startled her. Finny swished into the room.

"Finny." She stood. "Where have you been?" Cassidy had never seen the finely detailed rose-colored dress she wore. Finny dropped a matching hat and reticule on her bed.

"You know where I've been Cassidy." She dropped her chin, with dismissive eyes. "Just as I know where you have been. If you aren't traipsing around with Truitt Emerson, then you are riding off with Pierre Doré. What is he calling himself? Your manager? Really, Cassidy, everyone in town is talking about you."

Cassidy felt heat rise straight up her backbone. "What are you implying Finny Finnegan?"

"Kathleen O'Ryan," Finny leered. "If you don't mind."

"Maybe I do mind. My name was never to be associated with a tramp!" Cassidy spat.

"Oh, Sweet Mary, Mother, and Joseph!" Finny growled. "Here we go. Aye, like I haven't heard this before." Finny sat and pulled her boot laces apart. "You're such a charlatan, Cassidy, blimey. I help you to cover your pure, modest bosom, and then you bend and sway, enticing every man in the room into a frenzy. And if that wasn't enough, you suddenly gallivant off with Truitt Emerson dragging you by the arm. Are you going to stand there in all your virtue and tell me that man doesn't know how the lace and strings on your pantaloons feel?" Her eyes narrowed on Cassidy. "Or your skin underneath."

Gasping, eyes wide with shock and indignation, Cassidy lunged forward. She would take her by her chicken neck and swing her till it cracked. Rage rose in her breast in a white hot fury. Then she froze. Her feet seemingly nailed to the floor. Blinking back the shame and shock, she tried to contain her shaking limbs. Her ire centered in Finny's harsh but almost correct assumptions and the truth hit her like a brick. She *was* a hypocrite, living another lie, through and through. A full willing participant in Truitt's desires and she was helpless against his kiss, his touch. Her chin began to quiver and her eyes filled.

"Ahh, fimble-famble," Finny's voice softened. "Don't be spill'n them tears now."

"I didn't count on falling in love." Cassidy sucked in a breath. A hollowness stole over her and she swiped her sleeve across her damp face. "This was to work for you." She gulped. "And freedom for me." She searched her bed for her hankie.

"It still can. It's working fine. We've set a date — one month from Saturday." Finny came near and touched her arm. "We can do this. Just a few more weeks, then you can fiddle or sing or dance your heart away. Arnold already said he'd give ya a wage. That is good, eh?" She tugged on Cassidy's arm.

"Yes, that's wonderful." Cassidy blew her nose and sat on the bed. Looking down, she shook her head and caught a few more tears with her hankie.

"Are you cryin' cause your man's left?"

Cassidy's head popped up. "Truitt? He's left? Left for where?"

"I don't know," Finny shrugged and walked back to her bed. "Something about the land his father had bought. I think it's up where he picked us up from Mr. Coffey. Probably full of snow and Indians," Finny croaked.

"How long?" She swallowed the lump in her throat. "Did Arnold say how long he was to be gone?"

"No telling. He and Arnold argued in the middle of the street. I heard him say he quit. He was leaving."

Cassidy winced, feeling her body waver. "So he may not be back?"

"I can't say." Finny shrugged. "Maybe your dilemma will take care of itself. If he wanted you, wouldn't he still be here?"

"Not if I told him we had no future." Cassidy murmured, still dizzy with what she'd done.

"Aye, yi, yi, Cassidy, what am I to make of you." Finny dropped her fist on her hip. "You say you love him and the next minute you say there is no future. Devil may care, what is the true story?"

"I can't lead him on in a lie." Cassidy felt bereft and sick inside. "Truitt deserves the truth."

"What are you talking about?" Finny huffed. "You came here to make your own way. To play your violin, to entertain. Isn't that the truth?"

Cassidy stared long at Finny. The woman had little conscience. "I can't say...that I am you." She wiped her hand across her damp face. "I have to be me. I can't live with myself, or have a future lying to him."

Finny paced across the narrow room and back. "Now wait a grand minute. You are saying *I* can lie?" Finny spun and glared, only a foot away. "I can marry a man, lying about who I really am? But you cannot? Is that what you just said?"

Cassidy groaned, she was too tired for another fight. "It doesn't matter, and no one's asking me to marry him."

"But you pushed the man, the man you say you care about away...because you can't be Cassidy Finnegan?"

Cassidy needed this to be over. "Yes, there I said it. I couldn't keep who I am from him."

"Well it's a mighty fine thing he's gone now." Finny paced the room again. "Did you ever think, you could be Cassidy Emerson? Does that name bring you shame?"

"Finny please, your name doesn't bring me shame. It's the way I've—"

"So ya think it's been my pleasure to be you? Keepin' my nose in the air and trying to catch my Irish heritage by the tongue. A hard workin' grand heritage it is, tisn't it?"

"No, no Finny. I'm not saying that about you."

"Aye, yes you are." Finny scowled. "It's just grand for someone like me to lie and marry for advantage. But nooo." Exaggerating, she waggled her head and hips in disgust. "Not you. You're just like your father and step-mother. Always puttin' us hard workin' people in our place. Do this, do that."

Finny paced again, pointed her finger back and forth in the air. "That cloth has a wrinkle, iron it again." She snapped her fingers. "That soup is too cold, go heat it. You missed the crumbs under the table. You probably never knew I was the maid under the table," Finny's voice caught. Besides the Indians, Cassidy had never seen her break before. "I was the one down on my hands and knees like a dog while you sat eating your fine food," she spat. "Someone had to make sure those crumbs didn't grind into your fine carpets. Oh, nooo, didn't know that was me, did ye?" she mocked. "Your little sisters dropped more on the floor than into their spoiled mouths."

Cassidy winced. Finny's eyes were filling with hot, angry tears. "Did you know I was under there? Did you, Miss Kathleen O'Ryan? Of course, not. Nobody cares. Nobody ever noticed me. Nobody ever wanted me part of their family. So my ma left me with relative after relative, and then one day just never came back. Don't you think it hurts that I don't have my father's last name? Finnegan is my mother's name. My *unmarried* mother!" Finny shook. "Because my lovely mother couldn't remember who the bloke was."

Her jaw clenched, and she roughly wiped the tears off her cheek. "At least I know my man's name. At least my man is going to marry me and give me a home. And a fine home at that." Finny shook a finger in Cassidy's face. "Call me a tramp, go ahead, but you will not tell the truth about us." She growled. "Do you understand me, Cassidy? If you do, you will ruin my life and there will be no forgiveness from heaven or earth for you, even if I have to rot in the devil's hell… there will be no—no—forgiveness." Finny sucked in a strangled breath as she walked to her bed and laid down.

Trembling to her core, Cassidy sat for a long time watching the dark shadows overtake the room and listening to Finny's muffled sobs helpless to offer any comfort.

Twenty-Seven

ALL WEEK REMORSE encompassed Cassidy like a heavy blanket she could not shed. She'd thought of a hundred ways to apologize for the pain she and her family had caused the young woman, Finny Finnegan. But they all seemed trite and filled with lame excuses.

And what of the regrets she had in dragging her into this scheme. It was her idea. It was her deceit that Finny had agreed to. How does one apologize and turn from those wicked ways?

It was too late. Finny was just doing what Cassidy asked. Her guilt labored with her every movement as she left the Bedford Hotel and headed to the Snider house.

Surprisingly, Finny had returned to Bedford Hotel with Cassidy each day after Cassidy helped the Basque girls with schooling and English. Finny loved the backyard where there was a gazebo and a little bench swing. She would take a blanket and book and lounge most of the day there. After a spree of ordering everyone about and unpacking her new items she must have found her new role as lady of leisure quite agreeable. Each night, Arnold would come to take her to dinner and then she would return by nine. They spoke little and Cassidy didn't want to ask questions. Finny would read into every one as being judgmental.

Friday afternoon Cassidy practiced a few new tunes for the El Dorado performance as Finny readied her hair for dinner.

A knock at the door had them looking to each other. Finny opened it to take a card from Mr. Newton.

"It's addressed to both of us." Finny flipped it over. "It's from Arnold. He says Truitt has not returned and you need to be able to extend your performance tonight. He will not be able to take me to dinner as he is searching for others who will agree to a boxing match." Finny slapped the card against her palm and huffed. "Wonderful." She shook her head and sat on her bed. "This will put him in a fine mood."

Cassidy set her violin and bow into the case. "I could order us up a tray?"

Finny shook her head. "Mr. Emerson has not contacted you?"

Cassidy shook her head. "Nothing."

"I'm not worried about eating," Finny sighed. "Arnold gets very upset when anyone defies him. He told Mr. Emerson to take some time, but he expected him back. This will not bode well, aye. He'd best fire your strapping lumberjack like he would a street urchin, but he needs him for the removal of those miners who don't pay. The Friday night fights are just a side gig. His real job is to do the dirty work Arnold wants done."

Cassidy wanted to remind her that Truitt Emerson was not her anything. Maybe Truitt had come to his own change of heart about the work he did for Arnold. She began to open her mouth but shut it quickly, not wanting to make excuses. And to keep some level ground with Finny.

THE EVENING'S PERFORMANCE closed out well, and as soon as she could wrap her cape around her bare arms, Pierre Doré was by her side.

"Ma belle, lovely. Your sweet strains of tender cords are as lovely as you are, my dear." His hand rested on her back. "That last song was so touching. Many of the men, I think, were swooning," he laughed.

"'The Lovers Waltz' is one of my favorites. I'm glad they enjoyed something besides the wild and romping tunes."

"May I escort you home?" He stood passively nearer than he should.

She'd only looked around the crowded, smoky room a hundred times. She forced her eyes back. Truitt was not here. "Yes, thank you. But aren't you needed here?" She snapped the latch on the violin case. He took her arm and led her out the back door.

"Emerson has not shown, and word is Mr. Snider has found two others to fight. We will carry on without him," Pierre smiled.

Cassidy noticed the small woman, So Chen, pacing back and forth in front of her wash and bathing house. Cassidy wanted to look away, but the woman was in obvious distress.

"Pierre," Cassidy pulled from his grip, "could you give me a minute?" Cassidy walked across the street. The small woman looked at her and looked away.

"So Chen?" Cassidy asked. "Is there something wrong? May I be of service?"

"Nah, nah." So Chen scratched her dark, black hair. "One my girls missing."

"What is her name?"

So Chen shook her head. "It Jan-nee. Jan-nee Long."

"Oh," Cassidy piped up, "I know who she is. Would you like me to help you look?"

Pierre stepped up next to her. "We should get you back, Miss Finnegan. You gave a heartfelt performance." He pulled on her arm. "We have another full day to Coloma tomorrow."

"Thank you, Pierre." She pulled from his hand. "I know you have obligations tonight. I think I will stay and help So Chen look."

Frowning, he scanned the street and sidewalk. Glancing back to the El Dorado, he cleared his throat. "As you wish." His chin jutted to the side before he finally stepped away.

Cassidy turned to the petite woman. "Please tell me how I may be of assistance?"

So Chen opened her mouth and shook her head. "I think it bad." She led Cassidy inside the front door of her shop. "She been gone day and night. I put more wood on fire, then found on floor," So Chen waggled something from her hand.

Cassidy took the white garment from her and as she did it fell open with bright red blood streaked across the fabric.

"Oh, lolly," Cassidy gasped, "does this belong to Janny?"

So Chen nodded, pointing to the wall she grabbed a lantern. "Not know America marks well. These on wall above her slip." She held the lantern high as Cassidy looked close. Someone had scratched rough letters into the wood.

It looked like an E and M and Emerson. "It says Emerson did this." Cassidy jumped back. Swallowing hard she felt herself choking. "He—he—would never hurt her…"

"Oh no, no, no." The little woman swung her head back and forth. "He help the ladies. Keeps bad men away. But where did he go? I not eye him all week. Something bad happen to him, too. It not right! He good man."

Cassidy clutched her bodice, feeling her chest rise and fall. Would Arnold do something spiteful? Viciously spiteful? Is that what Finny was trying to warn her about? Cassidy scanned the simple shop and tried to find an anchor of reason. Somewhere she thought she heard a baby cry. "The sheriff. We need to go to the sheriff. I fear the worst has happened to Janny."

"Oh, no, no, no. He trouble. Not good man." So Chen's face creased. "He push and hit the girls here."

Cassidy gripped her neck and bit her lip. She'd convinced herself the west would be different. Lord above, the folk on the wagon train were more civilized than in this place. At least they shared the common goal of survival and compassion for one another. "I know someone I can talk to." She ran her hand gently down So Chen's arm. "I have to believe Truitt can take care of himself. He helped two defenseless women through mudslides, Indians, and from freezing to death."

"Ahh." So Chen leaned her head back. "You woman he told me about. You violin he burn."

Cassidy whimpered a half smile. "Yes. He burnt my violin and then bought me another one." She lifted her case.

"I see it in his eyes," her head bobbed up and down, "He love you. Sometime he dumb with words, but he not need speak. Eyes say it."

Unable to speak, Cassidy wondered if it was So Chen's broken English that stabbed those words through to her heart or a collision of undeniable dreams. After a few moments of silence, Cassidy found the words. "I can return in the morning to help look for Janny. But then I am off to Coloma."

"Eh," So Chen shrugged. "Truitt tell me about west man's God. He has the story of God in his little book in his pocket."

Cassidy nodded, she knew of that little Bible.

"He say. You can pray to this God in the Heaven. He will hear you and answer."

Cassidy had sat through Sunday mass all her life and never understood the ways of God.

"You," So Chen poked her in the arm. "You pray to this God. He help. He help Truitt and He help Jan-nee."

Cassidy reluctantly nodded as she stepped out.

"He find Jan-nee and Truitt. You ask Him." So Chen said before she dropped the plank over her closed door.

Cassidy rubbed her arm where the woman had poked her. Down the wooden sidewalks, the four, dark blocks to the Bedford Hotel loomed ahead. Over her shoulder, the El Dorado pulsed with men and revelry.

Not intending to test God, but just letting Him know her trepidation for her situation and how grateful she would be for His protection, she prayed. *Lord, if you can see me safely home, I'll pray every day for their return and believe that You do want to help people.*

She took a deep breath and started for the hotel.

Twenty-Eight

THE FOLLOWING WEEK, Cassidy tried not to let her resolve waver. Nightly, after her uneventful return to the Bedford Hotel, she had continued her small childlike prayers and yet there was no sign of Truitt or Janny Long. Likely God did not listen to liars and women that entertained for a living. After she finished the day's lessons with the Basque sisters, she would stop by and see if So Chen had any news.

The back door of the Snider house kitchen opened and Cassidy and the girls turned to watch Arnold Snider walk in. Cassidy felt her skin crawl. It was the same feeling she had every time he was near. Why had she not admitted it before?

He walked up to Emery and flipped one of her long braids off her shoulder. "I thought I told you to teach them genteel presentations. She's a woman still dressed like a girl."

Cassidy's blood boiled instantaneously. Both the Basque teens wore new sensible dresses with new aprons with ruffles. They were neat and clean, and...her chest squeezed painfully, how dare he force woman's attire into what he wanted — the same nasty thing he tried to do to her.

"Why is your face red, Miss Finnegan?" his expression sour.

"None of your concern, sir." Cassidy hated that like everyone else in this town, she cowered to stand up for herself and the teens. "Girls, would you be so kind as to check the garden for the last of the vegetables you can find. Then I will gather up my things and we can walk to the blacksmith to meet your father." Cassidy pulled the paper and books into a pile as they left.

"I'm making arrangements for them to take a room here," Arnold told her slyly.

Cassidy froze at his words.

"Their father doesn't have time to work the claim and run them back and forth to town." Arnold went to the stove and poured himself a cup of coffee.

Cassidy tapped the papers harder on the table than needed. "That would not be proper, sir. They cannot stay here in the evenings and nights. I highly doubt their father would allow that."

"My new wife will insist on it after we're married of course. They will be of assistance to her."

Cassidy wanted to scream. No wonder Truitt left. Arnold Snider was insufferable. "I've asked Kathleen to ask you," Cassidy said, shielding her anger, "if you have any knowledge of a young woman gone missing? Janny Long, she works at the laundry."

"At the laundry?" He snorted. "How naive are you? She's a dimwit whore who has worked this town for years." He shook his head. "Life expectancy is short in that business."

"So no one cares? The law has taken no action to find her?" Cassidy locked a steely gaze on him.

"Why don't you ask your man, Emerson, who came down with a sudden case of wanderlust—no thanks to you?" he smirked. "Without him around to protect the low life of Hangtown, things happen."

Cassidy gripped the wooden chair to keep her hand from striking him. Truitt's name etched into the wall. He was blackmailing Truitt, she could feel it in her bones. Could Truitt have stopped whatever had happened to Janny? Like a wind breaking off the ice, Finny walked in the back door with her blanket and book.

"Love, I thought I heard your carriage drive in," Finny smiled at him.

Arnold narrowed eyes on Cassidy and then lightly kissed Finny on the cheek his expression instantly turning from night to day. "I was just telling Miss Finnegan the plan to have the Basque girls take a room here. Much more convenient, allowing their father more time to mine."

Finny managed a thin smile. "We do plan on expecting our bundle and will need a nanny. This way with both of them staying on, I can oversee their abilities to care for infants."

Cassidy knew her eyebrows rose. Not yet married and now they need nannies?

Finny linked her arm around Arnold's. "You should see how well Cassidy's teaching is going. They can talk and understand me so much better."

He slightly nodded to his fiancée. "Wonderful. As you know, Miss Finnegan, the soon to be Mrs. Snider is the final word for the training and care of the domestics. With all the preparations for the wedding, she does not have time to oversee their education. We insist you remind them daily that without submission and obedience their employment will come to an abrupt end and their father's mining claim will be no more." He pursed his lips, squinting with insincerity. "Must be hard for the man to know the family's next meal is dependent on his daughters' employment."

Cassidy wondered if Finny also heard the slight emphasis Arnold put on the words submission and obedience.

Finny and Arnold turned to each other, and his hand slipped down her back and rested on Finny's full skirt covered bottom. Finny leaned in with admiration in her eyes and kissed his cheek. He gave Finny's bottom a squeeze and Cassidy felt her stomach roll up. How could Finny tolerate his touch? Was she playing the overt actress or did she honestly have romantic feelings for this weasel of a man?

"I will see the girls to meet their father." Cassidy couldn't move fast enough. "Would you like me to come back for you, Kathleen?"

Unfortunately, Cassidy had to see why Finny did not answer. Arnold was whispering in her ear as they nuzzled each other.

Shaking her head, she reached for the kitchen door like a prisoner finally escaping a suffocating cell.

STANDING WITH THE teens as their father gathered them up, Cassidy turned to see Pierre at her side. He removed his hat and dipped his head flashing his sizeable, white smile.

"Ah, my, how you say, *jolie colombe*? Ah, pretty dove! What perfect timing. I was hoping I could persuade you to accommodate me and my humble company for a light dinner?"

Cassidy didn't have a chance to form her excuse.

"I think you look especially lovely in that green frock." He lightly touched her sleeve. "But if you would like to change, *oui*? I will wait in the lobby at the Bedford?"

Cassidy thought of spending the evening sitting in her room alone since unescorted ladies were not allowed in the dining room in the evening. She would be pining over all the things wrong in her life. His humble company did sound diverting.

"We will discuss all things about your wonderful performance and this next trip to Coloma," he smiled.

The one thing she felt could hold her soul together was the music. The performance and outlet were all that had any meaning of late.

"I won't change if you will wait for me to talk to So Chen," Cassidy countered. "I have not heard any word of Janny Long."

"I did hear the sheriff earlier at the El Dorado. Nothing has been found. No sign of her. People assume the worst," he frowned.

"As do I," Cassidy sighed, looking up and down, considering the low gray clouds and the dusty streets of Hangtown. "I suppose I am still new here, but I feel like there is evil inside this town. Something that lurks under the floorboards and the skin of the silent citizens." She squinted at Pierre. "Am I speaking foolishness?"

He exhaled and looked away then back at her. "You are not a fool. There is an evil here," he paused a moment. "It is greed." He slipped his hat back on and nodded at her. "I was here," his eyes widened, "after the 1849 discovery. Quiet, little, peaceable farms and ranches turned into towns and roads, and the people came from everywhere. Every crackling stream is now crowded with men with picks and pans. There was no law but what beliefs they brought with them. Desperate men believe they can steal in the name of survival. Desperate men believe to kill is to protect their own. Mexicans kill the Chinese. White men kill the Indians. Many of my French patriots have been killed or run off. These are hard things, no?" His tone and expression were dispirited and he shook his head. "But gold seekers are not all desperate and evil. Now, look at this town." He swung his hand out in front of him. "That building over there is to be a church and school when it is finished. Now there is new business and more families are finding homes here."

Cassidy nodded. His words were painful and true at the same time.

"Monsieur John O'Sullivan called it Manifest Destiny." He looked back at her. "Is it a divine obligation to push the boundaries roughshod over everything stretching to the Pacific Ocean? You, mademoiselle, are an intelligent, outspoken woman. What do you think? Are we to kill and shove the Indians from their land, pushing them ever farther westward until there is no room for them? Are we to allow and accept all men from all nations to find their way here? Aren't we all from somewhere else?" He shrugged. "Do we have the directive from God to make all people in the north Christians? And what if they don't want to attend that church?" His shoulders rose in a typical Pierre pose as his eyes swept over the new construction. "And what if they want to hold tight to their own beliefs?"

Feeling challenged, Cassidy shook her head and met his eyes. "I have learned many things. Some, my gender was never meant to hear and see." She crossed her arms, rubbing her elbows. "I want to believe that God sees the hearts of good men. I think if someone was to harm my child, I might be prevailed upon even to kill another." She lifted one shoulder in a half shrug, "So how do we love and respect others? Isn't that what you are asking? How do we manifest love to those whose skin is different from ours? Those from a different country, or with different beliefs? And how do we secure retribution from those people who hurt us first?" She shook her head and saw the Laundry and Bath Shop out of the corner of her eye. "I suppose it's within each man and woman's heart to find and give away forgiveness, over the wrongs done against them. I'm not spouting platitudes." She thought of week after week living with Finny. "Love over judgment is extremely difficult. But when it comes to prevailing evil, we all have to stand together. That is a destiny worth fighting for."

Twenty-Nine

SUNDAY MIDDAY THEIR carriage clipped along the road from Coloma. Cassidy pondered Pierre's extravagant suggestions.

Maybe she should consider the trip to Sutter's Fort? His description of this large wharf where the America River joined with the Sacramento River allowed her to daydream of a proper music hall, other musicians, and well-dressed patrons.

Pierre had seen a steamship, the *Chrysoplois* that transported goods and people on these mighty rivers. Her mind envisioned the modern comforts of the port of Boston.

"Whoa, now." Pierre pulled back on the reins. It looked as if a large fallen tree blocked their narrow dirt road. A strange clicking sound came from behind her as she realized the man who rode backward had prepared and raised his gun.

"Pierre," she squeaked, looking around the tall grass and brush, clutching his arm.

"Stay calm, mademoiselle." He patted her arm before he pulled out a gun from his boot.

They waited, searching the landscape with bated breath. Unable to hear over her pounding heart heightened the fear that this fallen tree was no quirk of nature.

"Can you go around?" Cassidy tugged on his arm, searching left to right. "Please find a way! I don't feel—"

Pop! The sound reverberated off her ear the same time she saw the man in the back fly off his perch, thudding to the ground.

As she sucked in the breath to scream, Pierre pulled her off the seat and to the narrow floorboard. Crouching into a ball, she grabbed her violin and squeezed it with all her might. The horse reared with the same panic that Cassidy felt. His nervous dance bounced them around the buggy, and Cassidy's head knocked against the front of the carriage.

"Please! Please!" Pierre shouted with his gun in the air. "You may have everything! Please do not harm us." Cassidy wasn't sure what he meant, she couldn't breathe as her throat was closing up; dizzying terror rushed through her being.

Finally she heard voices shouting in Spanish. "What, what are they saying?" she cried. Taking a peek from her tight ball, she saw a man unhitching their horse from the carriage.

"I know not." Pierre rose an inch or two his hands and gun still in the air.

"Don't shoot him, don't shoot him," Cassidy cried and begged. Watching out of the corner of her eyes, she saw a Mexican man with a rifle motion Pierre out of the carriage. Cassidy didn't realize how much he hovered over her until he began to stand. Pierre pulled her by the arm as her throat ached straining to breathe and keep from screaming all at once.

They finally stood erect outside the carriage as one of them snatched Pierre's gun. Cassidy counted four men pointing their weapons at them. Bandannas covered the lower part of their faces, but not the menace in their eyes. She looked the other way hugging her violin like some sort of barrier, and shock hit her with a wave of nausea. She couldn't look at their escort laying in the dirt with blood pooling around him. Why would they shoot him? A whimper escaped. What could they possibly want?

Before Cassidy could gather a rational answer, Pierre pulled her by the arm as two of the men vehemently waved them to the side of the road. The other men began to rock the carriage, back and forth back and forth.

"What is going on?" Cassidy tugged on Pierre's coat. "I don't understand." She scrutinized his face, while he quaked, red with anger. "Pierre! What?"

"*Tu!*" One of the men shouted at her. "Mueves. Separado!" He gestured his gun between them, and Cassidy stepped away. Pierre stood so stoic Cassidy wondered if he was breathing. The man waved Cassidy farther, and she reluctantly sidestepped away from Pierre.

The rocking had caused such an imbalance that the carriage tilted with a loud crash on its side. Three of the men began to pull and jerk the black cushioned seat from its place. What did this carriage hold? Cassidy watched in horror as they pulled the wood flooring apart finding a hidden tin box.

The men cheered and clapped hands in the air. A vague shadow flitted in the corner of her eye, and Cassidy turned in slow motion. What she saw shocked her to the core. Pierre had slithered without notice around the upturned wagon, and now rode away on the back of their horse. One of the men raised his gun and pulled the trigger. Cassidy's scream was overpowered by the loud pop. Pierre laid so low on the galloping horse that she could not tell if he was hit. But her eyes did not lie, he galloped hard, leaving her abandoned and unattended with four bandits.

Before she could react, her wrists were quickly bound together with a thick, scratchy rope. The bandit with a red bandana had taken her violin, opened the case, searched it and threw it and the case into the bushes. He jerked her forward and twisted the other end of the rope around the saddle horn. Coming up behind her, he held the stirrup out and shoved her forward. Her hands were already bound to the saddle; she'd no choice but set her foot in the stirrup and mount. As she tried to shake the thick layers of her skirt over her ankles, the man snatched her foot out of the stirrup and replaced it with his own, pulling himself up behind her. Cassidy was assaulted with the coarse smell of sweat and unwashed skin. His arms pinned her unwillingly against him as he took the reins, jerking the horse around and into a gallop. Dodging the brush and trees, the bandits rode hard as Cassidy gripped the saddle horn fighting the shock of what was happening.

The ruddy oranges and pinks of a ripe sunset fell in a long line of sky behind her. West, the sun sets in the west, she remembered the talk on the wagon train. That means they were heading east. Twice the bandits had pulled their horses together to discuss something important.

Blast it. She knew no Spanish.

When they pointed to the tin box, she didn't need to understand the language to know that it was of value. Whatever was in there was worth the risk to kill and steal. When they took off again, she thought her ribs would crack under the rough pounding. Panic tears welled and fell. She wondered if Pierre Doré knew about the box. Is that what the man riding backward was about? Just like Arnold Snider said, she was so naïve, and with the revelation of being used again for his gain, fresh angry tears arose.

The horses strained and pulled around the last steep ridge. It was dark and getting cold. Cassidy felt the wind of the mountains cooling her chapped wrists and tear stained cheeks. At least there was no rain or snow.

The man with the red bandana jumped off and jerked her from horse and onto her feet. But her legs had no strength after hours of riding, and she collapsed into the dirt. Two of the other men walked by pointing and laughing at her.

Humiliated down into her bones, she gritted her teeth and pushed off the ground to stand. Keeping her eyes down but watching every move through her eyelashes, she saw they'd pulled the saddles from the horses and made an area for camp. Cassidy took tiny steps backward. How had Pierre done it? They were all so busy watching the carriage turn over that he'd snuck away unaware. Her legs felt leaden with atrophy, could she run? With the ridiculous layers of her skirt, could she outrun four of them?

Two of the men seemed to argue about making a fire. She stepped back a few more inches. One bandit started scraping his flint into a pile of twigs, while the other was making some sort of argument, reasoning points on his fingers to the oldest man.

Gathering the extra rope into her palm, she took a few more steps back. The older man waved him on and brought out a small scale and set it on a flat rock. A few more tiny steps back and she saw the little fire caught. The tin box was brought out by the rock, and all the men gathered to watch the opening. Feeling dizzy with fear, Cassidy took her hands, still bound together, and lifted the front of her skirts.

Go west, go west. The words pounded with the beat of her heart. She checked one more time as they all gathered around the tin box.

Then ran.

Her body strained to keep her legs moving. Her revitalized nerves somehow shook through her limbs and down into her shoes giving her legs strength she didn't think possible. Clutching her skirts higher, she jumped over a fallen log and dashed past a patch of thin trees. Another opening showed her the way in the darkness, and she finally felt the assurance that her swiftness was building with each leap and turn. The terrain was going downhill, giving her the— suddenly, something jumped on her back and knocked her to the ground. Crying out, she clawed the dirt and leaves to get out, but his weight was too much.

Roughly, he turned her over as he knelt over her. It was the same bandit she had ridden behind. With his bandana around his neck, she got full view of his dark, rough, patchy beard, and rage shooting from his eyes. Soon the others stood over her as they laughed and chided each other. Cassidy tried to move, desperate to get her legs out from under him. She tried to rise up and push against his chest, but he just pushed her back.

One of the younger bandits elbowed the man next to him and began to undo his gun holster. They all laughed as he undid his belt next. Motioning to the man sitting on her legs to move over. Cassidy screamed and swung her bound hands knocking her captor in the face. He came back so fast, Cassidy never saw him pull his knife until her head was against the ground and the blade rested against her throat.

The taunting and jabbing from the men silenced. The forest even quieted in order for her to make peace with this life. She'd rather die in this minute than have her body taken against her will. The older man nudged with his boot the man holding the knife, and he pulled the blade back. They spoke something in low tones as the men standing stepped back. Even in the shadows, Cassidy could see the red rage in his eyes and a trickle of blood from the corner of his mouth.

"*Loco. Muy loco.*" He licked the blood from the corner of his bruised lip sizing her up and down. Knife still in his hand, he watched the others retreat.

Knowing her lips were moving, she prayed some gibberish, begging God for her release.

"*No tomes mi oro.*" The bandit yelled over his shoulder and rocked back on his heels. He grabbed the rope between her wrists and jerked her to standing.

Cassidy tried to comprehend what was happening next. But it seemed he was taking her back to the camp area. When they reached the small crackling fire, he pushed her to the ground. He took the rope and rewound it around his saddle laying on the dirt. As the other three huddled around the scale, holding out their pouches, her captor seemed only interested in what they were doing.

Cassidy realized her body trembled head to toe. The sting of the rope burns made tears roll down her face along with the shock of what had nearly happened. The wicked desire for gold started all this madness. But the greed for what each Californian thought was their right, their due, made men into criminals. The greed Pierre Doré talked about, might have also saved her.

Thirty

THE BANDIT WITH the red bandanna dropped a round flatbread in her lap and walked away. Looking down, Cassidy remembered the Mexican woman on Main Street of Hangtown who would come out with a cart full of frijoles and tortillas. Daily, men would line up to eat this food. She lifted her bound hands and took a nibble. It didn't taste like anything. The men pulled out different colored peppers and ate them and hurriedly drank from their canteens. She remembered that Finny refused to drink from the Indian water pouch. What had she spouted off to Pierre? We all have the capacity to love and not judge. Groaning she closed her eyes. That was easy to say when her body wasn't riddled with fear and a hundred different aches. She tried to shift her weight to the other hip.

The men pulled their blankets out and innocently sparred with each other. Cassidy assumed it must be about their gold pouches as they all tucked them deep inside their shirts.

Cassidy timidly pulled back as her captor stepped her way. Squatting down, he jerked on the knots he had made around the saddle horn. She'd picked and pulled at them at every opportunity. He needn't worry. Unless she thought she could pick up the heavy saddle and run, they were secure. His eyes scrutinized hers.

"*Tienes frio?*" He waited, then pointed at her and rubbed his arms like someone who was cold.

"*Vamos.*" He pointed at her again then to himself. "Come. See. *Yo,*" he tapped his chest.

Cassidy had figured out his offer of wicked warmth and glanced away. He cackled gruffly before he jerked his saddle blanket from next to her and went to lay by the fire.

Thankfully, the robbers all looked too tired to accost her anymore. She felt the tension in her body ease up a pinch or two. Pulling her cape tighter around her, she remembered reading in the Penny Press about the problems in Texas. Mexicans were wanting to hold on to their land and President Polk had ordered American soldiers to go to war over what they believed was theirs. Then the same thing happened in California. The native people were forced to retreat. Maybe they believed the California gold was theirs all along?

Cassidy yawned, the fatigue of the day and the little crackling fire lulling her senses. The men's murmurs in Spanish had ceased. She shook her head quickly, blinking her drooping eyes. Feeling the pain in her wrists and body ease somewhat, Cassidy's chin shot up. One of the men snored and snorted loudly. Newly awakened, now she would not sleep, she would not...not...

A JERK AT her wrists awoke her, and she sensed someone looming over her and opened her mouth to scream. A thick hand covered her mouth, and she felt her body swiftly pulled to standing. Her arms flailed wildly in front of her, and she realized her wrists were no longer bound. Turning to push against the massive arms that pulled her backward she heard a sound in her ear.

"Don't fight. It's me." Now his arm was around her waist and practically lifting her over the dark, woodsy brush.

Like the awakening of the dawn, she recognized that voice as well as the strength to hold her and pull her off her feet. She nodded her head up and down and loosed her vice grip on his arms. Feeling the tension give way, she turned and saw Truitt lift his finger to his mouth to signal her to be quiet. She nodded and took his hand as they ran and curled through the dark woods.

They skirted around a large tree where a horse waited. Truitt grabbed her knee and lower leg and lifted her effortlessly as she swung her other leg over the horse. She held the reins taut as he jumped up behind her. Still without a word spoken they rode carefully with only the moon to guide them. As the horse slowed to a walk, Cassidy wound her arms and hands around his thick arm and buried her face against it. "Thank you, thank you," she whispered.

They rode on for what seemed like an hour before Truitt pulled the horse to a stop and listened. The forest was quiet. Cassidy didn't want to risk being captured again any more than he did. After listening for a few more minutes, Truitt jumped from the back of the horse and reached out to help Cassidy down.

Praying her legs would hold, she swung down and looked up at him. "Tie the horse and step away," she said.

<hr>

HIS EYES LOCKED on her as he wound the reins around a tree and she continued to move back in the dark. Curious and alarmed as to why she moved away, he went to open his mouth but before he could form his concern she came at him full speed and jumped into his arms. Cassidy peppered kisses over his face and temple. Murmuring his name, she kissed his hair and cheeks all while he held her suspended against him.

"I think you are happy to see me?" He pulled back, smiling. After a fast kiss to his lips, she nodded a yes a few inches from his face. Lowering her to the ground, her eyes shone with tears of happiness.

"I think we are safe." He still wanted to chuckle at her greeting. "And I don't think they wanted you."

"Humm?" She tilted her chin, and gazed at him wide-eyed.

"No. Not how *I* want you." He squinted and lifted a roguish smile. "I meant they were only after the gold." He drew his fingers softly across her cheek. If Doré wasn't such a no-account pantywaist of a manager...

"Truitt, tell me." She gripped his arm. "The extra guard in the carriage to Coloma. Was it always about protecting the gold?"

"Of course." He took her by the hand, and they sat on a fallen log. "The only reason Doré had permission for you to perform in Coloma was to transport Snider's gold to another bank."

Cassidy stood and Truitt felt the loss of her hand in his. "It was all a ruse," she sighed. "How stupid could I be? I was the pawn for the transport of gold." Crossing her arms over her chest, she sighed looking long into the night and shaking her head.

"Your talent and music are real, though, Cassidy." He came and stood behind her. "The folks you played for enjoyed the show." He brought his hands around her waist. "That was real."

"And you." She twisted and faced him. "You knew of this and did not tell me?"

"I wasn't sure." He scratched his neck. "He has a lot of money and he sends it to the bank in San Francisco, too. I'm not always privy as to how or when he makes transfers."

Cassidy stepped further away. "How is it you found me?"

"When you didn't return to Hangtown from Coloma, I knew something was wrong." His brow crinkled. "I came upon the overturned carriage and found your violin in the bushes. Four men on horseback weren't that hard to track." He let out a heavy sigh. "Someone from Coloma was at the wreck saying that Doré was getting a search party together."

Cassidy's shoulders slumped and Truitt could feel her disappointment and shock. The poor woman had been through Hades. "I wouldn't have let them violate you."

"What!" She turned wide eyes on him. "You were there! You saw them?"

"I had a clear shot to the one lowering his belt. But I'm glad I waited. Four dead rancheros bleeding out all over you might not have been good for you either."

"Ack." She grimaced holding her head. "Oh, Truitt." She walked in a small circle. "You, you were in Hangtown? You knew I didn't return?"

He nodded, understanding her weary confusion and took her hand in his. "You're tired, and I haven't slept." He led her a few feet away and sat at the base of a large tree. "It will be daylight in an hour." He tugged for her to sit in front of him. As soon as she relaxed back against his chest, a thankful stirring enveloped his being. He rested his head back and tried to close his eyes.

Her hand lay innocently on his bent knee, the warmth of her arm on his leg.

He knew his breathing quickened beyond his control, surely she could feel it. He bent his head and kissed her neck. "I couldn't stay away," he whispered, feeling her soft skin press next to his rough cheek. "I hate Hangtown, but I'm in love with you. I couldn't stay away." He captured her hand from his knee and surrounded both her hands in his warm ones, resting them around her waist.

She twisted her shoulder into his chest, trying to look at him. "Truitt, I want to say things from my heart too, but I…"

"It's okay. I know I made a mess with you in the closet at the El Dorado." He sighed. "I…I have more than enough confidence in the boxing ring. I am better at actions than words. I should have told you what I felt before I showed you. I understand why that was not right. Why it upset you."

Cassidy opened her mouth and closed it with a little frown. "It's not even that." Her head and shoulders fell.

Truitt waited, riding hard today and imagining the worst was exhausting. She seemed out of words. He took their intertwined fingers and separated them. Pulling his finger across her palm, he spelled S—L—E—E—P.

Squeezing his hand, she curled up tighter next to him and laid her cheek against his chest. An unbelievable bliss pulsed through his muscles. After almost giving up, he held his beauty again. He'd found forbearance with her and had actually told a woman how he felt. He closed his eyes. Had he done it right, this time?

Thirty-One

CASSIDY SAT UP from his embrace and stepped away from where they had slept. Truitt awoke, blinking back the full sunlight and felt the void of holding her. He stretched, rolled his stiff shoulders against the tree and watched her. She stood with her back to him, pulling the pins from her muddled hair, dropping them into her pocket. Fingering her long nutmeg strands, she pulled a leaf and twig from her mass of hair. Shaking her soft tresses loose she separated them into three cords and began to braid them. A crow cawed overhead to reprimand Truitt for studying her longingly. He drank in her beauty and grace, her slender fingers as they wove her hair.

In the years before Cassidy, his insides had turned to stale bread and his heart had acquired a tough, protective cover. He inhaled a deep breath of morning air. When did her voice, her laugh, her touch bring renewal to his being and somehow peel the tough scales from his heart? God was his reason for existence. But Cassidy had put meaning back where it belonged.

Would such a fine independent woman want to belong to him? He stood, brushing the leaves and dirt from his pants. She wound the braid into a circle at the base of her neck and used the pins from her pocket to hold it in place. She was so beautiful. He stilled. Could his stripped heart know what to do? Could he give her the life she deserved?

He'd told her he loved her last night, but they both knew the truth. She wanted to live where she could perform, a life with an audience, a stage. He wanted to live up on his property by the Big Blue Lake, the Tahoe, the Indians called it. Hunting and keeping to himself always suited him better.

Pulling out a few strands around her face, she turned and faced him. Her smile was sweet and shy and he felt something knock in his chest. "You slept some?" He asked, feeling a crazy blush coming up his neck. She nodded.

"I was wondering." He took a step closer. "What does it take for a man to court a woman like you?" He enjoyed watching a smile rise on her lips. "You mentioned not liking any of the suitors your father had chosen for you. Do I have to write a letter of intent of some sort? Mention my earnings, my worth?" He smiled, but after a moment of thinking her countenance dropped.

"I said something wrong." He waited for her to look at him. "Cassidy Finnegan." His eyes narrowed. "What is the nature of...of us? Do you see ever yourself married?" A cool breeze rustled the falling leaves around them.

"Lolly." She croaked, cupping her hand around her chin. "Courtship to marriage?"

He took another step and took her hands in his. "I'm bringing it up. You've slept in my arms twice now." He raised an eyebrow, trying to get her to smile. "Just wanted to do the honorable thing."

Her face softened and she touched his cheek. "You are honorable, but...I...I'm..." she just couldn't choke the words out.

"Is it that I burned your violin? Can you forgive me?"

"Oh, yes." She leaned against him and he drew her close. She fit perfectly inside his arms.

"It's not that." Her tone weak. "I just need some time." Her face rose up to see his. "Can you just give me some time?"

"Of course." He kissed her forehead and stepped back to see her. "Can we have an understanding then?" Squeezing her hands, he braced himself to speak his mind. "You'll take no other offers?" He thought Doré was ready to pull that trigger on marriage at any minute. He waited, fighting the quiet brooding surrounding her.

"No." She shook her head. "No other offers, Mr. Emerson, but can we keep this just between us?"

"I think that best." He agreed, wondering why her pleasure did little to match his.

"Truitt." She stepped back. "Janny Long is missing. I fear the worst. And—"

"She's dead."

Cassidy squealed, clapping her hand over her mouth.

"I found her in a shanty by the Eureka Mine. Rubin Zimmerman was one of her regular men. He must have done it. He's nowhere to be found." Seeing her trembling, he took her back in his arms.

"Truitt, I spoke to So Chen." She mumbled into his chest. "Someone left Janny's nightdress with blood on it at the laundry shop. Your name was etched in the wood." She drew her hand up his shirt and touched his collar. "Could Cousin Arnold be this vicious?" She moaned. "Is he getting you back for leaving Hangtown?"

"Possibly. The man hates to be dismissed. You called him Cousin Arnold?"

"Oh, lolly." She swung out of his arms, shaking her head. "What is to be done?"

A squirrel stopped a few feet away, peered up at them then scurried up a tree. A light breeze of pine and cedar wafted in the air.

"Vengeance is mine sayeth the Lord," he said, exhaling a gruff sigh. "Far be it from me to do to others what was done to my father." He turned to grab the horse's reins. "Though, right now it sounds like an acceptable and an upright thing to do."

⌐⁓⁓⁓⌐

CASSIDY RODE THROUGH the woods with Truitt holding her inside his arms, safe and protected. In all her attempts to stay awake and alert in the last twenty-four hours, she hadn't allowed herself to dream that he would come to find her. He'd been gone from Hangtown leaving her heart seared in half to think of him never returning. As soon as the bandits had tied her to their horse, she believed she was utterly alone. Again. All those simple little prayers for Janny and Truitt's safety said little about her faith.

"Truitt, you read that little Bible for yourself?" She turned and tried to see his face.

"I do." He pulled the reins to the left. "I was a grown man when my father and I left Russia. I'd never really missed my mother, but after my father died, I guess I missed her. Knowing she wanted me to have it and that I was in such a bad state, I suppose I needed it. Where my sin and despair ran deep, the truth of His words ran deeper. I read it every night."

"Every night." Cassidy considered his devotion. "I tried to pray for Janny and you, but I've never read the Bible. I suppose that helps when you pray to God." She tilted her head to the side. "And now knowing Janny's sad fate, I can conclude that God doesn't listen to someone like me."

"Someone like you?" He chuckled. "We are all sinners. We all need the grace of God, for we all fall short." He pulled the horse around a large grouping of brush. "Jesus of the Bible took all the sins of mankind on the cross."

"I've been in some beautiful churches in Boston with stained glass and large crosses. I could admire the artistry, but I never understood the man who hung on them with pierced hands and feet. I knew he deserved reverence but he looked so sad to me."

Truitt nodded. "One of the chapters I read said Jesus is now at the right hand of the Father praying for us. He's no longer on that cross. The sin of the world was satisfied, once and for all. And now He is preparing a place, a home for Janny in heaven where there will be peace and joy for all eternity."

"And for my mother, I suppose." Cassidy murmured. "I don't really remember her. My grandparents told me of her goodness and kindness."

"I'm sure she was a lot like you."

Cassidy leaned into his arm, squeezing it like she had last night. "Thank you." Her mouth burned with the desire to tell him the truth. That her name was really Kathleen O'Ryan, but her mother's parents had always called her Cassidy. They told her that was the name her mother had picked out before her father changed it. For as long as she could remember, when anyone asked her name she said Cassidy. Her father had finally given up correcting everyone. Her father. She straightened picturing his face. He was the reason she'd left home and traveled across the wide land of America.

"Truitt, do you believe God brings people together? That there is a reason for everything that happens to us?"

"I know I've been awake many a night trying to justify why that can't be true. But I think it is. I know I want good things for good people and bad things for bad people. But sometimes it happens quite the opposite way. And I still think God knows what he's doing, even if I can't figure it out."

They came to a clearing laden with long, green grass. He stopped to let the horse nibble. "Do I believe a stunning woman called a lady's companion could travel all the way from the east to the west just to meet me and give her heart to me? I fear that's a bit farfetched."

Truitt slipped off the back of the horse and took out his canteen. Cassidy swung her leg over, dropped down, and took a drink after him.

"But yet," she waited for his attention, then winked. "It has happened." She filled her hand with some water. Just as his smile rose, she held her hand over his head, dribbling the water over him. His eyes flashed wide, and she squealed and took off running in the tall grass.

"Running from back east." He replaced the canteen and yelled after her. "Running from mudslides." He came around another tree and easily blocked her way as she dodged him left and then right. "Running from the El Dorado or me after a fight in Hangtown, you said." Smirking from his teasing, she stepped backward and then skipped across the grass and hid behind the horse. "Running from four gold thieves. Amazing Cassidy." He snuck closer to the horse. "These legs that walk, and dance, and..."

She saw him close in and circle the horse after her. Laughing, she tried her best to keep the horse between them. After he'd circled the horse without reaching her, Truitt pushed on the large neck, easily making a way to grab her by the arm. "Running off with Doré and bandits." He pulled her close. "No more running, Miss Finnegan."

Their chests rose and fell as Truitt's eyes dropped to her lips. Meeting the desire in his down turned gaze, she rose up on her toes. As his lips fell onto hers, he was the same thirsty man she had kissed before. He never did anything halfway. All his body, hands, and kisses consumed her, robbing her of her senses. She gripped his face and hair, feeling the water that had started the chase. Unexpectedly, he sat down to lay back in the tall grass and pulled her on top of him. More frantic need encompassed his kisses as she rested on his wall of a chest. He was a fury in battle and in love, her hope was to be his and match all her—

"Ahh!" she squealed and quickly rolled away.

Truitt laughed without a trace of concern as the horse took a step and leaned in close with wide whiskered lips and grass sticking from his teeth. The wide chomping muzzle bent low to nuzzle Cassidy and she rolled further away. "He tried to eat my ear." She stood brushing off her dress.

"He's just jealous." Truitt stood and grabbed her hand, pulling her close to kiss her neck and ear. Shaking her head, she tried to twist away, but he wrapped his other arm around her hips and easily lifted her over his shoulder. Walking as if he did this rash behavior often, he sidled close to the side of the horse and held the stirrup for her foot.

"Enough running and rolling in the grass, Miss." As she settled in the saddle, he held his hand on her leg and squeezed it. "It's time to get back to town."

Thirty-Two

CASSIDY SPIED THE outskirts of Hangtown, knowing she looked like a ragged dog. "You are used to taking me in the back way. Yes?"

"Yes, I am." Truitt turned the horse down a side trail and came upon the back of the Bedford Hotel. "Swing your leg over the front." He held out his hand for her to hang on to as she swung down. "I will tell Newton to send you food and water and then I'll send a runner to Coloma to call the search party off."

She squeezed his hand. "The searchers likely want to find the gold."

Raising their hands to his face he kissed her hand. "And here I already found it." He winked, let her go and led the horse around the large building.

Cassidy smiled, feeling the flattery down to her toes. Her stomach growled and she went up the back stairs and found her room. Holding the handle she paused. She would have to be brutally honest with Finny. Arnold Snider was a corrupt man. Voices came from the hallway so she slipped inside. The room was empty. As soon as she had eaten and bathed, she would find the right words.

An hour later, Cassidy combed and towel-dried her wet hair. Looking in the long mirror, her own reddish hues shone brighter than the fading color she'd dyed into her hair. She wrapped her bathing gown tight around her waist and spied her bed. A warm stream of sunlight lay across her covers. A nap would be wonderful, but too much churned in inside for sleep to come easily.

She thought about Truitt and his touch, his kisses melding with hers, and the deep bond she felt with him. Courtship, marriage. She blew out a breath. Those thoughts would allow little sleep. How could she persuade Finny to reject Arnold? Their wedding was to be in a week. Finny was impossible to move once she had her sights set. And how to tell Truitt the truth about who she was? A letter to her father, asking for her hand? To Mr. O'Ryan? "Oh lolly," she sighed.

A strange new desire pecked at her heart. She knelt down next to her bed, the sunlight warming her damp hair. "Dear God, I've seen your buildings and I've seen your book, but I'm not sure how to see You or know You, or if You want to know me." Cassidy nodded. That was honest anyway. "But I need to be forgiven for the folly I've committed and allowed. The folly and shame I've put others through. Truitt says that is what happened with Jesus on the cross. He's sad because he's taking away the harsh sin for all of us. So if you could ask Him to take mine, I would be very appreciative." Cassidy wondered and waited if she would feel any different. Did it work? "And then if it's allowed to ask one more thing, could you see Truitt and me to finding a road to marriage? And rescue Finny from Cousin Arnold." Cassidy grumbled. "I guess that was two requests." She fingered her loose hair. "Thank you and Amen."

Later, Cassidy set her tea down as Finny rushed into the room.

"I just heard." Finny stood before her, wide-eyed, shaking her head. "You were kidnapped?"

"I was on the wrong carriage." Cassidy tried to curtail her sarcasm. It wasn't Finny's idea for her ride to Coloma to be robbed. Cassidy held her hand forward. "Finny, please, come sit a minute."

Finny's full skirts filled Cassidy's bed. "You don't look any worse for the wear." Finny looked her over. "I heard Truitt telling Arnold they didn't hurt you."

"No, they didn't." Cassidy chewed her bottom lip covering her chapped wrists. "I need to tell you something difficult. You won't like it so…so…I'll say it fast." Cassidy sucked in a quick breath. "You can't marry Arnold Snider."

"What?" Finny rose off the bed. "Blimey, did you fall and bump your head in the ordeal?" Her thin face turned red.

"Before you start in, just let me finish." Cassidy pleaded. "Just five minutes, can you listen to me for five minutes?"

Finny crossed her arms over her chest and gave her the death stare. "Go ahead."

"I…I take responsibility for this, but…but I didn't know what kind of man Arnold was. Finny, please listen. He's all about dishonest gain. I don't believe he's honorable. Possibly, he's a corrupt shyster and I don't like the way he looks at the Basque sisters. He has lust in his eyes."

"Ohh, nooo." Finny waved her hand in the air, mocking her. "What man doesn't?"

"A gentleman who is betrothed to you should not, for one!" Cassidy snapped back.

"Oh, Mary, Mother, and Joseph, here we go." Shaking her head, Finny circled over to her bed. "You and the devil don't have nothin' to judge but me day after day?"

Cassidy rose off the bed. "No, Finny. Listen." She huffed. "I'm not judging you. It's Arnold, my own cousin. He's not the right man for you."

Finny turned with fire in her eyes. "Not for me, aye? Is this your demented plan? Now that you've sat in his kitchen, seen his grand home, his servants, wealth. Now, this new blimey plan comes out—to have him for yourself?

"Heaven's above, no. No, Finny. He's been creating devilry wherever he goes." Cassidy exhaled, lifting her face to the ceiling and rolling her eyes. How could the woman not see the true nature of the man?

"Well, you'll just have to excuse me," Finny said smugly. "I suppose I will need to find another to stand up with me on Saturday. We are getting married at the new church. All the best people in town will be there. I had hoped you would share in my good fortune. But obviously not." She hesitated. "And your Mr. Emerson better watch his step. I tried to warn you. Must be drowning he's after because there's always a millstone." She shrugged one shoulder. "Arnold will not be dismissed by anyone. Arnold showed him great generosity only to be countered with a refusal of employment. And Mr. Emerson got paid very well. Such disloyalty is not tolerated."

"See, see how you defend the man?" Cassidy cried out. "He does not own Truitt. America is a free country. Truitt can come and go as he wishes."

"Oh, and now who is defending who? A bit two colored shouldn't we say?" Finny pulled her bag from under her bed.

Cassidy stood back speechless as Finny pulled her things from the wardrobe. "To think I was truly worried about you." Finny flung her drawers and petticoats in the bag. "To think after all that we've been through—living out of a wagon, the wind, the rain, the Indians, the desert, poor Mr. Dingle." Finny paused in her packing doing the sign of the cross. "God rest his soul."

She looked under the bed and pulled out a pair of stockings. "That in this week of my first true happiness, you have to spoil it." Finny shook her head and looked around the room. "I don't really care what you think of Arnold. He means *me* no evil." She jerked the heavy bag off her bed and walked to the door. Turning, she glared at Cassidy. "And come Saturday, the money that your family sent, it goes to Arnold. The wedding makes it official. I will be Mrs. Arnold Snider, wife of the most prominent man in town."

"Finny." Cassidy's voice faltered, the regrets crushing her. Her long time, red-haired, short-tempered, and obstinate friend. Her dreamer companion, willing to walk over blistering sands with her, yet blind to the truth. Once again, she'd wounded her through and through. She took a step toward her. "The money will be there, as I will, if you will allow it?" Cassidy waited. How many of these tiffs had they had and later found forbearance for one another?

"To your own doing." Finny shrugged.

"And then you will be gone on a wedding holiday?" Cassidy asked.

"Not right away," Finny sniffed. "We want to travel by one of his ships. It gives Arnold a chance to oversee the shipping too. Something about getting them manned with hearty sailors soon."

"Very well," Cassidy said softly. "I'm sure it will be a delightful…trip." Cassidy wondered how the town would fair without Mr. Snider's rule and influence.

Finny went to turn the knob.

"Wait." Cassidy took another small step forward. "I understand you don't want to share a room with me anymore. But Saturday will be here before you know it. Please, just believe one thing." Cassidy waited, but Finny would not look at her. "All my meddling and unrequested opinions…they come from a deep place in my heart. You're right, we have been through so much together. I…I… love you, my dear friend. And I want you to be happy and… rich…" She chuckled at how that came out and thought she saw Finny do the same. Something her grandmother in Ireland always said rose up in her. "Blessings on you. May love and laughter light your days,

and warm your heart and home.

May good and faithful friends be yours,

wherever you may roam.

May peace and plenty bless your world

with joy that long endures.

May all life's passing seasons

bring the best to you and yours!"

Finny looked down and nodded thanks for the blessing before she walked out and closed the door behind her.

Thirty-Three

TRUITT SAT IN the hard chair at So Chen's table. Leaning his face into his palms, he listened to the heavy rainfall. Except for the small woman and her sons working to keep the water buckets emptied of the rainwater, he might have drifted off to sleep. Why had he been tired all day?

So Chen struggled to lift a full bucket. He jumped up from the table, easily taking it from her and pouring it into the black pot she used for heating water. Going out the back door, he placed it where the water ran off the building.

"What you do?" She asked as he walked back to the table.

He sat again, leaning on his elbow and scratching his head. "Quitting the work for Arnold has put a mark on my back." He rubbed his palm into his forehead.

"No, you get job any town." So Chen placed an iron on the hot stove top. "What about violin woman? What you do with her?"

Truitt stilled. What personal intimate moments he'd had with Cassidy would always remain between the two of them. After he settled his pulse, he realized she didn't mean the details of his affections. "I want to marry her. Is that what you mean?"

"Oh marry…" So Chen dragged a long sheet over the ironing board. "You love her?"

The question made his chest tighten. "I do." He dropped his chin.

She stopped what she was doing and came close, squeezing his neck with her tiny hand. "Then what is this?" So Chen pointed at his cheek while she made a sad frown. "Why you so sad of face?"

Truitt lifted the corner of his mouth into a smile. So Chen had seen him inside and out without looking too closely. "I've never been good at any of this. Should I dress nice and ask her to step out? I bought her a new violin. Should I bring her more gifts?" So Chen had returned to her ironing. "I didn't really ask her to marry me." Thinking back, what was the tumbled mess of words he'd said? Did he tell her he would fight until he was black and blue to make her happy? "Umm," he growled. She didn't like his fist fighting.

"She asked me to wait." He remembered his antsy days at the Damonte Station. "I suppose I'm no good at that." He stood and gazed out the rain-blurred window. "This rain might keep up for days. The Arnold Snider wedding is soon. I think things will change for her after that."

"The girls and me," So Chen said, breaking into his dreary thoughts. "We want see Janny grave. Say a few words. You take us?"

Truitt turned, looking at her. "Yes, I will take you." He stepped over to where she worked on the ironing. "So Chen, you have enough money? Enough food to feed you and your sons? I know you keep feeding all of the women who need a place to stay."

"I got money and gold. Plenty for needs. No good keeping in store with big box. Anybody come around with gun and take it. I hide it."

"The bank?"

"Ya, don't like that place."

Truitt nodded with a small smile. "The thing is, I don't work for Arnold anymore. I have my own place I'm building up the mountain. There is a lake so large you can barely see the other side, and trees as tall as the sky. The colors are breathtaking. The water is so clear and blue you can see the fish on the bottom."

"A good place for you?" she asked.

"I think so, but…I won't be here. I won't be able to check on you and the girls. And look what happened when I was gone. I don't like that. Not at all."

"Ahh." She waved her hand at him. "You need me more. Who will sew skin back together? Who tell you what to do?"

Wavering, Truitt shook his head at her. He was not the savior he thought he was. Like what happened to his father, the things he couldn't control were the hardest part to swallow. Being on the wrong side of Arnold could prove deadly.

⌒‿◡

THE PATTER OF the rain helped Cassidy sleep longer into the next morning. The warm bed lulling her to doze from crazy dream to crazy dream. There was small knock at the door and she noticed a card pushed underneath. Flipping her covers off, she grabbed it.

I'm in the foyer, don't hurry. I will wait all day if needed.

A large smile covered her face as she kissed the card and began to dress. A few minutes later she smoothed her hands down her deep blue dress. The note from Truitt made her heart beat wildly out of her chest. Fanning the heat in her face, she took one more spin in front of the long mirror. Her hair was coiffed nicely at her neck with a few loose curls hanging around her face.

"Breathe," she said aloud, trying to gain some composure. This solid man and his touch, his words, his intentions had her more fluttery than she'd felt in years. Then, just as fast as her excitement had escalated, it left her being. She had to tell him the truth. Truitt needed the truth. Truitt deserved the truth about who she was. Loving someone is telling the truth. How would he respond?

Closing her eyes, she exhaled. Would it end the hope, the joy, everything she ever pictured with him? The rain tapped into the stillness. Biting her lip, she went to the door and turned the knob.

Before she got to the foyer, she let out a long breath then took the two last steps. Searching for the man whose giant frame was beyond noticeable, Pierre's fine suit turned and walked swiftly to meet her.

"Oh, *ma jolie, tu es vivant*."

Before Cassidy could open her mouth, he had her hands and drew her to the middle of the foyer. Pulling her hands to his lips, he kissed them and muttered half French and half English. Every other word contained apologies and sorrow and something about her beauty she guessed.

"I feel my tears form in such gratitude," he said fervently. He released her hands and wrapped his arms around her. Cassidy could smell his heavy cologne as he held her cheek against his starched collar. Pulling away, she tried to interrupt his display. "Pierre, I'm fine. I'm alive."

"That you are, *ma belle*." He had her hands again gripping and massaging then inside his. "Please, please, I was in such shock. I could not think straight." He closed his eyes, shaking his head. "I should have never left you like that. My actions were unconscionable."

Cassidy wondered how to politely agree with him. "We both were in shock. You thought to go get help. I suppose we both should be thankful to be alive."

"*Oui, oui*. Our guard was not well trained, I suspect." He sighed.

Cassidy felt something stiffen up her back. "Was he trained to guard a shipment of gold from one town to another or to guard a performer and her manager from ruffians? Since he is dead, it's a bit hard to ask him."

Pierre's wide open mouth pinched into a tight circle. "I…I cannot speak…say for him."

"So let me hear from you." She pulled her hands free of his. "How did it come to be that the carriage to Coloma was really about transporting gold?"

"The carriage belonged to Mr. Snider. He is the one who wanted you to be safe, have a guard. Wait." He held his hand up. "That is not true. Above all, I wanted you to be safe. When we were surrounded by men with guns, I knew there was nothing I could do. I saw the horse left alone and all I could think was to get away and bring help back to find you." He shook his head and touched her cheek. "I could think of nothing but you. My heart was fading, my blood thinning. My only hope—reason for living —was to see your striking blue eyes, your face again." His lips crinkled a pained frown. "It was all right and all wrong. Can you please forgive me? I beg of you."

Cassidy went to open her mouth but no words would come. Truitt had called him a coward. But what did it matter now? She took in a deep breath. "Right now I need to see my mistress to the church altar. I will be busy with a wedding and will have no time for Coloma or the El Dorado. I...I...forgive you Pierre."

"Oh, *oui, mon amour.*" His relief showed over his whole body. He took her hands again and brought them to his lips. One of his hands let go and he hugged her against him. "You mean the world to me." He nuzzled her cheek to his and whispered into her ear.

Someone cleared their throat and Cassidy raised her eyes over Pierre's suit coat to see Truitt looking smug and wide-eyed at her.

Oh, lolly.

Thirty-Four

CASSIDY MOVED BACK so fast that poor Pierre fell forward awkwardly with suddenly empty arms and his moment of tenderness cut short.

"Truitt." Cassidy skirted around Pierre and came near the large man whose eyes were assaulting Pierre black and blue.

"Pierre," she sighed, dropped her head to the side. "I mean, Mr. Doré was apologizing for what happened on the road from Coloma."

Truitt still assessed him like a badger waiting to bite. "Uh huh."

"It was just the most horrific thing imaginable." Pierre shook his head at them. "And you, Emerson, with those useful primitive hunting and tracking skills. I'm…we…all are so thankful you were there to find her alive."

Truitt's eyes flickered with roguish humor and then settled into aggression.

Cassidy went to touch his sleeve and changed her mind. "Yes, how thankful we all are that Truitt was so close on the trail." She tried to hold the awkward silence without cringing, Truitt was not happy and it pulsed from his body. Pierre's untoward affection toward her couldn't have been worse in timing. They stood in a silent triangle with Truitt's chin lowered, a locked jaw, and fire in his eyes, reverberating between them.

"I must go." Pierre nodded and headed for the double doors of the Bedford Hotel.

"Ahh," he spun on his heal, "I almost forgot to ask you..." Pierre's eyes flashed to Truitt and he straightened his cravat. "There is a wedding party tomorrow night at the Snider residence." He took a deep breath. "If you are not previously engaged, *s'il vous plait*, I would be honored to... to escort you."

Cassidy slowly smiled and blinked. At least the man showed effort in the face of the enemy. "Thank you, Mr. Doré. I will likely be engaged helping Miss O'Ryan. I'll have to look forward to seeing you there."

"*Oui*. As I will also." He bowed quickly and left the hotel.

Cassidy carefully swung around to Truitt. He was still looking out the door, chewing on the corner of his bottom lip. She, herself, was a bit rattled, wondering if—

"I don't know if I should chase him down and knock the stuffing out of that shiny suit," Truitt said as he finally looked down to her, "or shake you."

"A shaking is probably not..." She looked around, her voice trailing. "...appropriate for this fine lobby."

"So." He took in a breath. "This is what you needed time for, what you didn't want to tell me." His expression was so tense, so somber, Cassidy felt her throat constrict.

"No," she croaked out. "There is nothing between Pierre and myself." This was the complete truth. Never had she been attracted to Pierre. "He's been managing the El Dorado and Coloma performances and the traveling." She pursed her lips. The list was increasing. "And the robbery was just just...."

"Trust me, Cassidy." He released a short huff. "That's more than enough for a man to have strong feelings for you."

She went to open her mouth and closed it. What had she done now?

He raked his fingers through his hair. "Something strange happened to me the moment you fell from the wagon and landed in my arms at Damonnte Station," he released a heavy sigh, "and I was sure you were Kathleen O'Ryan, Arnold's fiancée."

Cassidy felt her body waver. Why was it so stuffy in here?

"And then in the cave," Truitt said, dropping his eyes on hers.

The recollection, she couldn't help linger lovingly on his face and eyes. That was the moment her heart had quickened for him—without meaning to. Her hand gently touched his cheek. Hearing Finny's words, you will be Cassidy Emerson, came to mind. No one would ever have to know. It was a fine name for sure. A grand name. Could she take this identity switch to her grave?

"Truitt Emerson, Acushla," she whispered. She felt his hands on her waist, pressing her close to his thick body. "I know you are the man for me." Basking in his gaze, she pulled her hand down his cheek and neck, fingering his collar. Whether he was clean and pressed, or rough and unkempt, there was no mistaking the intense attraction she felt for him.

"Good." He pulled a few loose strands behind her ear. "Acushla. What does that mean?"

She lifted a coy smile. "It's a word used in Ireland between two people who love each other. My grandfather used it to speak of my grandmother. It means you are the beat of my heart."

The corner of his lip he had been chewing lifted in a smile and his gaze softened. "Acushla. It's a good word." He glanced back at the door Doré had exited. "And because of the beat of *my* heart, it would be prudent for Doré to keep his hands off you." His eyes demanded she understand. "I say it because of this book." He tapped his pocket. "I have to forgive. I believe the Almighty has done that for me." He shook his head. "But the forgetting," he shot a solemn gaze at the door, "that is my weakness."

"An admitted weakness?" Cassidy gripped his sturdy arm and gave it a squeeze. "How can that be in here?" Drawing a finger across his chest, she smiled trying to lighten the moment.

Truitt cleared his throat, "And did I mention to you? You're my most beautiful, talented, enchanting weakness." He rested his large hand on the back her neck, narrowing his eyes on her. "But I feel something." He drew his other hand down her arm. "Something is not right. Humph, even if I could knock a few of those pearly French teeth out." He squinted, waiting, watching her. "I don't think that would settle this unease I feel." He squeezed her hand. "Cassidy, tell me what it is."

He was so close, almost nose to nose and Cassidy's heart skipped a beat and her countenance saddened. What could she say? She wanted to tell him. She needed to tell him the truth. But she feared that tender expression turning into cold fury at the deception. She turned to the only thing she could do. She hesitated.

"I told Finny." She ground her teeth in regret. "I mean Kathleen." She stepped back until his hands slipped away, so she could better concentrate on diverting his question, "that Arnold was not the right man for her. I felt I had to point out his lifestyle of dishonest gain." She shook her head. "It just made her spiteful. She believes I judged her."

"You two are very different. I suppose she doesn't take well to the hired help stepping out of their station and speaking their concerns."

Cassidy lifted a weak smile. "Yes, the help. I need to be of help. I'll go now to her and help with the preparations." Cassidy tried to keep her chin up. "This Friday is the wedding party. Will you be there?" She squeezed his hand.

Truitt scowled and scratched his chin. "Arnold and I are not on good terms. I knew I would create discord when I quit working for him." He paused and drew his finger around her chin. "But with Pierre on the loose, waiting in the wings for another moment to tell you how sorry he is," his voice dripped with sarcasm, "I think I'm going to invite myself."

"I would like that." She inched closer and glanced side to side at the empty lobby. Pulling up higher on her toes, she searched his face and was rewarded when he bent close and met her lips with a light sweet kiss.

"That was nice." She whispered as his forehead rested on hers. Eyes aglow on each other, then closed, they shared another enticing kiss.

A sound behind them brought them apart. Finny and Emery, the oldest Basque sister, walked into the lobby.

"Public display, Cassidy?" Finny droned. "Didn't have the nerve to tell him our room is empty?" She tilted her head to the side. "Or from the flush on your face, maybe you've already been there."

Cassidy felt the jibe through her gut and out the other side. Even poor Emery looked away embarrassed. Cassidy remembered quickly how to handle Finny Finnegan. "I was just saying goodbye to Truitt and was about to come to the house to help you." She would give the woman no satisfaction. Why had she tried so hard to help her see the light? Finny had been rude and disgraceful at every turn. Her father's money—her own dowry—was a minuscule price to pay to be free of the woman. "What can I do to help?"

"I'd made some notes and left them in my room." Finny started up the stairs with Emery following. "I will get them and then we need to see what the mercantile can put together for food. I suppose you can help with that and the place settings." Finny stopped and came back down a few steps. "Oh, and Arnold wants you to bring your violin. Have a few of your tunes ready for entertainment."

"My violin was…" Cassidy saw Truitt shake his head.

"Someone found it at the wreck and brought it to Snider," he murmured.

Heat rose up her back. Instantly she knew why Truitt had to quit working for him and why things had to change. This new couple and their dominant, superior attitude was revolting. "Yes, I'd be delighted to play at your wedding soiree," she lied. No response returned, as Finny and Emery reached the landing and turned.

Exasperated, Cassidy shook her head and tried to bite back her flaring words.

"Listen, Cassidy." Truitt's hand cupped her arm bringing her back to the moment. "It's certain Miss O'Ryan has told Arnold we are together." He sighed and stared out to Main Street. "I don't trust him. He enjoys getting even. Just stay away from him at all costs." He gave her arm a shake. "Are you listening? He knows the best way to get to me is through you."

Cassidy blinked, having the most overwhelming desire to hide in his arms and beg him to take her away. Oh, lolly, she was so close—the reason she'd traveled from Boston to California. Only two more days and Finny would be settled and she would be free. "Yes, yes, I hear you. Stay clear of Arnold Snider at all costs." A strange thought hit her. "Truitt, you are free from this town, you have no work to keep you here, no reason to stay."

He rolled his lips, squinting at her. "No reason?" his tone was incredulous. "Cassidy, Acushla, I have every reason. I love you and don't ever want to be long away from you."

Finny and Emery reappeared walking down the stairs, talking. But Cassidy pushed every sound away, pressing to her heart this man before her and the momentary happiness of Truitt's sincere confession.

Thirty-Five

THE FOLLOWING EVENING, Arnold Snider's grand Victorian home glistened at the end of Main Street, Hangtown. Nothing in this mining town could compare with the lights and finery flowing from every window. The dining room table was laid with giant candelabras, fine china and tiers of finger foods and sweet delicacies. Cassidy had worked with Arnold's staff to make sure every detail was to his and Finny's liking. The sweet Basque sisters donned full-length black service dresses and crisp white aprons. After Cassidy had fixed the girls' hair up in soft coifs, they were transformed into astute, mature servants. An hour after drinks were refilled and the crowd had all complemented and congratulated the couple, Cassidy was told to play one of her soft melodies and sing only one Irish lullaby.

Donned in her best deep blue dress, she tenderly finished the last note. The people clapped and smiled while she curtsied. She spotted Truitt outside on the large porch talking to some men. He was inches above the others in stature and strength. From the first night when she cried on his shoulder, he was without hesitation the gentlest and kindest man she'd ever met. Funny how she had thought her future and her freedom would be on the stage.

She smiled to herself. Playing small soirees like this, weddings or gatherings, felt good and right. Maybe one day she would play for their children. Face flushing, Cassidy smiled back at the admirers gathered in the parlor. It was an interesting revelation. She wanted to be with Truitt, more than on the stage or performing with the Pacific Minstrels.

She placed her violin back in the case. Even San Francesco had lost its appeal. She'd never been in love before. Who would have known love was always meant to be her freedom, her freedom of choice; to love someone without puppet strings, and without a business arrangement. She had come west and found a golden treasure. An honest man who loved her and risked everything for her. She looked about the room as people stood in groups talking and laughing. Tomorrow Finny would marry Arnold and Cassidy would have a brand new day to call her own.

Emery walked by balancing a tray of cups and saucers. "A bit of coffee, Miss Cassidy?"

Cassidy smiled. "No, thank you, Emery. You and your sister are doing a wonderful job tonight."

"To you, thanks," Emery smiled. "I understand the English more I speak it, more it comes to me."

"Wonderful."

"I never see a woman play like that. Your deep love in the notes and the songs," Emery chuckled. "Those right words, yes?"

"Those were perfect words." Cassidy saw Pierre Doré coming toward her. "Just remember, Emery, never settle for anything less than a job or a man or a life that makes you happy. I don't care what you've been told. It's America, it's a new day. You find what makes your heart sing and never let it go."

"You say beautiful words. Thank you, Miss Cassidy." Emery gave her a small dip of her head and turned to serve others.

The instant she left, Pierre took her place. "Ah, *ma belle*, even in such a small venue, your skillfulness and beauty fill the room, the entire house, I believe." He took her hand and kissed it.

"Pierre," she searched for a gentle beginning, "I want to thank you for all your help in these last weeks. I know it is unusual for a woman to…to find a place to perform."

"*Oui, oui*. It is unusual unless the woman is greatly gifted in such a way many here in the west have never heard. I think some came to stare at your beauty and we cannot penalize them." He smiled, all white, bright teeth aglow.

"Well, that's—" Through the window, Cassidy saw Truitt still talking. "I need to say something and you make it difficult." She clutched her violin to her chest.

His smile faded and he straightened, blinking at her.

"Mr. Emerson has made a declaration for my hand in marriage." Cassidy wondered if that sounded truthful, but it made the right point. "And after my mistress and Mr. Snider are settled, I said I would accept."

Pierre jolted back. "This is not true."

"No, no, it is true." She looked away, hoping his voice hadn't carried to the other guests. "I...I love him." She finally looked again to see the pale confusion on his face.

"But he is a ruffian. A fighter who...who threatens and takes and..." Pierre shook his head. "I know you are a domestic but that doesn't bother me. I would give you a home and security. You do not have to settle like this." His face creased.

Cassidy pressed her lips flat. How thankful she should be that he would overlook her station in life. She caught the groan in the back of her throat. "And for many women, they would be...thankful." But not me. She held back. "I don't think I can explain it to you. But I just wanted to say thank you for the opportunities and earnings you gave me."

"So, you will run off to the woods with that willful man." Pierre scowled. "Leave all that you've worked for behind?" He shook his head. "What a waste of your talent."

Cassidy couldn't let his words penetrate far under her skin. She had left her grandparents in Ireland and never been encouraged or accepted as a musician. Now someone told her she was wasting her talent. Likely, she would never make others happy.

"I must leave you." She pulled in a deep breath and bowed. Walking through the parlor to the front door, a few of the finely dressed women watched her from the corner of their eyes. Yes, she would tell each of them; she would trade all the fine gentlemanly offers and fancy dresses to be home. Home on a prairie, being free to kick up her heels with a group of sodbusters and gold hunters or home in the woods with her husband, Truitt Emerson.

Truitt held the conversation with the town blacksmith and watched every move Cassidy made while conversing with Pierre Doré.

From the look on Pierre's face, the bright-toothed man didn't like what he was hearing from her. Good. It was time to cut the cord on that association. Even outside, the sound of her violin had beckoned every conversation still, every ear quickened to listen to the clear penetrating notes. She had a gift from God, no doubt and though he didn't know how, he would have to give her reign to live her dream.

Would she agree to marry him, and live on the land his father had left him? Would he move to San Francesco to find work while she performed? God would have to give him strength for that. He patted the blacksmith on the back and stepped forward as Cassidy met him on the porch.

"You'll be cold." He squeezed her hand.

"And you have been my warmth." She smiled coyly and tucked the violin case behind her.

A hearty laugh escaped. "I won't burn it, I promise." He pulled on her hand and kissed her cheek, not caring who saw them. "You played beautifully tonight." He looked into those soft, sparkling, blue-gray eyes. "I was thinking I would like to be in your audience every day of my life." Her smile matched his longing and she squeezed his arm.

A well-dressed man walked up the porch stairs and removed his derby. A ruffle of gray hair stood up and he flattened it as he took the last step up onto the porch. Folks standing around nodded and Truitt heard Cassidy gasp as the man came into the light of the house. Her violin case hit the floor and she suddenly covered her hands over her mouth.

"Welcome, sir." Truitt reached out to shake his hand and Cassidy cowered behind him.

"Kathleen?" The man shook his hand and looked closer. "Dear Lord lass, come into the light."

Truitt turned to face her and saw her pale stricken expression. Who is this man that had her trembling? How did she know of him?

"I...I...am Miss Finnegan, sir," her words wobbled as her voice quaked. "Kathleen is inside." She turned to the large front window. "There, in the yellow and pink dress."

The man rubbed his nose with his knuckle and leaned toward the window. "That woman is not Kathleen O'Ryan. What kind of parlor game is everyone playing at this party?" Two men on the other side of the door resumed their conversation and only Truitt and Cassidy remained to answer his question.

"May I introduce Miss Cassidy Finnegan. She is Miss O'Ryan's companion." Truitt could feel her hands gripping his arm like a vice.

"All right, all right, Cassidy it is," he nodded. "I'd forgotten you insisted on being called Cassidy."

"Please to meet you, sir. I am Donavan O'Ryan. I am Arnold's step-father and Kath—Cassidy is my niece."

Truitt stood still. His mind raced at the confusion.

"Please tell me, dear niece," the man addressed Cassidy, "did I miss your wedding?"

Thirty-Six

CASSIDY FELT HER stomach roll up and swallowed hard not to be sick on this finely painted porch.

"Uncle Donavan, I...I...will not be marrying Cousin Arnold." She tried to loosen her fingers from digging into Truitt's arm. "He has fallen in love with another woman. And it's not me. I believe it's for the best all around." Fear dripped in between her words. "I...I also have chosen someone else. Arnold and I were just not suitable for each other."

Her uncle jerked his head back. "That makes no matter. Did you not understand that this was the purpose for your trip from Boston?"

"I was." She held her mouth open, searching for any rational words. She had to keep talking to keep from looking at Truitt. "I don't think you or my father understand what it was like to travel across these many states. It was hardship month after month. Poor Mr. Dingle died in the desert. It was by the grace of God that we made it and it should be of no difference who we choose to marry." She tried to control her erratic breathing. Desperation overtook her manners. Never before would she have spoken to her father or uncle in this manner.

"Of course it matters." Eyes narrowing, he shook his head. "I wondered about the prudence of this arrangement. You have always been a flighty child, picking your name and sneaking around with that old violin attached to your back." He pointed to her case. "The money is only to stay in the family, silly girl. Arnold is the only male heir. Even though he is not my blood, he has a fair business head on his shoulders."

"Wait. " Truitt stepped away and the cold air of his missing presence sliced into her. "You said your last name was Finnegan?" He licked the center of his bottom lip and shook his head. "You are Kathleen Finnegan?"

"Dear Lord, man," Uncle Donavan said. "What games has she been playing on you all? This is my niece, Miss Kathleen O'Ryan."

Before the truth could hit Truitt, the door opened, and Arnold stepped out.

"Father! What an amazing surprise. I wrote that we would love to have you, but I never imagined." Arnold shook his hand.

"I took the Harrison Ship from Port Charleston."

"Of course, very well," Arnold said.

Cassidy felt darkness flickering in and out of her eyesight. If she fainted now…

"Please, come in sir." Arnold held his front door open. "How opportune. You are just in time to enjoy the wedding tomorrow."

No one moved, and Arnold's face flushed. "Please, sir, this is my home. I look forward to introducing you to the businessmen of Hangtown."

"I think it best we converse out here," Donavan's jaw twitched to the side. "Kathleen has explained that you've decided to marry another rather than her."

Cassidy couldn't feel her toes or fingers and the blood was rushing from her limbs. Truitt leaned close. "What's happening, Cassidy? Tell me now." The cold up her spine was like nothing she'd ever felt, yet close to the moment she handed over her grandmother's violin in that tiny cave.

"I am marrying my cousin, Kathleen O'Ryan." Arnold puffed his chest and let loose of the door. "She is in there." He gestured toward the window. "The lovely redhead with the yellow and pink dress."

Donavan O'Ryan held his hands up in the air. "Now who's fooling whom?" He demanded. "That is Kathleen." He pointed to Cassidy. "Don't expect me to stand here and believe that you did not know her."

Arnold's mouth fell open and a vile expression covered his face. His slow gaze at Cassidy was like the slipping of a guillotine blade, thin threads of his anger holding the blade over her neck. "You...you are Kathleen?" His nostrils flared. "You purposely tricked me, betrayed me?" His hatred lingered on her. "You will go to hell and back for this."

"There must be a reason for the mix-up." Truitt stared him down.

Cassidy took a deep breath in between her heart pounding from her chest. "This is my fault, Uncle." She bit her bottom lip and took another breath. "Arnold and I last saw each other when I was but ten or eleven. He was already a young man. He never paid me any mind and I..."

Everyone turned as Finny stepped out the door. "Dearest, what is keeping everyone out on the porch tonight?"

Arnold's face turned bright red and his lips were pinched into a white line. "You," he fumed, "how could you do this to me? You lying whore." He shook his head, seething. "Where did you pick her up, Cassidy? Some saloon tramp with red hair and just enough resemblance that I could be duped? Made a bumbling fool by both of you!" His jaw ground tight. "Now you can all have your grand jest at my expense in front of my father and this entire town!"

"No, no Arnold, oh God, no!" Finny lunged for him but he pushed her off.

"You will never touch me or see me again. Get your things and remove yourself from my sight."

"It was her!" Finny screamed, pointing to Cassidy. "She made me do it. Please Arnold, please, I never wanted to hurt you. I fell in love with you."

Cassidy caught Truitt from the corner of her eye, pressing his head with large hands he looked to the ground. Shaking his head, he shoved his hands in his pockets and walked down the steps of the grand house. Everything in her being wanted to call after him to beg him to understand her plight. But this oak of man lived in his right or wrong world. Truitt's truth was that she was a lying coward not to tell the man she loved the entire truth. Her lips parted to call out, but she would sound as desperate as Finny did now, crying and sniveling empty promises.

"I said get out now!" Arnold roared, pointing to Hangtown. "I've changed my mind. Everything you have is what I gave it you. To the burn barrel with all of it." His lips pressed in a thin line. "And the Bedford is closed to the both of you."

"I hate you, Cassidy!" Finny blubbered. "We're on the dirt street 'cause of you and your wicked schemes. Woe betide ya, Cassidy. May the devil prepare a boilin' fire for you. To the devil with all of ya." She flung her arm in the air and stomped down the steps cursing and spewing.

Scarcely paying Finny any attention, Cassidy wondered how a body could go from full haste to barely breathing. Her legs felt like they were wedged in the thick silt of the Missouri River. She turned but couldn't look at her Uncle. A disgrace and embarrassment to her family, her father would hear about this soon enough.

"I still have my dowry," she murmured. "We never touched it. It was to go to Arnold tomorrow. I will have someone bring it by." She picked up her case and took each step down like a descent to darkness.

"Kathleen." Her uncle called after her, coming down the first tier of steps. "We've all made mistakes in our youth. I can give you some time to reconsider Arnold's proposal."

Cassidy paused and then took another step down.

"Or you may return with me on the Harrison. We can be back in Boston in five or six months."

Cassidy could find no words, no response. Every bit of life was drained from her. She should have told Truitt everything when she had the chance.

"Party's over!" Arnold's scornful voice roared on the porch, "Get everyone out of my house."

"I'm so sorry, Uncle," she whispered, descending the rest of the stairs.

Cassidy trembled against the cold as she walked toward the Bedford. The manager was still at the party and could not kick her out before she arrived. She needed to force herself to be calm as she crossed the hotel threshold. Finny would likely jump out and beat her with any object she could get her hands on.

The true crushing of her chest hit when she saw the empty lobby. Truitt was nowhere to be seen. Hadn't they just had a tender moment yesterday in this same room? She took the stairs and saw the empty hallway. He was not waiting there and why should he? She had lied to the only man she'd ever loved. Her feet refused to move, and she dropped her case and crumpled on the top step. How? Why? Was this how God pronounced His judgment to the sinner?

The look on Arnold's face; had she ever considered what his wrath would be like? Groaning, she pulled herself up and walked to her door. Finny would be inconsolable. She turned the knob to see a blackened room. Striking a match to light the wick, the shadows revealed an eerie absence. What other connections did Finny have? Where would she have gone? As she placed the glass over the flame, she saw the paper on her bed. It was a creased and worn notice of some kind. Pacific Minstrels it said at the top. Auditions being held at Bayside Music Consortium, 150 Third Street in San Francisco.

"What?" she whispered. Then the writing on the bottom caught her eye. It matched that first note from Truitt she had found on her bed. "Take the eight o'clock stage in the morning. Go to San Francisco and don't come back."

He wanted her gone. There was no forbearance coming from the man. From their first moments, she had lied to Truitt Emerson about who she was. If she was ever to hear him forgive her, it would not bring the needed repair to his heart nor to her own.

The man said he did not forget.

Thirty-Seven

SUNLIGHT INFUSED THE white lacey curtains of the room at the Bedford Hotel. Cassidy arose, surprised she'd slept at all.

Pulling the curtain back, she peered at the movement of the town and sighed. Likely it was past the eight o'clock hour and the stage heading to San Francisco had pulled out. It made no matter; she wasn't going to leave her selfish mess and skip town. She pulled her dresses from the wardrobe and laid them on the bed.

Each one mocked her with memories. The gray and red stripes from the escapade at Damonte Station to Hangtown. The deep blue gown from her travel and performances in Coloma. The serviceable brown from sitting at Cousin Arnold's table while she'd helped the Basque teens master their English. Closing her eyes, her soul sank under the weight of her actions.

How long into the night had she rehearsed the words she would say to Truitt. But laying in the dark, she could never picture him finding tolerance for her lies. A strong man in stature and in pride, he would see the lies as her betrayal, as self-regarding, and indefensible. Every time she'd looked into his tender gaze, she'd felt compelled to tell him the truth and every time she'd shrunk from the consequences. What she had imagined would happen had finally happened. She was rejected.

He was surely back at his property in the woods by now. Pulling out her bag, she flopped it on the bed. Something rustled under the door, and she looked down to see a note on the floor.

His last words to her were to leave town. Could there be any hope in this new day?

Dearest Kathleen,

Would you meet me in the next hour at Arnold's home? So many things were said in shock and haste. I'd like to have a peaceable conversation.

Thank you, Uncle Donavan.

Cassidy pulled the stiff mattress up from its wood base. Her dowry was still tucked in a worn envelope there in the corner. She would need to return it anyway. Her shoulders drooped as she pulled the brown dress from her bed.

CASSIDY STOOD ON the wide porch and knocked on Arnold's door, reliving the nightmare of last evening. Emery swung the door open and greeted her with a weary smile.

"I wish you were here for lessons, Miss Fi... ah, Miss O'Ryan." Emery stepped back allowing Cassidy to enter, but she looked to the floor not at Cassidy.

"I wish I was too." She felt a sudden wave of nausea, smelling the lingering smell of cigar smoke. Looking around the parlor, she asked, "By any chance have you seen the other Miss Finnegan?"

"No, ma'am." Emery scurried away as Cassidy's uncle came around the corner.

"Kathleen," he took in a deep breath, tugging on the tweed vest under his jacket. "Thank you for coming."

The awkward, cold breeze of his personality rushed into her bones. He was much like her father, never showing affection or giving expressions of goodwill.

"Let's sit," he pointed to the settee.

Cassidy sat carefully and pulled the envelope from her reticule. "This is the dowry that was to go to Arnold at the wedding." She looked around hoping Arnold would not interrupt them. "I'm sure I look rebellious and sinister to you and Arnold," she passed the envelope to her uncle, "but I assure you, money was never a motive for this trip. I left with the intention of finding my own way. I resented my father for picking a marriage partner based on the benefit it would be to his own business. I—I—" Her words sounded even too perniciously selfish for her ears. She dug her fingers into each other not able to look at her uncle. "I know that sounds ungrateful and wanton of a daughter who was raised with every convenience."

"You can still make this right," he said. "I am one who knows that we all make mistakes. We have the responsibility to make amends and straighten out what we've wronged. Do you agree?"

Cassidy felt her mouth go dry. "Yes. I...I should take responsibility. But..."

"Good," Donovan cut her off. "I've spoken to Arnold. It was with great influence on my part to find a solution to this debacle." He rocked closer to her in his seat. "Without the family and the business, none of us would survive. So he has reluctantly agreed to the marriage."

Cassidy opened her mouth and rose to stand. Her uncle pulled her back to sitting.

"Just listen, Kathleen."

"He cannot fathom your disloyalty to the family. So he has agreed to a marriage in name only. This is a fine house. Large enough for two people to live and carry out their responsibilities. I didn't suggest this to him, but maybe one day an heir will be born. That would be a grand blessing to the family. I'm sure you would love a baby of your own. Most women do. You will run a full household, and he will run the shipping business."

"Shipping business?" Cassidy sat back, shaking her head. "Do you know anything of Arnold— of Hangtown? He runs this town." She prayed Arnold didn't lurk around the corner. "The gold rush has changed everything." She stared into the distance for a moment then she turned back to Donovan. "Word is that San Francisco Bay has boats floating abandoned. The sailors all want a chance at the gold. Arnold runs the hotels, the bank, the stores, and probably the livery and blacksmith." She tried to control her shaky tone. 'I know very little of this phantom shipping business, besides what my father does in Boston."

"Kathleen," her uncle's lips tightened into a thin line, "I am trying to be patient with you. You have overstepped your feminine station. This is your weakness and you must take responsibility and overcome it." His eyes narrowed. "You said you would make amends for your mistake. As a young woman, it is not your place to question a man or question his business workings. Ever."

Cassidy's shoulders slumped. She sounded like a brat who was tattling on a brother. "Yes, sir. I apologize to you and my family. I don't mean to slander Arnold. But—" the thought of marriage to Arnold started to squeeze her throat closed, "I will not... no, I could not ever marry Arnold."

Donovan O'Ryan stood quickly and stared out the large bay window overlooking Hangtown. "This is a fair offer of security." He marked each word with the firmness of authority. "I know Arnold will not take kindly to another rejection. I used great care to sway his opinion of you." He raked his hand down his face. "Kathleen, be reasonable," he coaxed. "You will never have stability if you refuse."

In the heavy silence, he finally looked at her. His nose flared as he shook his head. "And what am I to report to your father?" He pulled out a white handkerchief and swiped his face. "That his daughter is cursed with rebellion? You would ignore the wishes of your family?"

Somehow his words did not crush her heart as they should have. "I thought of this for eight months as we crossed the country. The longer I was away from home, the more I felt like myself. It was scandalous, but I might as well tell you. I knew Arnold would never allow me to be a musician.

"Many a night on the prairie, we would build fires and I would play my violin and sing. Others would sing along, sometimes they danced and clapped." Cassidy dropped her head to the side. "I don't expect anyone to understand. But my heart found freedom and love — something I haven't known since my childhood in Ireland. I loved to see others smile. For a few moments, we could let go of all the pain and disappointments we all carried, and my music played a large part in that"

"Ireland," Donovan heaved a sigh. "Whence stems the problem."

"You're right, Uncle. The O'Ryans never wanted to speak of the old country. My father would never talk about my mother or my grandparents. You all wanted to leave it far behind. All I wanted was to take it with me." She stood. The quiet between them and his hands on his hips signaled their impasse.

Cassidy took a deep breath and said, "I wish you well on your journey home." Her tone was resolute.

He finally turned to her as she curtseyed. "Here." He took some bills from the envelope. "Arnold has more gold than his grandchildren can spend." He put the money in her hand. As your Uncle, my better sense is pricked by your tenacious independence." He growled. "If you only knew how stubborn your father is…you're an apple fallen not far from the tree." He walked with her to the door. "I will be off to San Francisco tomorrow. Spend a few weeks on what is left of the shipping business." He scowled, "If you change your mind to return home, I will be staying at the ship docked off Pier 1. You can contact me there." He patted her back, and Cassidy reached in for a stiff hug.

"Thank you, Uncle Donovan." She posed a weak smile and stepped out. Feeling like an adult finally locked out of the nursery, she lifted the front of her dress a few inches. Pulling in a deep breath, she stared ahead at Hangtown and slowly descended the steps. *Tenacious independence*, her uncle said.

Two wagons passed each other in front of the El Dorado. This was still Arnold Snider's town. She opened the gate and stilled. Had she deceived herself once again into thinking she could have her music, her freedom? She looked down at the money in her hand. If she split it with Finny, it would only last a few weeks.

Then what?

Thirty-Eight

M R. NEWTON, AT the Bedford, had graciously held her bags and arranged for her things to be moved to a room at the Miller Boardinghouse. Thankfully, it was at the other end of Hangtown, opposite of the Snider mansion and the El Dorado. She would have to walk a block and some just to catch sight of the mercantile and So Chen's laundry. She stood debating in front of the simple, chipped, white-painted house. Maybe being away from all that was familiar would help her adjust to this despairing future.

"Look who the cat dragged in."

Cassidy recognized that snide tone. "Finny."

Miss Ethel Finnegan stepped from the boarding house door. Still wearing one of her fancy Arnold gowns from their old room, she looked striking, yet entirely out of place. "I knew the moment Mrs. Miller said they were putting up a cot in my room it was probably you. Someone my age they said."

Finny still blocked the door, and Cassidy wondered if they would even be able to share the same boarding house, let alone a room. "Of course I recognized your bag and violin when it came in."

"I had wondered where you'd gone off to," Cassidy didn't want to fight with her.

"It was your grizzly bear beau," Finny smirked, and Cassidy felt her pulse quicken.

"When I came back to the room, the door was open, and he was leaving a note on your bed. He helped me find this place. Aye, then paid for a week for me out of his pocket, he did. Not you, of course."

Cassidy thought she saw her head twitch to the side. Finny loved to antagonize her. "That was kind of him." Cassidy held herself rigid.

"I told him everything, aye, I did," her smile was more a glaring smirk. "Told 'im how you talked me into your crazy schemes. How we practiced and planned this up and down the wagon train. How Mr. Dingle and Mr. Coffey were the last people to know who we really were. But Mr. Dingle conveniently died before we got to California. God rest his soul." She tapped each shoulder, her forehead, and chest, but her voice held no remorse. "Mr. Coffey is long down the trail away from us now."

"That was no convenience, Finny," Cassidy growled.

"Oh, but it was for you and your wily ways."

Cassidy felt her jaw clench. Poor Mr. Dingle, she'd tried everything in her power to help him recover. She met Finny's snarling expression.

"I feel for Truitt to have to hear your pitiful excuses. You were no victim. Aye, just poor Mr. Dingle. All those sips of water you asked me to give him. The very sips I took to keep me alive."

Cassidy felt hot flames burning her skin. "You—you—are—" Her words wedged in her constricting throat and she paused before she could spew any accusations. With heart thudding, she realized that desperation was at work here both in Finny and herself. Who was she to point the finger? She'd lied and manipulated to get what she wanted and she'd given Finny free reign to do it, too. Deception had met its evil match.

She swallowed her anger and tried to breathe. "I suppose we are both paying the consequences."

"Did you accept Arnold's proposal?" Finny's harsh tone softened somewhat.

"How did you…that was but an hour ago." Cassidy's mouth hung ajar in shock.

"Those Basque teens still work for me. I can make better promises than Arnold ever can."

Cassidy felt a wave of exhaustion. She'd forgotten the fate of the Basque teens. What would their family do now? She rubbed between her eyes. "No, of course not."

Finny stilled, seemingly at a loss for words. "What do you plan for us now, Cassidy or *Kathleen*? Are you leaving for San Francisco?"

Us? Cassidy fought against the rolling of her eyes. "I…I…can't say." Cassidy was dazed that Finny needed her to make yet another plan for them. Stepping up on the porch as Finny held the door. She sighed. "All I want to do is speak with Truitt." They stepped into the small parlor and took the narrow steps up to a landing with four doors.

"It's not the Bedford," Finny huffed as she opened the first door on the left. The room was even narrower than the one in Damonte Station. A thin bed with an old quilt and a small white cot covered what free space there was. Cassidy saw her bag and violin case under the cot. Without any walkway, she could barely put one foot in front of the other. Pulling the pins from her hair, she sat on her bed and pulled the pillow to her chest. Drained and numb, she hugged it and leaned forward.

"I think it best we leave town," Finny said.

Cassidy hoped her hair would cover her in darkness and everything would go away. "You keep saying we," Cassidy murmured into her pillow.

"Yes, we. Arnold will get back at both of us."

"My Uncle Donovan has been talking to him. He will help cool Arnold's wrath."

Finny huffed, "You really don't know him, Cassidy. He has shared confidences with me that would make your blood freeze. We are on the wrong side now. We are the enemy—an enemy to be dealt with."

Cassidy didn't like how somber Finny had turned. She vacillated between her fatigue and that the woman made sense for once. "What would you have us do?"

"Truitt said we must leave town. I think we should be gone in the morning." Finny stepped past her feet and sat on her bed. "Do you have the family money?"

"No, I gave it to my uncle." Cassidy sighed, rubbing her temple. "If the men in my family have only sights for their coin staying in their own pockets, then I've done my part." She wouldn't tell Finny of her uncle's help. "I have some money from my performances. It will last us until we find work."

"Mary, Mother, and Joseph." Finny scoffed. "We were so close. Aye, that fine house was to be mine. Only a day away." The silence hung in the air like the smell of burnt beans. "I'm not sure how long I can work," she whispered.

Cassidy straightened up and pulled her hair behind her ears. "Why is that?"

Finny stared at her clutched hands before finally looking up with anguish in her eyes. "I'm likely in the family way."

Cassidy dropped her face into her pillow groaning. "Oh, Finny. No, no, no. Not that too."

Finny sucked in a deep breath. "I've looked at it a hundred different ways." She closed her eyes and rubbed her brows. "I don't think it will do any good to tell him. He was so angry. He hates me. I find little comfort that Arnold would marry me. It might bonny well make him fume to the ocean and back."

"Oh lolly, oh lolly." Cassidy squeezed the pillow and rocked. "A grand state of affairs we find ourselves in now, Miss Ethel Finnegan."

"We can get to the city." Finny hesitated. "Say my husband died in a mining shaft. That happens all the time."

"I can't lie anymore," Cassidy grumbled. "I've ruined everything that was good by lying. I just can't do it." She wrapped her arms around her head and squeezed.

"Well, that's easy for you to say now, you're only out a boyfriend. But it leaves me an expectant unmarried woman, shunned and despised, just like my mother. Blessed Mary,

Mother, and Joseph, I should have married the dandy from the wagon trail. But no, we had to see your plan out — all the way to California."

Cassidy was too bereft of emotion to offer the woman any sympathy or explanations. "Maybe you should have."

TRUITT COULDN'T ESCAPE the antsy feeling in the atmosphere. Hangtown was restless. He'd tried to dismiss it as his imagination, but things were moving differently. For two mornings he'd watched the stage come and go. Neither Cassidy nor Finny had booked passage. Finny, that was the woman's name. No wonder Cassidy had let it slip a time or two. Kathleen O'Ryan, the shrewd woman who had planned for her maid to take her place in California, had almost succeeded. If she was that clever, then why hadn't she followed the advertisement and gotten on that stage?

Truitt gritted his teeth and watched the wagons roll past So Chen's. From the first moment Cassidy fell from that wagon and he'd held her in his arms, he knew she was no ordinary woman. She came from wealth and security and likely told him the truth when she said that she didn't want a life with the suitors her father had chosen for her. Maybe it didn't matter, her station. She was still the softest and most beautiful woman he'd ever known.

He tried to remember the words spoken on Arnold's porch. Hadn't she stood up to her uncle and said clearly she'd wanted to marry another? She had chosen him. Her kisses had proven as much. It was flattering, but how could he say he would choose her in return. He couldn't take a liar for a wife; one that had plenty of chances to explain herself. It was liars in Hangtown who had killed his father. He shook his head. Mistrust and anger crawled through his skin.

Had he ever really known her?

Thirty-Nine

MOODY AND DEPRESSED, Finny had overslept the last two mornings. Pale and feeling queasy this morning she could barely touch her late breakfast. Cassidy had tired of the tiny space closing in on her. "I will go to the mercantile and see if they have any ginger tea." She announced, hooking her boots closed.

"I don't know." Finny leaned back against the wall. "It usually passes." She blew out a breath. "I don't think you should go out. I know you want to talk to Truitt, but if he hasn't contacted you yet he's long gone."

Cassidy stood and rubbed the back of her neck. She'd thought of that every hour herself. The fresh air was better than sitting in this matchbox. "Do you need anything else?"

Finny shook her head and lowered onto the quilt.

A few minutes later, Cassidy stepped from the Miller's simple home and onto Main Street. The streets seemed more dusty than usual. Something eerie ran up her spine, and she couldn't help but look left to right as if she was being watched. Was it safe to be out alone? A strange thought flickered in her mind; Pierre Doré. He was the closest thing to a gentleman and he'd made her a fair offer. It seemed unlikely he would lend her his mannerly elbow now that he knew who she really was. She shook her head, walking past the Bedford. Oh lolly, her distraught brain, agitated nerves, and this uncivilized town was getting to her.

Seeing the mercantile ahead, she went to cross a side street but stepped back as a large wagon rumbled in front of her. Bumping back into someone, a hand surrounded her arm and pulled her farther back. Before she could look through the maze of dust, she recognized the hand, the strength of the grip. She would know it anywhere.

"Why haven't you left?" Truitt growled in her ear and stepped her back from the street.

"Because I could not leave without seeing you." She pulled her arm free from his grip. His face glowed with the same anger she heard in his voice.

"Now you've seen me. Now you can leave." There was dismissal in his tone.

"Truitt, I know I have wronged you."

"Are you apologizing so you can move on and marry your rich cousin?" He glared at her.

"What? No! I swear this town has ears for half-truths and little else. I said no. I would never marry Arnold. I only want to marry you. I love you."

His jaw cocked to the side and he shook his head.

"Truitt, will you marry me?" Oh, lolly, that came out fast. He looked so good standing there in all his angry handsomeness.

His face curled up in confusion. "You can't ask me that. I have to ask you."

"So will you?" She tried to breathe through the shaking of her limbs. "Ask me?"

"No." He smirked. "You've lied to me from the first moment I met you."

"I lied about me," she said wearily. "I never lied to hurt you. It was my lie. I used it to give me hope. Hope that I could have a new life in California."

"Many a folk have come to California without living a falsehood."

"And I wanted to tell you. Every day I did. But you worked for Arnold and Finny kept warning me not to do anything to upset the cart." She dropped her head and squeezed her ears. The excuse sounded pitiful, especially after all Truitt had done for her.

"I have no stomach to speak in circles with you. Nothing in this town ever goes right." He raked his hand through his hair. "How stupid can I be to stay and take the dishonesty here?" His eyes fired into hers, and he swiftly gripped her upper arm, giving her a shake. "Get on that stage. Tomorrow." His tense face came closer. "I swear, Cassidy, if you want to show me you love me, get on it and never look back."

"Truitt..." Desperation lodged in her throat. "Please. Please forgive me."

"If I say I forgive you will you leave this town?" His eyes narrowed.

Cassidy felt the rock turn in her gut. "I...I—"

He slowly shook his head and released her. "You are stubborn and headstrong to the bone. Why didn't I see it?" He huffed. "A woman who travels across the country planning to dismiss the wishes of her family and talks her maid into switching names just for her selfish, foolish dreams. Who does that?" He scoffed, jerking his head back. "Marianna left me without a goodbye. You know my father was hung unjustly, but I am who I am before the Almighty. I would never change that. And never lie to the people I love." He looked away rolling his tongue inside his cheek. "I was taken with you from the first moment I saw you. I shared things with you and I—I—didn't even know you. I believed God had— God had—oh, forget it." He closed his eyes and rubbed his temple. "And," he said, jerking back to her, "I had a feeling. I always had this uneasy feeling, but no—" He twisted and massaged his fist in agitation. "Your beauty is blinding, Cassidy. Your kisses ignite fires in my body and I turned into a brainless dog to be led around by a rope." His chest expanded with anger and he licked his flattened bottom lip.

"I'm done being your fool. Done with being Snider's fool and this town's muscle-headed fool. No more of that." He stepped back nostrils flaring. "I'm taking an ax to the Hangman's tree in Elstner's Hay Yard and then I'm gone for good." He took another step away from her. "I've tried to do the last kind thing, the Pacific Minstrels flyer should help you to leave. But if you won't go there, I have nothing more to say." He turned on his heel and strode away.

Cassidy stood speechless watching him until he disappeared around the corner. Every word that tried to call after him refused to come out. The man was solid, resolute to the bone, and she wondered if her legs would hold her another minute. Her greatest fear had come upon her. To keep her sham alive, she'd risked losing Truitt. To keep Truitt, her sham had to die like the burning of her grandmother's violin. When all that was precious was gone, there was no bringing it back.

Another wagon rolled down the side street and jarred her back to the present. Why was she even out today? Her brain was stunned by Truitt's words, her tears felt dried and callous inside her eyes. Of course, she'd hoped to see him. Talk to him. She stood looking lost and alone. Could she make her feet move? Finny. She was out for tea for Finny. The next crisis in her life.

Cassidy entered the store and tried to fathom the harsh realities Truitt's words had brought. She purchased the bag of tea and exited from the store lifeless. If she loved him, should she move on? Wasn't her only hope in Hangtown to be with him? She waited for the street to clear and walked across to the livery station where the stage picked up and dropped off. There was a simple handwritten note on the door with the stage's schedule. The other stops and times. A man carrying a large barrel came towards her, and she barely stepped out of his way avoiding a dangerous collision.

The town seemed more hectic than usual or perhaps it had been awhile since she'd paid much attention. She looked toward the end of Main Street; the Snider home stood in all its grandeur. Her uncle had said he was going to San Francisco. She sighed. Truitt was right. She was overly stubborn and independent. Her uncle would have helped her if she had asked.

Someone grabbed her upper arm again.

Oh, heavens above, "Trui…" His name halted on her lips as an unpleasant, large man with dark hair, gruffly yanked her back.

"Snider wants to see you." The brutish man smelled like he'd hadn't bathed in a week.

"You may unhand me, sir. I can walk without your assistance." Cassidy turned from his grip. Disappointment weighted her duped heart. It wasn't Truitt. "I have a delivery to a friend, and then I will come."

"He said now. At the house." He closed in on her backside until she had to quick step to keep from touching him. Suddenly wondering if she could persuade Arnold to have mercy on Finny, Cassidy reluctantly walked toward the house. Was her uncle still there? Should she say anything about Finny's condition in front of him? Finny's melancholy certainly spoke of some genuine feeling she had for Arnold. Could Arnold find a sliver of forgiveness? It had been a few days. Maybe she could pave the way. This baby would need a family. If he wanted to talk to her. It must be for a reason.

Cassidy walked up the first set of stairs to the house.

"He said to come in the back door." The man took her arm again and led her around the home. First thing upon arrival, Cassidy would tell Arnold that she didn't need to be pushed and punished like a child. They all needed to be adults and move on. Unfortunately, the gazebo where Finny loved to read and rest brought memories of better days. Not waiting for her escort to open the door, she let herself in.

The ornate home felt cold and gray with Nelson and the Basque girls nowhere to be seen. Without Finny and her ever-revolving wants, she'd pray he'd let the teens go. Waiting next to the kitchen table, Arnold came around the corner and leaned on the opening.

"Kathleen O'Ryan," his eyes drooped with seeming indifference.

"Please call me Cassidy, Cousin." She looked around the kitchen. His presence was unnerving.

"Cousin. Humph," he smirked, "I don't think so, Kathleen."

"Is Uncle Donavan still here?" She could only hope.

"No." he frowned. "After being told how negligent I am—scarcely a finger in the O'Ryan shipping business someone told him." Arnold crossed his arms across his chest. "He's found it necessary to take a significant amount of money from my bank." His pause increased the discomfort she felt. "He has gone with my inheritance, to right all my wrongs." His finger pulled at his stiff collar and necktie.

Cassidy's heart beat erratically, and she took a deep breath. "Cousin, could I speak to you of Miss Finnegan? I know her well...as you...do... and I know the feelings she still possesses for you might warrant a second look for a suitable wife."

"Save your shrewed lying breath. You will be marrying me." He held his finger up, pointing at her. "And before you spew from those open, deceiving red lips. Remember, we are perfect for each other."

Forty

CASSIDY STIFFENED AN inch taller. "I had hoped we could talk like adults. But I've already answered this marriage question with Uncle Donavan. It will never happen." She turned to walk back out the door, but the large-framed man stood with his back against it.

"Could you ask your bodyguard to move, please?"

Arnold moved closer, and Cassidy could see the beads of perspiration on his balding forehead. Arnold's thug must've obeyed her words. She turned back to the door, and he was gone.

"Good day. I will let myself out." She pulled the door open and stepped outside. The man with dark hair was standing on the corner of the lawn looking down at Hangtown.

He turned and frowned at her, then looked past her. "Something is going wrong at the bank, sir."

Sure enough, the frantic ruckus and commotion stopped Cassidy in her tracks. People were swarming everywhere around the bank. A shot fired in the air and she jumped. "What is happening?" she absentmindedly addressed Arnold.

"Take her to the basement." Arnold spun and ran back to the house. Before she could protest, the bodyguard bent at the knee and swooped her up over her his shoulder. Like a sack of potatoes, he carried her to the outside stone stairs that led to the basement.

"I don't need a place to hide. I can find my way home. Let me go!" She struggled against his grip as he carried her down the narrow steps into the damp dirt and stone-walled room. "I will not stay here! Do you hear me?" Just as her feet touched down, he was already up and out the basement door.

A long narrow beam of light shown through a glass window. She moved a small barrel over to the window and tried to peer out. Growling, she stepped down. It only faced the other side of the yard.

"This is ridiculous." She yanked up her skirts and took the narrow steps back up to the door. She twisted the handle but nothing happened. "Oh, lolly." She pounded her fist on the door. "Arnold! Let me out!" She pushed and pulled the door handle in every direction. "Let me out! Now! I insist you let me out!" she called, pounding her fists with fervor and anger. After her arm could take no more pounding, she went back down the stairs and looked around. An old simple butcher block table sat in the middle with three mismatched chairs. Empty barrels and crates full of hay lined the dark areas from all his many household expenditures no doubt.

Shaking her head, she peered back out the window. Another pop, pop rent the air. Gunshots? What was happening at the bank? Had it been robbed?"

Cassidy paced and dug around until she found a box of old matches and a crooked candle to light. She tried to reassure herself Arnold or his thug would be back after seeing to the trouble. Would Arnold do something so protective to keep her from harm? Was there a side of him only Finny knew?

An hour later it was getting cold. Cassidy curled her shoulders as she rubbed her arms up and down for warmth. What would Finny think about her absence? This would be the last place Finny would come to look for her. Besides yelling for the butler, Nelson, and repeatedly banging on the door, Cassidy could not think of anything else to do. The house remained empty. What a fine kettle. Cousin Arnold's offensive remark about them marrying irked her almost as much as this locked basement door.

Cassidy awoke from where she had rested her head on her arms at the table. The sun was setting, and the candle was burning low. She thought she heard voices. The door at the top of the thin stairs rattled, and she rose quickly.

"Thank you, God." She stopped at the bottom of the stairs as Arnold and his man marched down toward her.

"Cousin!" This is no way to…" She heard the door slam behind them and stepped back. Her mouth went as dry as the desert. Their faces were red and sweat covered.

"We have a problem here." Veins protruded from Arnold's neck. "The people are rioting with the bank closure." Arnold paced around the table looking high and low. We have to leave tonight, within the hour. You won't be able to get your things. We'll send for them later." Arnold tapped a few of the stones holding the foundation of his house.

"I'm not going anywhere," Cassidy spouted, watching as he pulled a large stone loose and pulled heavy flour sacks from their hidden spot. Handing them off to the large man, she was sure he hadn't heard her. "Do what you must, Cousin, but I told you I am not marrying you or leaving." Her foot hit the second stair before Arnold grabbed her and threw her down into a chair.

"I don't have time for this, Kathleen!" he seethed.

Cassidy began to tremble, her body and mind reeling with his rough handling.

"And you *will* marry me!" He leaned inches from her face. "My step-father would never give me the O'Ryan name. He has treated me like an unwanted bastard from the moment I met him." My real father died at sea, leaving my mother a widow. I didn't choose to be in your pristine family." He stood straight grinding his teeth. "And you, the fairest offering from the O'Ryan's, could it be true? Could our blood mix, our children have the favor I never had? Because of you—only you—not some floozy you found in a saloon to betray me." He nodded with crazed eyes. "So yes, you will agree to marry me," he stared her down, "as planned."

Cassidy found her breath over the pounding of her heart. "Never," she whispered. Before her next breath could be found, a crack sounded as the back of Arnold's hand sent her head spinning blindly to the table. Her hand covered the painful sting on her cheek and with blurry eyes she could see the large man snickering. She jerked backward to jump from the chair, but Arnold slammed his hand on her shoulder, pushing her back down.

"It doesn't have to go this way." He gripped the thickness of her bun and looked back at the man. "Show her the choices."

Cassidy tried to squirm from his grip, but to no avail, as the two men closed in on her.

"Tongue?" the smelly man smiled.

"Good choice. No husband wants to hear a lying, harping wife." Arnold yanked her head back.

The thug roughly grabbed her cheeks and squeezed till her jaw opened. Quickly he stuck the butt of his knife in against her back teeth.

Cassidy felt a whimper escape, and the back of her tongue unexpectedly touched the dirty handle. She carefully shook her head no.

Arnold nodded, and his thug pulled the knife from her mouth.

Cassidy dropped her head trying to find air. "How...how could you be...so...cruel?"

"It's up to you, my deceitful beloved." Arnold patted her head. "You will come along in perfect obedience or you will lose something."

"But Finny loves you." Cassidy gasped, her heart pounding in her ears.

"She only loved me for what I could give her. With the bank going belly up, she would be gone in a moment. You have dismissed the family's birthright. It seems the family wants to dismiss me. That's one of the things we have in common."

"Cousin," Cassidy's mind raced trying to find the right words, "you deserve love. I am in love with someone else. That is not fair to you." She panted, her eyes shifted to the staircase exit. The men still had her trapped against the table. *Please Lord hear my cries.* Her eyes pooled.

"I don't have time to talk of love and betrayal with you. We must go. You will do as I say."

Cassidy felt her body waver. She thought she might faint until she pictured Truitt's smile and his penetrating eyes on hers. Remembering the way her skin tingled when his finger drew out letters on hers, the strength of his large arms holding her close and safe. The recollections, like the first notes of a soft Irish ballad, settled serenely on her. A calming, *yes*, a feeling of being held in God's comfort. What were his last words? Something about her being stubborn and headstrong. Likely so. She took in a deep breath. If she was to surrender it would only be to him. A worthy man.

Arnold gripped her wrist and raised it skyward. "These are the fingers she uses for the violin." He slapped her hand hard down on the table. "Want to keep these Kathleen?"

She tried to jerk back, but he held her wrist solid against the table. Tears filled her eyes and convulsions came from deep within her as she clawed her fingernails against the wood. Through the blur, she saw the man with a large knife hover it over her fingers.

"Now! Decide now!" Arnold's fury ricocheted in her ear.

She closed her eyes and remembered the man who held her tight in the little cave as she cried. Every fiber in her stilled with conviction. "I will never be yours," she murmured.

"Do it." Arnold hissed.

An excruciating pain divided her body, a crushing that took the air from her lungs. Before she could release her own scream, deep darkness pulled her under.

Forty-One

TRUITT CAME IN the back door of So Chen's laundry store and found her folding crisp sheets. "This doesn't surprise me." He shook his head. "The town is falling apart at the seams and you are folding the laundry."

"Ahh," she said waving her hand at him. "They get over it and still need clean sheets at Bedford."

Truitt shifted his weight and shook his head. "No money of yours in the bank, I recall."

"Nope." Arms raised, she snapped the white linen in front of him. "Who is so dumb to put their gold in someone else's big box? That not smart." After folding, she set the square fabric on a pile. "Oh, you dumb?" She glanced up at him.

"No." Truitt peered out her tall window. "Not me either." He watched two old miners with whiskey bottles in their hands stagger across the street. "Looks like everyone handles it differently. The sheriff says Snider is to blame. His father made a large withdrawal and someone said the bank is out of money and gold. Now everyone wants to get theirs out." He felt restless turmoil deep in his gut. Things in Hangtown were known for going to the extreme—fast and ludicrous within minutes. The lantern lighter moved his ladder to light the next wick. Truitt noticed a woman peeking out from the El Dorado.

"Are all the girls safe? That you know of?"

"Yes. Three already up and gone to work. The others I saw at noon meal."

Truitt turned from her and looked again. In the shadows, it looked like reddish hair. A stab of concern pricked in him and his curiosity would give him no rest.

"I'll be back later," he said. "And keep your boys in close." Pointing at her, she nodded and he went out the back door.

He jogged around a group of men and across the street. Coming around behind the Blue Bell Café he saw her leaning against the back side of the building looking in every direction. It was Miss…Finny.

She gasped. "Oh, sweet Mary, Mother, and Joseph." She clutched her chest. "You scared my heart from its station."

Truitt frowned. "Is everything all right?"

"I hope you'll be telling me right now that Cassidy is in your care?"

"No," he stepped closer. "Why would she be?"

"Aye," she groaned. "I asked someone earlier. They saw you together and saw her going into the mercantile. But she's not returned."

His eyes widened. "You have not seen her all afternoon or evening?" He ran his hand over his face, pulling on his jaw. "I left her before noon."

"Where would she have gone?" Finny whined. "I feel as if I could faint."

"Come with me." Truitt took her by the elbow. He knew first hand this woman fainted easily. "I need to leave you with So Chen." They crossed the dirt street. "I asked Cassidy to leave Hangtown. Are her things gone?"

"Neh. She would never leave without her violin. She loves that silly thing."

Truitt knew the feeling. The same reason he'd everything packed but couldn't get out of Hangtown. How could he leave the thing he cared for behind?

The bank going belly up didn't help. It'd distracted his plans for sure, but it was his heart that tricked him into staying. Now suddenly he felt remorse for the harsh words he'd left Cassidy with. *Lord, grant me strength.*

He barely had the door to So Chen's open before he spun around and ran to the Snider offices. Finding the key under a rock, the office looked dark. But he and a few others knew about a back room where the dirty work happened. Spinning from door to door, they were all empty. Everything was cold. No one had worked today. The evening air hit his sweaty skin as he ran up the street to the mansion. Had Arnold taken her with him? He turned the knob on the front door; it opened easily.

"Cassidy? Snider?" He called and took the stairs two by two. Snider's room looked disheveled. His wardrobe was bare. Searching from room to room, he locked his jaw; the house was obviously empty. He stood in the parlor, hands clutching his head and looked down Main Street. Where had they gone? The angriest part of the mob today had threatened to burn Snider's house down if he didn't put their money back in the bank. Of course, he'd hightailed it out fast. Someone must have seen them leave. The secretary, Mr. Hanson knew all of Snider's business. It was time to pay him a call.

A travailing desperate feeling punched Truitt's mind and gut after no one answered at Mr. Hanson's or any of Snider's thugs. The night his father died, he'd started to fight with anyone who looked at him cross-eyed. Teeming with frustration, his fists and maybe more were going to fly tonight if he didn't get some answers. Walking back to So Chen's, the town had finally settled. What could people do? There was no money left in the bank to take.

What could he do? Wake up everybody in Hangtown and threaten them? Elstner's Hay Yard stopped him in his tracks. The Hangman's tree stood tall mocking his loss. Ever since his father died, he'd been going alone—until he met Cassidy. The only person that made sense in his life, allowing him to dream of a home, a future. To think each night he thanked God for such a rare gift, bringing him something beautiful from all the anger and loss. Growling, he turned into the back of the laundry store. He needed to take Miss Finny back to the Millers. Sitting for a moment on a large rock to catch his breath, gripping his knees, he shook his head.

"Where God? Where is she? After I pushed her away, did she go with Snider?" He rubbed his hands up and down his face. His prayers felt paltry and insincere. He never saw himself as a pray-in-fear kind of man. God had always been more real, more trustworthy. Maybe he was duped there, too.

He stood and circled once around So Chen's large, black, hot water pots. Every muscle turned tense and taut. The helpless feeling crushed down the strength in his being, and that same uneasy feeling he had had for a while now settled in his chest like lead. All he could do next was take Finny back to the Millers. Maybe Cassidy was there.

Walking in the back door, two women slept on pallets with curtains hanging from the sides. The baby he'd seen weeks ago, was sleeping tucked inside one of the women's arms. So Chen and her sons slept in a small room with a door. He lightly tapped on it and waited until it cracked open.

"What?" She snapped.

"Did the woman with red hair go? I don't see her."

"Ya, ya. She take some water and want to go. I had Lo take her to her house."

Truitt nodded.

"No wake me up."

"Yes, ma'am," Truitt said, as the door closed.

He carefully let himself out and headed toward the Miller's boarding house. It was late, but he had to know if Cassidy had returned.

He stood on the porch and debated a few seconds, then knocked. He'd wake the house and hopefully two crazy women from back east.

Mr. Miller came to the door in his nightshirt and cap.

"What? What's happening? Is the town on fire?" He tried to look around Truitt.

"No. No fire. I need to know if the two ladies made it home tonight. Could you check the room? One is Finny. The other is Kathleen or…Cassidy."

Mr. Miller began to frown, rubbing sleepy eyes. "Two." Holding two fingers up, Truitt tried to keep his voice calm. "Check and see if two are in the room."

"That is highly improper at this hour. You may come in the morning. I will check then."

As it was closing, Truitt stuck his large boot in the door. Grabbing the door jam, he pushed the door open. "If you don't go do it, I will." Intense intimidation dripped from his voice.

"Ahh…" Mr. Miller exhaled, "never take in the single women." He grumbled but went up the stairs.

Truitt came off the stoop and looked around the square dirt yard. She needed to be there. He would talk to her in the morning. He didn't know what he would say, but something would come to him. This alarm was like nothing he ever wanted to experience again.

Mr. Miller appeared in his doorway. "Just one, named Finny. She said the other woman is missing."

Truitt was back on the porch in two broad steps. "Have you seen the other one? Today? Did she come in or out here?"

"I don't think so. The missus and I been around all day."

Truitt closed his eyes and stepped back. He had no one to blame but himself. I told her to leave, but why would she not take her things? The question was stabbing his gut.

"We saw her play at the El Dorado." Mr. Miller's words jerked him back. "She has quite the talent. We'd never seen or heard anything like her."

The El Dorado, Pierre Dorè, Truitt thought, ignoring the jealously arising. Please Lord, let her be with him.

Forty-Two

"NO, NO," PIERRE answered, coming from around the bar inside the El Dorado. "She is not here."

Truitt's nostrils flared, looking around the empty room. "Don't lie to me, Doré. I'm tired and I want to hurt something and you look available."

"I tell no lies, Emerson. You may look room to room, she is not here." Pierre scratched his head. "No one has seen her? This worries me."

"Not since I left her before noon." Truitt shook his head. "If she went with Snider, I believe it was against her will. Her things, her violin, are all still in her room."

"Ahh," Pierre sighed. "This does not sound good."

Truitt looked to the entrance. The back staircase to the El Dorado rooms were on the outside of the building.

"Despite what a coward you think of me, I do care for her. I will help you look." Pierre threaded his arms into his suit jacket. "The night at the Snider house. The wedding party?"

Truitt watched him as they stepped out and Pierre locked the front door. "I made a declaration of marriage."

Truitt felt his heart slam against his ribs.

"But she turned me down." Pierre swung his head, frowning. "She does not love me," he sighed. "She had the courage to tell me. She loves you. She wanted only you." Pierre looked up and down the dense night fallen on Hangtown. "So I can understand this search. I can't imagine if her heart was mine and I couldn't find her."

Her love for him was true. The knowledge of how foolhardy he'd been to reject her made him groan aloud. Truitt nodded at Pierre. "Start at the top of town. Snider's new wagon is missing. Look for tracks or ask anyone awake if they've seen which direction it went."

Pierre nodded and they separated into the night.

Hours later, Pierre offered Truitt a cot in his back room and he reluctantly agreed to get some sleep. At dawn, he would check with Finny and then gather provisions and head to San Francisco. It was the only possible explanation. He closed his eyes while the memory of Janny Long haunted his heavy sleep.

A dog barked and Truitt sat up quickly, forgetting where he was. Daylight. Thank God. People were up and every fiber in him was ready to take action. Stepping from the back door of the El Dorado he looked around town rubbing his fingers back and forth through his hair. A young woman with dark long braid scurried up to the Snider gate and opened it. One of the Basque sisters going to work. "Thank you," he prayed aloud, jogging to her. She might know something.

"Miss Emery," he called after her and she turned.

"Mr. Emerson." She looked to the ground. "I left my sweater in the pantry. There was a terrible ruckus in town yesterday. Mr. Nelson told us all to go home."

He nodded and walked with her up the steps. "Miss Cassidy is missing. I've looked and asked everyone. Do you know anything?"

"No, sir. I never saw her." She walked in through the parlor and Truitt followed. "Can you think of anything? Did you overhear anyone talking about her?"

"I did hear Mister—ahh, the father," she smiled. "My English has gotten better. No?"

"Yes." Truitt tried to keep calm. "What were Mr. Snider and his father saying?"

"It was a bad talk. They were angry at each other. It was about Miss Cassidy tricking Mr. Arnold. Mister...the father, said for him to marry her anyway."

Truitt pounded his fist into the kitchen wall. "Sorry." He shook his head. "I had a feeling."

Emery grabbed her sweater off the pantry peg. "I should go. And I tell you one more thing. Mr. Snider owes my sister and me money for our work. He said he gave us a room, clothes, and food. But our father needs money to keep his payments to the bank." She stopped and squinted. "Now what do people do? The bank is closed. This is very confusing for us."

"I'm sorry for what has happened to your family," Truitt said with sincerity. He was the one who tried to help them with jobs. "Here." He pulled the bills he had from his pocket. "Take this and hang on. Tell your father, many struck gold the day they were going to quit."

"Thank you, sir. This is very kind." She held the bills in her hand. "May I tell you one more thing?"

Truitt nodded. Anxious to be on his way.

"I saw Mr. Snider take a flower sack down to the basement one day. If it held gold, could you take it to the bank and help more people have their money back?"

The teen was a kind girl. "I think if Mr. Snider is gone, that bag will be gone." They walked out the back door and turned to the small door to the basement. Truitt turned the handle and found it locked. He walked around to the side yard and peered into the thin window.

"Good Lord Almighty!" He jumped up and ran to the locked door. "I think Cassidy is in there!" He took a few steps back and rammed his shoulder into the door. It rattled and splintered in the middle. He turned and found a large rock. He held it in front of his chest and rammed into the door again. It cracked open under the impact and he had to catch himself from falling down the narrow steps. Seized by horror, he saw the layers of her dress puddled around her body, something laying on the table, but it didn't register as he knelt and pulled on her shoulders gently and rolled her to face him.

"Cassidy. Oh, no, Cassidy." Pushing her copper locks back, her face was covered in blood and dirt. She was pale, cold and limp as a wet rag. He wrapped his hand around her neck and leaned close. He felt a tiny whisper of breath and a light tap from her heart beating came from under her chin. "She's alive!" He looked back to Emery. "Can you find the doctor and meet me at So Chen's laundry?"

Emery nodded yes, her hand shaking over her mouth.

"Cassidy. Love, please. Come back to me." The pool of blood was from something. Beside dirt and dried blood, her face seemed uncut, yet a large red bruise swelled her eye. He cradled her in his arms, looking over her neck, chest and down to her belly. What had happened? Both arms seemed in place, her... He sucked in a deep gasp — her fingers. The tips of four fingers were missing. Quickly, he swung his head. The other hand was intact. "Oh, God."

He carefully pulled her closer. "No, no, no." Kissing her forehead, he felt his eyes fill with tears. "Hang on love. I'm here. Nothing else will happen to you, I'm here, I'm right here." He choked out the words and quickly wiped his wet face on his sleeve. Gathering her close in his arms, he stood. For a regrettable split second, he glanced at the horror and cruelty of her severed finger tips laying on the table. His blood boiled and surged. He knew Arnold was savage, but hadn't thought he was capable of this kind of atrocity. He carried her up the basement stairs.

⌒

EMERY RAN INTO the back door of So Chen's laundry. Face red with tears, her chin quivered. "The doctor said he won't come. He's been drinking since he lost all his money yesterday. Said he'd be of no good."

Truitt felt the fury rise and tried to find release through his clenched fists. Breathing hard, he turned to watch So Chen. She gently washed the dirt and blood from the open wounds.

"We try this." She shook her head at Truitt. "Doctor can't sew back on anyway. You try give her water."

Truitt took the cup and tried to steady his shaking hands.

"You hold her head," Emery said, taking the cup from him. Carefully, he held her head and shoulders above the wooden folding table. Emery spoke gently and brought the cup to Cassidy's lips.

"Miss. Miss Cassidy. Here, ma'am. Here is some water." The drops rolled past her mouth and around her chin. "Can you take a drink?"

Truitt saw movement from her mouth. "Cassidy we are here. We are with you." He leaned closer.

"Truitt." A wisp of sound came from her lips. "Where…where am I?"

Before he could answer she began to writhe and groan. "It hurts. Oh dear God, it hurts. Why, why…"

Truitt tried to steady her movement. So Chen gestured for him to block the sight of her fingers.

"It hurts! Someone help me!" She tried to roll up.

"Lo, get my bark tincture and make a tea," So Chen said to her son.

Truitt blocked the gruesome hand as he held her arm close to his waist and came close. "We will help, hang on. Remember you are a tough girl. You can do this."

"Truitt!" She began to cry. "He cut my fingers… off!" She bellowed in between sobs. "It hurts, it hurts so bad." Her eyes rolled back. "But I love you so much." She reached up with her good hand and touched his face. Her drooping blurry blue eyes found his. "If I die…I…I love you."

Truitt smiled, feeling his eyes mist. That was the woman he loved. "I love you and I'm sorry for being so angry, for pushing you away."

"I forgive you," she cried, her voice shaking. "Can you…forgive me?"

"Yes, Cassidy O'Ryan." Careful with her bruises, he gently wiped her tears. "Nothing will separate us, I promise. We'll be fine. You'll be fine." He swallowed hard. The words sounded assuring but yet not truly believable.

SO CHEN GATHERED sheets and blankets for Cassidy on the floor. Truitt gathered her off the folding table and laid her down. Throughout the day patrons and working women came and went in the laundry shop. Cassidy would doze off and then be startled by the baby crying or a door shutting. She would focus on his face for a few minutes and then begin to writhe under the pain. As soon as Emery came back to check on them, he'd ask her to go for the doctor again.

The doctor came an hour later with his bag. His face was bright red from the alcohol, but his words seemed understandable. "She's not running a fever—yet." He began to unwrap her linen bandages. "Once that happens, you've got an uphill battle." He looked up at Truitt. "You a prayin' man?"

"Yes, sir." Truitt had given little thought to his earlier faithless prayers. Yet, if it wasn't for Emery getting a sweater and mentioning the gold hidden in the basement, Cassidy would have died alone in the dirt while he stood in the house right above her. The mystery of God's ways dumbfounded him. Cassidy groaned. "She's in terrible pain." His voice pleaded. "Is there anything we can do? We tried tea."

"Amputation hurts like the devil. Tea will do little good. If she lives, she'll have phantom pain. Maybe for years."

Truitt shook his head. "I don't understand."

"The missing body parts throb with pain even though there is nothing there." The doctor examined all around the stubs. Her pinky was missing the top and nail. The other three fingers gone above the middle knuckle. "You're a big man, can you hold her still?"

"Yes, sir."

Cassidy's face waxed pale, her watery red eyes begging for mercy.

"Just hold on to me." Truitt locked eyes with her.

"No, no more," she cried as he held his hands around her arm.

"I'm sorry," he whispered. The doctor held cotton to a brownish-red liquid. "I'm so sorry." He tried to steady his breath as he leaned over her, holding her still.

Cassidy screamed as the doctor dabbed the carbolic acid on the open wounds. "Hang on child. I've got some laudanum and canary wine to give you next." The doctor finished his treatments.

Truitt felt a wave of weakness as she cried, bucked, and scratched against his hold. The doctor pulled back in time for him to find needed air."

"Now, drink this." The doctor held a small cup to her lips and she took sips.

"She might sleep into the night. Give her a few drops when the pain gets unbearable."

Cassidy's sobs and hiccups began to settle down. He closed his eyes and pressed his hands down his face and over his rough stubble. Helpless to comfort and heal her, the horrendous vengeance done to her proved unbearable. Blowing out a heavy breath, he noticed two other women from the saloon, So Chen, and her sons all stood around Cassidy's pallet on the floor. Soon everyone in Hangtown would know what happened.

"When can I move her?" he asked the doctor.

Forty-Three

EMERY AGREED TO stay as Cassidy slept. Truitt owed Finny the news that she had been found. He walked toward the Millers' fighting the conflict of God's goodness and wanting revenge. Since it was her man, Snider, who mutilated Cassidy, Finny had better feel remorse or he would…he'd what? Hurt her? He let out a long breath, before knocking on the door. How did God have patience with His fickle senseless creation?

Mr. Miller answered the door. Now in denim pants and a red shirt. "You're back. And I suppose I have worse news."

Truitt shook his head, confused. All he cared about was that he knew where Cassidy was.

"The other one left earlier," Mr. Miller said. "She took her things but left the other woman's." He opened the door and Truitt noticed the violin case he'd bought and a leather bag waiting by the stairs.

"I have found the woman I'm looking for. These things belong to her."

Mr. Miller handed Truitt Cassidy's belongings.

"Did someone come for Miss Finny?" Truitt asked. "What did they look like?"

"Can't say." Mr. Miller scratched his head. "The Missus found a note. Said she had moved on."

Truitt stepped back and thanked Mr. Miller. Now even more sure of what he had to do, he tucked the violin under his arm and picked up his steps back to So Chen's.

PIERRE DORÉ WAS in the back alley holding Truitt's horse. He had met Truitt at the back door earlier and, after hearing the violent details, he'd volunteered to find a suitable wagon to get them out of town.

"Where will you go?" Pierre asked helping Truitt load supplies.

"I'd rather not say." Truitt dropped in a box of dry wood. "If Snider comes back, you can stay clear of his intimidation."

"After seeing what he would do to a fragile woman, I suppose no one is safe." Pierre dragged his hand over his face. "She will never play the violin again. To be so heartless, so cruel. A heart scorned is a terrible thing. No?" Pierre shook his head. "I believe she will be safe with you. You know this land, these mountains."

"I do." Truitt laid the blankets in the middle making a soft place for Cassidy to rest. "We must go. You never saw me." Truitt said walking in the back door.

Pierre stood outside. Truitt hugged the little Chinese woman and reached for Cassidy. Lifting her off the floor, he carefully walked her out. Her thick white bandaged hand held to her chest.

"Pierre. Is that you?" she squinted from the bright sun.

"Yes, my *chère*. I peeked in on you earlier but you were asleep."

Truitt sat her down and climbed in the wagon bed and gently pulled her backward.

"Pierre, thank you for your friendship." Cassidy's face flushed pink against her pale cheeks.

"You are most welcome, mademoiselle. *S'il vous plait*, please, I am so sorry for what has happened."

She lifted a weak smile and settled back in the blankets.

"Cassidy, I want to cover you and the bed of the wagon with a canvas, just till we leave town." Truitt pulled it secure, side to side.

"All right," her voice was slow and drowsy. "Goodbye."

Pierre slowly raised his hand. *"Au revoir,"* his words were lost under the rumble as he stood and watched the wagon roll from town.

THANKFUL FOR CRISP air and blue skies, Truitt led the wagon out of town and into the foothills. The irony was not missed, this was the same road he had taken to bring her to Hangtown. A week after they'd arrived, he'd heard a team of freighters had cleared the mudslide area. Now, he prayed for continual clear skies and hapless travels. Tapping his horse to pick up the pace, he swung back and saw her eyes closed as the wagon bumped and rambled up into the mountain. The medicine the doctor had given him for her helped to numb the sharp pains, helping her sleep on and off throughout the day. Taking a deep breath of pine and mountain air, he let it out. He had no qualms about his ability to protect her. But he was no nurse. He'd needed So Chen just to keep his skin together after a Friday night fight.

After two hours they made it to his first stopping point. Truitt grabbed his canteen and climbed into the back of the wagon. Cassidy's eyes opened and a small smile curved her perfect lips.

"Here take some water." He held it for her. "Can you eat a few bites? She nodded and he pulled out some cheese and bread. Breathing in another quick prayer of thanks, he watched as she ate. "I know I didn't really ask you. But I hope you don't mind. We are leaving Hangtown. For good."

"I thought that was what was happening." Her glossy eyes looked at the provisions all around her. "Will we be returning to our cave?" The lilt of her voice held a sliver of a tease. And Truitt felt his heart quicken.

"I had something a little bit bigger in mind for us." He waited and helped her take another drink. "That is, if you want. If you want to sing on a stage in San Francisco. Say the word, I would take you anywhere you wanted to go."

"Where are *you*... going Truitt?" She gave him a quizzical look.

"I'm going home, to my land. It has a road and a foundation for a house. I want to show you the large pale blue lake nearby."

"I would like that," she said slowly, her tired eyes lingered tenderly on his.

Relief and pleasure collided in him and he had to avert his eyes. "Good." This was the longest conversation they'd had since he'd found her unconscious. It was like meeting her all over again. Yet his heart was already hers and she was his heart's—what did she call it? Acushla. Yes, that was it. How could he expect her to know his prospects for a home. His future had never felt so hopeful. He rubbed his bristly chin, covering his grin. "Are you warm enough?"

"Mmm, yes, thank you." Her eyes began to droop and then opened. "Truitt, what about Finny. Did she want to come with us?"

"When I got to the Millers, she was gone. Left a note, they said. She had moved on."

"Moved on?" Keeping her injured hand raised, Cassidy tried to get comfortable on her side. "How could that be? She had no connections beyond me or... Arnold..." She stilled and her chin began to quiver.

"Don't think about that." Truitt massaged her arms and shoulders. "Maybe he came back for her. Maybe he didn't. I don't know if we'll ever know." A lone tear ran down her cheek and he wiped it with his thumb. "Are you hurting, can you take the bumps for the rest of the afternoon?"

"I can." She sucked in a choppy breath and her body shuddered. "I'm just sad for her." Another tear ran free. "She is carrying his child," she whispered.

Truitt froze. "Did Snider know this?"

Cassidy groaned and inched back into her blanket bed. "I don't—think so."

Truitt tucked her in tight and checked the ropes around his load. Snatching the reins from around the handbrake, he shook his head and jerked the horse forward. The best days for him from now on would be never to hear that name again.

Forty-Four

AFTER ANOTHER CRISP day at a slower pace and with needed stops, Truitt turned the horse and wagon a sharp right and wound back on a thin path surrounded by a forest of tall pine trees.

Noticing every tree, bush and curve, his eyes widened. "Cassidy, we made it." He grinned, pulling the horse to a stop. The land was roughly cleared and his foundation of logs and wood was just as he had left it. How could he explain why this place felt like home, like heaven on earth to him.

"I can't wait to see it," she whispered.

Truitt jumped down to the pine needle-covered ground and lowered the back wagon gate. She rose up on her own and he held her waist as she pushed off the wagon.

"Can you walk?" He braced her firmly.

"Please, I need to walk." She grimaced with pain as she wrapped her good arm around his waist and he supported her back as they tried a few steps. "Thank you, Truitt, for your help." She spied the clearing, the rock and log foundation. She looked up at him, curious.

"That will be a house, I promise." He chuckled. "With a big stove and a fireplace that could heat the deep woods." He moved closer to the flat structure and she feebly followed, glued to his side.

"And over there, a big window." He pointed. "On the left there's a place for a garden. The barn will go back there." He chewed his bottom lip. "I had only thought of a one room cabin for now. But I suppose we should have a proper bedroom with a door." He scanned the area and finally looked down to see a blush over her cheeks.

A laugh bellowed out with pure joy as he looked down at her. "What if we were to have guests? I won't forget your sense of eastern propriety."

Cassidy released a broken sigh, rubbing her right hand down her cheek. "Oh, lolly."

Truitt felt like God had just given him a miracle in this living, breathing, smiling young woman. Swinging her up into his arms, he brought her back to the wagon and helped her sit on the bench seat. "I can't wait till tomorrow, I have to show you one more thing." He jumped up next to her and led the wagon around in a circle and back down a long side road.

CASSIDY WAS EXHAUSTED, her arm and hand throbbing, but Truitt's excitement was giving her strength minute by minute. She leaned in as he sheltered his arm around her, holding her steady. His land, his home, his purpose; she could see it practically beat from his being. She drew her large wrapped hand in closer as they swayed back and forth on the rough decline of the path.

He wanted to take her far away from Hangtown and she understood why. The horror of that basement drifted in and out of her nightmares hourly. Just seeing the house, the porch, the kitchen in her mind's eye, made her weak and nauseated. Just like Truitt, one day, she might be able to forgive, but now she was deformed and would never be able to forget. The slicing of her thin bones and flesh into the wood table—the recollection caused her to feel dizzy and shivers to run up and down her body. At least when she was awake she could look at the man beside her. She stole a glance at him just as he had done at her as they traveled up into the mountains. How many times could she feel his eyes on her? That face, that manly man was the only image she wanted to retain.

"How are you fairing?" He gripped her tighter. "We're almost there."

From a weary state, she lifted her eyes to the most massive vibrant vision she had ever seen. "Am I dreaming, Truitt?"

"No, it's real."

"Oh, lolly." Her mouth hung open. "How does the sky and clouds dip those blues into that glassy clear water? These huge mountains encompassing the skyline, capped with snow. It's breathtaking."

"The Washoe Indians call it Tahoe. It means 'the lake'."

Truitt jumped down from the wagon and reached for her. Cassidy smiled, thankful to stand and have Truitt's warm arms around her. The vivid colors, the sky and trees, the surrounding splendor would be her new vision—brilliant new sights to fill her troubled mind.

"I had something else in mind here." Truitt looked down and swallowed hard. "I can't believe how close I came to losing you." Turning to face her, he held her undamaged right hand. A cool, snowy breeze came up off the lake and she felt it awaken her from her haziness.

"I...ahh. I can't believe...that...ahh...this." He huffed a smile and squeezed his forehead. "This is harder than I thought." He took in a deep breath. "Cassidy, Kathleen O'Ryan. Oh." Shaking his head, he knelt down on one knee. "Would you do me the honor of being my wife?"

She had to bite her smile between her teeth. This big, burly man was so nervous and so adorable looking up at her. Keeping her grin and eyes narrowed on his, she took his hand and turned it over. As long as she had these fingers left to tell, to touch, to weave through his hair, the answer was clear.

She set her finger to his palm and spelled. Y—E—S.

He rose up slowly, watching her and placed a soft, tender kiss on her lips. "I love you and don't ever want to be apart."

"I love you, Truitt Emerson. And I will hold your dreams for your home, land, and this area, like my own."

He hugged her gently and pulled back. "Cassidy you are not foolish as I said. I was hurt that day and I misspoke. Your dreams are just as important as mine."

She shook her head and looked away; the lake entrancing. "They are gone for good. I should have heeded the warning when my violin burnt in that little fire hole." She tucked her wrapped hand against his chest, feeling another icy breeze blow up from the lake water. "Your harsh words that day were, unfortunately…the truth."

"No, listen." His breath fell soft on her ear, "I have a notion, God has given you a special gift. The violin was just the surface tool." He searched her eyes. "Like a pick when the miners mine for gold. They know the gold lies beneath the rock and dirt. Many, many layers down. That is how God is with us. Sometimes our lives just have to spin and circle like the water around the miner's pan, getting rid of everything we don't really need. But look in deeper, Cassidy, what's left is what matters. The gold is there. Your gold is your love and how you care. The way you love to see people smile and forget their cares for a moment."

Cassidy sighed, remembering the families along the wagon trail. Her heart had swelled to see people happy and carefree from the weight of life.

"That isn't a violin." Truitt scanned her face and placed a gentle kiss on her bandages. "That's the true gold in you Cassidy and God is faithful. I know He will bring it to the surface." He watched her. "Have you lost your faith?"

"Quite the contrary," she whispered. "To live a lie is to live without God. When I finally spoke the truth, I had to trust Him with every part of me and now even through the pain, I see clearly His faithfulness in my hapless life. When I see you, I see the love and faithfulness of God. When I see His creation, like today, I see the glory of God." She leaned her head to his chest. "You have given me something to think about. There is gold in each of us, waiting to be unearthed."

"I believe it's true." He pulled her close, kissing her hairline. Looking over the expanse of water and trees, Truitt stilled.

"Finally, I'm here. You're here. Cassidy, I'm home."

Epilogue

Five years later

CASSIDY LEANED OVER her settee and tickled the squirming child with her right hand. "What have you done with my gloves, little lady." Her sweet, red-haired girl, giggled and spun off the settee, revealing a pair of leather gloves.

"Get your coat, love. Daddy will be taking us to the inn shortly." Cassidy carefully pushed her gloves over her deformed hand. Stiff cotton held inside represented her missing finger tips.

"Are da girls come to play the v'lins?" the four-year-old asked.

"Not tonight. Mama helps them to play on Wednesdays. Tonight is Friday and Mama will sing some pretty songs to the people who stay at the inn." Cassidy brushed her hand down her royal blue dress.

"I like your pretty songs. Sing the one where you do a jig." She kicked her foot forward.

Cassidy laughed. "I do enough jigs chasing after you and your father." She bent down and kissed her soft cheek.

"Cassidy? Katie?" She heard Truitt coming through the door of their two bedroom cabin. "Is everyone ready?" He stopped and looked her up and down. "Mmm mmm." He shook his head. "That dress is a show in itself. If you want to trip off the wagon and fall into my arms, I promise to catch you." He grinned.

"Performers do have standards, a stellar reputation you know." She dropped her head to the side. "No drinking, fraternizing, and no carousing with the owners."

"With one exception. The owner is your husband." He pulled her close and kissed her neck.

"Sir." She tried to wiggle free but he held her tight. "This is not businesslike."

"It's never been business to me." He kissed her until she felt her knees buckle. She hadn't seen him all day and holding his broad, muscled shoulders and thick chest reminded her of the strength and care he took in building the Tahoe Inn for her. It was a place where the weary would find rest as her voice, her songs, and the beauty of the lake took them away.

"Daddy!" Katie ran into her parent's legs.

"Hey, little miss." He pulled her up into his arms. "Are you ready to go watch Mama?" He smiled at Cassidy. "The inn is full. A few businessmen up from the city, some couples traveling, mostly hunters and fisherman, and a few Indians from the tribe."

"Wonderful." Cassidy took her coat from the peg. She'd never dreamed of large sterile music halls. This small stage, almost eye to eye with her audience, was perfect. With her family's beaming encouragement, tonight she would take requests, sing with love and joy, and ask them to join in so she could relish the faces of all that God brought.

The rarest treasures of life are found in His truth. That's why I prize God's word like others prize the finest gold. Nothing brings the soul such sweetness as seeking his living words. Psalm 19:10 TPT

Author's Note

I hope you were able to escape with a little love and adventure. Panning for gold in 1850 might have been easier than trying to pan the beauty, the gold, from our souls. I know it's not the main take away (read it in Matthew13 for context) but I can relate to the parable of the seed and the sower. Truth has to find deep soil to change our lives. Not only in the way of the Truth and Life of Jesus Christ, but also the truth of what God calls us, tells us who we are, our true identity. Something Cassidy didn't believe she could obtain without lying. Some of those truths fall by the wayside and get walked over. (I've lived years with the big shoe over my truth-ugg, how about you?) Some truths are evident for a season, but with the next season of heat, they crumble to a crisp. (My lack of soul temperature control.) Other times the toxic things in our lives poison the truth.

The truth of who we are in Christ takes a fair amount of nurturing. It likes to reside deep and full in the soil of our spirit like gold, pure and refined. I know I'm not there because, daily, I have to resist the lies of not good enough, smart enough, talented enough, or the worst, spiritual enough.

But the truth of our significance and belonging to the God of the universe always prevails and it is the only way to live a prosperous gold-laden life. Remember, you have the truth. You have ears to hear, eyes to see and a heart to believe.

Got to find my sunglasses. Madam Goldy. You are shiny, shiny, shiny!

Thank you for your time.

The Lord Bless you and Keep you-

Julia

It was so fun to write about Hangtown. Because I was that bouncy, author woman, eating ice cream and walking the actual streets, taking pictures of everything and anything.

Hangtown is now Placerville, California. The name changed in 1854 when the locals wanted something more "friendly." (*Even though today they have a mannequin hanging by the neck in Elstners' Hay Yard*). In its 1854 incorporation, Placerville was the 3rd largest town in California. Centrally located between Sacramento and South Lake Tahoe it is a truly charming California gold-rush town with some of the original buildings still standing.

Lake Tahoe was named Lake Bigler in 1850 after California's third governor and then renamed Lake Tahoe in 1862. One of my favorite places to camp and get away, I have experienced that gorgeous crest-blue snow water myself, after accidentally falling off a swim tube. Burrrrrr.

Alaska (Truitt's homeland) was purchased from Russia in 1867. (I've never been there.)

The Damonte Station was first a boarding house owned by Peleg Brown in 1864. My dates are off. But since I have family in Reno, Nevada who are good friends with the real, third generation of Damontes they got fictional billing.

Just another fun take away from the history of over 300,000 folks coming to California during the 1849 Gold Rush. They were RISK TAKERS, (1 in 12 died from disease, crime, and cultural clashes) but we have to give them a high five. As a native Californian, I can't help but think about some other modern-day gold seekers. All the computer dot-coms, the entertainment industry, biotech entrepreneurs with those crazy ideas that turned into bizillion dollar companies. Yes, some dig and get a rock, some dig and get gold. But they took the risk and kept digging.

Stop by and sign up for my very infrequent newsletter (enters you in all my drawings) and inside info on my books.

www.juliadwrites.com

Now off we go to the next mining town!

Morgan's Medicine

Loves Pure Gold, Book 2

When Emery is kidnapped, mistaken for Arnold Snider's wife, a gang of miners wanting retribution don't believe Emery is just a servant. Dropping her off with a reclusive doctor from the war to guard her, they leave her to arrange the settlement with Arnold Snider to get their gold back.

What will be Emery's fate when they find they've taken the wrong woman? Can her feelings for her handsome, but unusual, doctor ever turn from something besides mistrust? Will Emery's own shame claim her very life?